THE BOWNESS BEQUEST

REBECCA TOPE

LARGE
PRINT

First published in Great Britain 2017
by
Allison & Busby Limited

First Isis Edition
published 2018
by arrangement with
Allison & Busby Limited

A catalogue record for this book is available
from the British Library.

ISBN 978–1–78541–609–5 (hb)
ISBN 978–1–78541–615–6 (pb)

Published by
F. A. Thorpe (Publishing)
Anstey, Leicestershire

Set by Words & Graphics Ltd.
Anstey, Leicestershire
Printed and bound in Great Britain by
T. J. International Ltd., Padstow, Cornwall

This book is printed on acid-free paper

THE BOWNESS BEQUEST

Winter has arrived in the town of Windermere, and has brought with it the death of Frances Henderson, the best friend of Simmy Brown's mother. Having known the Hendersons all of her life, Simmy must cope with the loss of an important figure from her childhood — as well as surprise at being bequeathed something in Frances's will. Then, when Frances's husband Kit is violently murdered in his home, Simmy must face the fact that this family she was once so close to as a child holds some dark and sinister secrets. How will Simmy react to seeing their son Christopher, her childhood sweetheart, after so long — and could the rumours of Kit's infidelity provide a clue as to who killed him?

SPECIAL MESSAGE TO READERS

Another one dedicated to Sue,
even if she never reads them

Author's Note

The towns and villages in this story are real, but the
auction house has been invented.

Prologue

As funerals went, this was a low-key one, in Simmy's view. The family had lost a wife and mother, and were accordingly bereft and bemused, but they had not been flamboyant in the manner of her send-off. It had been a sad and shocking death from pancreatic cancer. "The one they have no clue how to cure," said Simmy's mother sourly. "Or prevent," she added for good measure.

A formulaic cremation, followed by tea and cake in a modest hall in Bowness, had been all the family could manage. There were perhaps sixty people assembled, including Simmy's parents. Frances Henderson had been sixty-three; an ordinary woman struck down by a fast-working cancer. Friends, colleagues and offspring were seated around the formica tables. The average age appeared to be below fifty, which perhaps made the occasion unusual, but in every other respect it offered little worthy of note.

Simmy carried her little plate of cakes around, in search of a seat. The one she had left to collect her food had quickly been nabbed by a man who looked eager to talk to Angie, Simmy's mother. There was a table

1

containing three women of roughly Simmy's own age, and she diffidently joined them.

"Hi, I'm Simmy," she said. "My mother was one of Frances's oldest friends."

"June, Cheryl and Hannah," said one of the women, pointing to each in turn.

"Oh — Hannah! Of course, it's you. What a fool I am." Simmy was deeply embarrassed. "I only saw the back of your head at the crematorium. What is it — twenty years since we last met? But you haven't changed."

She paused, her mind full of memories of a shared childhood with the five Hendersons and their parents. A series of flashbacks had been assailing her for the past hour, and still had her in their thrall. The three boys, each with his own individual habits and preferences, arguing with the two younger sisters, ignoring their parents on the sporadic occasions when there was an attempt at discipline. Simmy, with her mum and dad, trying to join in, and mostly failing. And now, here they all were, so oddly different from their adolescent selves, with their mother dead and their father cocooned in an invisible wrapping of shock. He had spoken a few words to Angie, nodded at Russell and frowned at Simmy as if unsure of who she was.

But Hannah was remarkably the same, with her cloud of thick hair framing small features. There was no possibility of failing to recognise her, face-to-face. "Simmy," she said now. "That's okay. You've changed a lot. Were you always so tall?"

2

Simmy laughed. "Pretty much, I think." She took a seat next to the woman introduced as Cheryl. "Have I met you before as well?"

"No, I don't think so, although I know who you are. We live just over the road — I think we know everybody here. Neighbours, workmates, family." She looked around the room, not appearing to take any pleasure in her social knowledge. "I've known the Hendersons for ages. I worked with Kit in the carpet warehouse. It was my first job from school. June too, for a bit. She knows everybody as well."

Simmy focused on the other woman. "Hello, June," she said.

"Hiya," said June listlessly.

Cheryl was a colourless creature, wearing a bulky dark-blue coat. Plump, pale and clearly not very interested in Persimmon Brown. Her friend was prettier, with long bleached hair and a full mouth. Both looked to be in their early forties.

"A man stole my seat," said Simmy, waving a hand at the other table.

"That's my husband," said Cheryl. "Malcolm. He insisted on coming, but I don't think he knows anyone, really. He doesn't like me to go anywhere on my own." She preened slightly at this, as if it were a source of pride. "You not married?" she added carelessly.

"Divorced. Your husband's chatting to my mother as if he knows her," Simmy observed.

"He does that. We were in the row behind you at the crem, and he recognised your mum. He'll be checking it out. I told you we know everybody, just about."

3

"I remember your mum very well," said Hannah. "She was always great on our seaside holidays. Full of all those stories about the swinging sixties. I loved all that. I was sorry when everybody got too old for them and we all drifted apart."

"Where's Lynn?" Simmy asked. "I only saw the back of her head as well. You two were always so alike."

"Still are, according to most people. She's doing the tea, in the kitchen. Can't let anybody get on with their job without interfering. She's still furious with George for bunking off right after the cremation. Says he has a duty to be here."

"Poor old George. He'd hate all this, wouldn't he?"

"Time he grew up and got over himself," said the man's unfeeling sister. "But, if anything, he just gets worse."

"Oh, well," said Simmy, still immersed in early memories of the Henderson family. "Eddie makes up for it."

"Not to mention Christopher," said Hannah. "Three brothers, all as different from each other as anyone could imagine."

Simmy nodded in agreement and sipped her tea.

CHAPTER
ONE

The shop door pinged huskily at two o'clock on the Monday afternoon following the Friday funeral. *Must see what's the matter with it*, thought Simmy. It wasn't electronic, but a simple old-fashioned bell above the door. Perhaps there was some fluff caught in the works.

An unmistakably familiar man was walking through the shop towards her. Brown eyes, hair with a hint of auburn in it. Tall, with big hands and a hesitant smile, he combined features from both his parents. Something quick in his movements conjured his father, while the big head and long chin were from his mother's side.

"Christopher," she smiled, mentally running through potential reasons for his being there. Yet again, the sight of him revived sweet memories of sand and salt and fried fish, combined with an easy intimacy that had existed from her earliest days.

"Have you got a minute?" He met her eyes with a look she had seen on men countless times before. A look that said, *Just how well do we really know each other?* She wondered whether a grown-up brother would have asked a similar question, if she had ever had one.

She spread her hands to indicate the empty shop. Early November had to be one of the quietest points in the year as far as a florist's business was concerned. "Very much so," she said.

"I thought it would be better to come in person. Much better than a letter from a solicitor."

"Pardon?"

"My mother left you something in her will. I thought you might know about it already."

She was bemused. "No, I had no idea."

"Well, our families have been friends forever. She approved of your new life. It's not so surprising, is it?" He seemed impatient, even mildly irritated.

"But . . ." The dead woman had five children, and had not been wealthy. The modest bungalow in Bowness had always needed painting or pointing or roof tiles replaced. A widower remained there with his memories. His offspring were all still in the area, three of them married.

"She was fond of you," he repeated.

"Yes. And I almost never went to see her, since coming here. She was my mother's friend much more than mine. Did she leave Mum anything?"

"You'll have to ask her," he said uncomfortably. "It's supposed to be confidential."

"Are you an executor?" Simmy was very hazy about the way such things worked, but she was under the impression that people's wills became common knowledge once the person had died. Her parents had never yet discussed their own end-of-life affairs with her, but she had a suspicion that they might get around to it before much longer. When they did — if they did — then being an only child would presumably make everything nice and simple.

"Oh, yes," he sighed. "Eldest son, and all that. It's us three boys, actually. Lynn and Hannah are sulking about being left out, but they'll soon realise they've had a lucky escape."

"Sounds complicated. I can't imagine that George will be very useful."

"George is a law unto himself, as always. He's going to take a while to settle down, after losing Mum. But actually, the business side of things is all fine. Eddie and I are cracking on with it quite happily so far. And Dad's okay with it all. He only wants to be left to get on with everything the same as always. He hasn't really taken on board that he's on his own now." He sighed. "He's really not in very good shape mentally. I hadn't realised just how far he's sunk. He'll need somebody to watch out for him from now on. And everybody seems to think it'll be me."

"I like your dad," she said, with a degree of exaggeration. "I always did." In truth, she had seldom been able to feel anything for the man. She couldn't get closer than liking the *idea* of him, rather than the reality. He had been a detached sort of father to his large family, but basically harmless, as far as she knew. He maintained a steady income and never hit anybody.

"You'll have to visit him, then. He'd be thrilled if you did."

Simmy entertained another rapid kaleidoscope of childhood memories in which the Straw and Henderson families had holidayed together, year after year, in North Wales. Christopher and she had always been good mates, swimming together and pootling in the rock pools. They had been born on the same day in the same hospital, which explained the friendship. The two new mothers had become welded together, despite the subsequent move of the Hendersons to Cumbria when the children were in their teens. Ten years later, Angie and Russell Straw had followed them, and ten years after that, Simmy too had moved north.

"So what have I inherited?" she asked again.

"Come down to the house, and I'll show you."

The Hendersons lived at the southern end of Bowness. It would take twenty minutes to walk each way from Simmy's shop in the middle of Windermere. Longer coming back, in fact, due to the uphill climb. Perhaps she'd take the van and save the time. "After work," she nodded. "Is that okay?"

He looked uneasy. "I suppose so. Can't you come now?" He glanced around the shop, evidently searching for a deputy.

"Sorry. Bonnie isn't in today. She takes Mondays off, in lieu of Saturdays. I can't just close up for an hour or more, can I? Shouldn't you be at work yourself?"

Christopher's career had always been a source of fascination to the Straws. He had gone to university for a year and then dropped out, spending the next two years working on an organic farm and fighting against a variety of perceived ecological threats. At twenty-two, he then switched track again and took part in an epic voyage on a sailing ship, down to the Straits of

8

Magellan and up the western side of the Americas. None of his friends or relations saw him again until he hit twenty-five, got married and settled in Solihull working for a stonemason. At no stage did he have any reliable income; a fact that his wife eventually found intolerable. She wanted children and an easy life. "Why in the world did she ever marry him?" Angie Straw repeatedly demanded.

"Because she loved him," said Frances, his mother. "Obviously."

Christopher was unarguably lovable. Women melted under his charm. The past ten years had seen him mostly based in Cumbria, albeit with regular absences. The stonemasonry fizzled out, and he took another swerve into antique dealing. Here he finally found his niche. After dabbling in china and glass, then stamps and postcards, he settled into a post as second in command at a thriving auction house, gaining a reputation for straight dealing and bottomless knowledge. He did most of the high-profile work as auctioneer, while his boss sat in a small room and offered valuations and expert identifications of a vast range of objects.

"Mondays are quiet for me, too," he said. "We had a big sale on Saturday, so I've earned a day off, same as your Bonnie. The girls are always crotchety on the Monday after a sale. People forget to collect their purchases, and then phone in a panic. The staff have to keep their wits about them, in case anyone tries to claim the wrong things, accidentally on purpose. And it's all got to go on the website. I'm best out of their way."

"Is it an antique, then? My bequest?" Her curiosity was starting to blossom, after the initial surprise.

"Wait and see," he insisted with the first proper smile since he came in. "I'll be there if you come at five or soon after. Dad's going to want to talk to you as well."

He left awkwardly, his brow furrowed as if burdened with a long list of tasks to complete. Other people to inform about an inheritance, perhaps. Simmy watched him thoughtfully, her head full of questions. *Had* Frances left anything to Angie, Simmy's mother? Did anyone in the family resent this apparent generosity to an outsider? At the funeral, the widower had held himself straight and stiff and nodded randomly at anyone who approached him. He was seventy-four, in good physical health. Angie Straw had reported that Kit was wearing rather better than her own husband, afflicted with an abrupt decline into a type of paranoid neurosis. The two wives had enjoyed regular sessions, in which they appeared to fortify each other through the disappointments and tedium of stale old marriages. Angie would pass on a few snippets to her daughter, generally along the lines that she might not be missing a great deal by being single again.

But then everything collapsed with Frances's cancer and Angie lost her highly valued friend. From diagnosis to death had been five weeks. "And that's a lot more than some people get," said the visiting Macmillan nurse.

10

Mr Henderson was another Christopher, but was known to everyone as Kit. Frances had a sister named Christine, shortened to Chris, which meant that the firstborn son was always referred to by his full name. "Why in the world didn't you think of something else for him?" Angie had demanded, on the very day the child was born. "It's a family thing," Frances had replied. "There's no ducking it."

Angie had been almost as scathing about all her friend's subsequent children's names. "So dull," she said. Simmy always winced, with her own exotic "Persimmon" more burdensome than she liked. Hannah or Lynn would have suited her very nicely.

The afternoon drifted by, with a single customer searching for an African violet that would be guaranteed not to die. Simmy was the soul of patience, explaining the plant's preference for water from beneath the pot, as well as adequate warmth and light. "The clue's in the name," she smiled. "They're from Africa, where conditions are very different from here." She hoped, by the end, that at least a few of her hints had taken root. So many people seemed to be unaware that plants were living things, with all the same needs for nourishment as any other creature.

Accustomed to spells of quiet in the shop, she occupied herself with ordering new stock, and making plans for the Christmas display that Bonnie was due to create in a month's time. The girl had a flair for design and colour, already dismissing any notions of wreaths or poinsettias, suggesting all kinds of alternatives that would catch the eye of anyone passing their window.

She intended to make liberal use of gold paint and glass baubles, she warned her employer.

"It'll be amazing," Ben Harkness had approved. He and Bonnie were a closely entwined couple, bonded by each being seen as unusual, if not downright bizarre, by the world at large. Ben was just eighteen, Bonnie a few months younger. He was studying for a clutch of A levels, and she had abandoned any further attempt at passing exams, having had an interrupted school career that left her with a pathetically meagre set of GCSEs. Nobody doubted that she would make a success of life, regardless of formal qualifications.

Simmy had been running her Windermere flower shop for a year and a half, slowly learning her way around the Lakes, and discovering the different characters of the various small towns: Ambleside with its confusing streets and legions of hotels and guesthouses; Coniston with its Old Man lowering protectively just behind the houses; Hawkshead, with its timeless little huddle of odd-shaped buildings. She loved them all, as well as the fells that surrounded them. Windermere and Bowness were both a lot less distinctive, on lower ground, with the fells away in the distance. The water lapped gently at the edges of Bowness, and a patch of tame woodland sheltered Windermere from the worst ravages of the winter weather. "Soft," people said of these two settlements. You were safe and warm, down here — unlike on the unpredictable heights of Kirkstone or Grasmere.

And although Simmy found the wilder regions thrilling and beautiful, she had to admit she spent almost all her time in the lower reaches. Her home in Troutbeck might sit on rising land, closer to the fells than it was to the lake, but it was very nearly as hospitable as Windermere for much of the year. Troutbeck, she had concluded, was as remote and adventurous as she was ever going to feel comfortable with.

The first few months after moving north had been devoted to establishing the shop, a process involving mountains of paperwork and rapid learning. By the end of the summer of the previous year, she had everything in place and a growing stream of people wanting her flowers. Assisted by Melanie Todd, a local girl of considerable ability, she had supplied weddings, funerals, birthdays and other momentous life events with suitable floral embellishment. And along the way — at a wedding, then a birthday and after that three other commissions — people had been violently killed. Simmy had been drawn into investigations and personal danger, merely by virtue of delivering flowers. The first occasion was just over a year ago now, and she profoundly hoped that the anniversary would mark a change of fortune, leaving the whole business of murder far behind her.

The fact of an unexpected bequest seemed to add weight to this hope. It had never happened to her before. Even when her grandparents had died, they had left their meagre savings to the generation above Simmy. Not so much as a silver candlestick had come her way.

Visions of jewellery, or a picture, or a handsome piece of china filled her head. Something that Frances had kept tucked out of sight — because Simmy could not remember ever seeing anything of the kind on display in the house. One thing she was sure of: it would not be money. How could it be, when the family had always been struggling to find cash for holidays or a new car, or a replacement television? Kit Henderson had worked as a carpet fitter for most of his life, earning little more than the basic retainer during the big recession nearly ten years earlier, without the added commission for jobs done, since few people saw a new carpet as a high priority. Although the situation improved, he had seemed glad to retire on a very modest pension at seventy, leaving his wife to keep them afloat with what she earned as an administrator in Barrow Hospital. "I'm really just an office clerk," she would say, "but everyone calls themselves administrators these days."

The hours finally passed until five, at which point Simmy hastily locked the shop and went to the van parked on a tiny paved area behind the shop. Her car was somewhere out on the eastern side of Windermere, where parking was free and unrestricted. She would leave it every morning, and have to try to recall exactly where in the afternoon. When she got back from Bowness, she would have to locate it in the dark, damp streets where all the cars looked the same.

Eagerly, she turned the opposite way from usual, and headed southwards towards Bowness. *I've got a beque-e-est*, she sang softly to herself. It made her feel oddly blessed, as if an angel had brushed her with its wings. Within a very few minutes, she would discover exactly what it was that Frances Henderson had left her.

CHAPTER
TWO

Bowness was a linear little town, following the eastern edge of Lake Windermere for a mile or so. It had opted very early on for a particular brand of tourist appeal that had been sustained for well over a century. It boasted a promenade, manicured gardens, large and handsome hotels, and many more shops and restaurants than Windermere could offer. Boats could be hired and small lake cruises embarked upon. Just south of the town was the ferry across the lake. South again was Newby Bridge and a whole different kind of landscape.

Traffic was comparatively light, but it was never a smooth business to drive through Bowness. Simmy's destination lay past the promenade with its swans and kiosks and to the right into Glebe Road. A road that had been steadily colonised with a variety of houses over the years, it looped past a cemetery and a small park, and back into central Bowness. The Hendersons had probably the least attractive property in the street, deprived of a view of the lake and suffering all the noise and disruption of the substantial tourist trade, being close to the Ship Inn.

"It was all they could afford," Angie had said. "And you have to admit they've made the most of it." The house was kept tidy outside, the woodwork painted regularly and the garden forbidden from escaping human control; with a large lawn, frequently mowed, and easy shrubs, which flowered on schedule. Simmy glanced all around, sighing at what she felt was a false image, created entirely to placate neighbours and town councillors. There was a soullessness to it that a florist could not fail to notice.

Christopher had evidently been watching out for her, and was standing in the doorway as she approached. "Good timing," he said.

She followed him into the small shadowy hallway, then through to the sitting room at the back, which had been chosen as the quietest and lightest room, by a small margin. It looked south-west, where tiny glimpses of water could be had between buildings and trees. To Simmy's great surprise there were three people sitting there, all obviously waiting for her.

She had seen them all only three days previously. She had spoken to them, and eaten cake with them, after Frances Henderson's cremation. It felt strangely unsettling to see them again so soon. It had been as if the funeral of their wife and mother, with the release of tension that came after it, was the end of the story. Even though she knew that life had to go on, she had not expected to be part of it right away, if ever. She looked to Christopher for an explanation.

"We've been going over the will this morning, you see," he said. "We knew what was in it — nothing very

17

complicated — so now the funeral's out of the way, we have to deal with the details. George and Eddie know what we're doing. Hannah and Lynn came over this afternoon to help us get clothes and a few other things sorted."

"I see," said Simmy uncertainly. "Well, hello, everybody. Kit . . ." she faltered. What did one say to a man still numb from the death of his wife? Could you even assume he *was* numb? Anything was possible. He could even be planning a Mediterranean cruise, for all she knew.

"Simmy," he nodded, not even making a token effort to get up from his chair. There was none of the old-fashioned gentleman to Kit Henderson, and never had been. In that respect, he was altogether different from Russell Straw. But Kit didn't need to make courteous gestures for a woman to see the twinkle in his eye. He had something roguish about him, with brown eyes and a skin tone darker than most Cumbrians. Once or twice Angie had likened him to a gypsy. Always a slight man, with thin limbs, he also had something of the monkey about him. He moved quickly, and it was easy to imagine him crawling across newly carpeted floors, nailing down the edges and ensuring all was neat. Frances had, since Kit's retirement, complained that he was impossible to live with, telling Angie Straw how unreasonable and demanding he had become. "Expects me to wait on him hand and foot," was a recurrent theme. "And I swear his wits are going. He asks me the same question a hundred times."

The two sisters were together on a shabby sofa. With only fifteen months between them, they had frequently been taken for twins. Now in their early thirties, they had gone their separate ways, and Simmy had little idea of the pattern of their lives. It had been twenty years or more since she last saw them. Pausing to take proper note of their expressions, she found them to be singularly unfriendly.

Again she turned to Christopher for reassurance. He gave her a weak smile, but said nothing.

"What's the matter?" she asked, slightly too loudly. "I've got no idea why Frances should have left me anything. If it's a problem for you, I'll be happy to give it back — whatever it is."

"Huh!" snorted Hannah. She had bushy straw-coloured hair that dwarfed her face, which had similar small features to her father's, creating a resemblance despite the very different colouring.

"Wait till you see what it is," added Lynn. As if to break away from the likeness to her sister, she had cropped hair that sat springily on her skull like a reluctant wig. It was of a texture more often found in Africa, the colour of both it and her skin somehow wrong. She seemed less inclined towards hostility than Hannah, perhaps remembering how Simmy had babied her in the past, helping her with sandcastles and shell collections. There had been a close bond between them in those early years when Lynn had been little more than a toddler.

"So tell me," Simmy begged. "The suspense is awful."

"Come and see for yourself. It's on the table," said Christopher. "It's easier than trying to explain. I'm not even sure that any of us quite understands it, anyway."

There was a small round table in a corner of the room, covered with a cloth that someone had embroidered flowers on, many decades previously. An empty ashtray and a pair of woolly gloves shared it with a large book. "There," said Christopher.

She was tempted to lighten the mood by pretending to think her legacy was the frayed gloves, but she restrained herself. The book was plainly the object in question. "This?" she said, touching it lightly.

"Right," said Christopher. He gave a deep sigh. "And I of all people ought to know if there's something special about it. I can see it's been carefully made by hand, but that doesn't make it valuable. Look inside," he urged her.

She picked it up and opened it at random. It was a substantial case-bound volume, quite heavy. The paper was far thicker than the pages of a normal book, and they were all interleaved with fine tissue. "It's gorgeous," she breathed. "Where did Frances get it from?"

"Her mother did it," came Kit's smoky old man's voice. "She always kept it in the bottom of the wardrobe. I've only seen it once."

"There's a letter with it," said Hannah, her tone still sulky. "Inside the front cover."

Balancing the book on her left forearm, Simmy extracted an envelope. Awkwardly, she put her new possession back on the table and opened the letter.

"Are you sure you want to read it now — with all of us here?" Christopher cautioned her.

She frowned. "Why not? It can't possibly be secret, can it? Even if it is, I wouldn't keep it from you. You're her family. I'm not important. I can't think why . . ." But she could, of course. The moment she had opened the book, she understood why it had been given to her. Because it was full of watercolour paintings of flowers, and flowers were her thing. The execution was competent rather than brilliant, the colours not quite natural. But she had already fallen in love with it, three seconds after realising what it was.

Dear Simmy, *the letter ran,*

I wanted you to have this because you understand and appreciate flowers. My mother made this when she was expecting me, in the 1950s, and a friend of hers bound it for her. She said it was to pass down the female line of the family, as long as there was a daughter to inherit it. And yes, I know I have two daughters, neither of them you. But they don't care about this sort of thing, and quite honestly, Simmy, you're the daughter I always wished I had. Awful thing to say, I know, but in my situation, it feels dangerous to avoid the truth. As if I might bring yet more calamity down on myself.

So keep it nice, and get it out now and then and spare a thought for me, just as I did for my mother. And be nice to Christopher.

With very much love, Frances

"Well?" demanded Hannah. "What does it say?"

"Leave her alone, will you," snapped Christopher.

"She said it couldn't possibly be secret. So why not read it out to us?"

Simmy barely heard her. Tears were threatening, along with a burning wish to escape. "Sorry," she sniffed. "It's rather personal. Listen — I'll have to go. Thank you — all of you. I will come and see you, Kit, if you'd like me to. And my mum and dad will ask you over there when they're not too busy with the B&B people."

She gathered up the beloved book, and turned to leave. Christopher stood in her way. "Are you all right?" he asked.

"Oh yes," she assured him. "Don't worry about me. You're the ones who've lost a wife and mother. I'm just sorry this has all been a bit awkward." She felt desperate to escape and give herself time to process what had just happened. From feeling unexpectedly blessed, she was now consumed by a strange sense of guilty embarrassment. A woman she had only known as a child, who had no reason to think of her at all, had snubbed her own daughters by favouring Simmy. It felt more aggressive than generous, as she cast a last look at Hannah's face. Its expression remained hostile and suspicious. "Thanks, everybody," she blurted. "I'll be sure to take very good care of it." She held up the book, and then hugged it to her chest.

Not even Christopher went with her to the door. She drove back through the town, heading for the only person she knew who might make sense of what had just happened.

"P'simmon! I didn't expect you this evening." Angie Straw was carrying a mug in one hand as she opened the front door to her daughter. She waved it expressively. "We haven't got very much for supper," she said.

"Never mind. I can have an apple or something, if you've got it."

"Why are you here? Your father's going to think it's Wednesday. He'll be all confused for the rest of the week now."

Simmy had developed the habit of calling in after work, midweek and again on Saturday afternoons. In the past few months, she had found herself being called upon to help with the B&B work, much more than before. Where Russell had changed duvet covers, loaded and unloaded the dishwasher, gone shopping for the large quantities of food required, he now made little more than a token effort to share the load. The regularity of Simmy's visits seemed to work best with her father, despite Angie's dislike of predictable routines.

"I've just come from the Hendersons' house. Did you know Frances had left me this?" She stepped into the hallway, pushed the door closed with a foot, and proffered the book. "Have you seen it before? And did she leave *you* anything?"

Angie blinked, and headed for the kitchen. "Come and sit down, and tell me properly," she said.

Russell was sitting by the Aga, his dog between his knees as always. "Good evening, daughter," he said solemnly, with a slow nod. "The nights are drawing in. Dark at five. Every year, I wonder how we bear it. But we do, of course."

"Pity the poor Icelanders," said Simmy. "It's dark all day there."

"They should emigrate south," he said.

"I think most of them did, didn't they? A few centuries ago."

"Perhaps so. You might recall that I was reading a book by Halldór Laxness last week. I learnt a good deal about how the poor wretches lived until not so long ago."

"I do remember," said Simmy. "That's why I mentioned Iceland just now."

"Of course it was," he said, nodding with satisfaction. "Good girl."

"P'simmon has come to show us something," said Angie. "It's not her usual day."

The elderly man shrugged. "Who cares?" he said crossly.

Angie turned away from him. "Let's see it, then," she invited Simmy, who laid the book on the table, which barely had space for it. Piles of crockery occupied most of it.

"What are all these plates and things doing here?" she asked.

"I'm checking them for chips and cracks. I thought I could try and get to the auction up in Keswick at the weekend and get some replacements. You can get lovely

24

stuff for almost nothing. Christopher gave me the idea, when I was chatting to him at the funeral."

"It's a long way," said Simmy doubtfully. "Would you have time?"

"Probably not," said Angie with a frustrated sigh.

"Anyway — have a look at this. Have you ever seen it before?"

Angie leant over the book and turned a few pages. "No — never. Flowers," she murmured. "Who did them?"

"Her mother, in the 1950s. Isn't it gorgeous!"

"All hand done. Even the binding. So why have *you* got it? I don't understand."

"She left it to me. There's a letter. She said I was a more suitable person to have it than Hannah or Lynn. They're not very pleased about it, understandably. So you didn't know anything about it?"

Angie shook her head. "She never talked about that sort of thing. I kept trying to make her say how she felt about everything — dying so young and all that. But she wouldn't. And no, she hasn't left me anything, as far as I know."

"I'm not surprised she wouldn't talk about dying. You are awful, Mum. From what I heard, Fran was actually very grown-up about it. She wrote that letter to me, for a start. She might have done them for everybody, for all we know. What did you expect her to say, anyway?"

"I'm not awful at all. I was trying to help. Poor Kit didn't know how to talk to her, so I thought I could make it easier for them both. All she would say was she'd had a good life and wasn't scared at all."

"Well, what else *was* there to say, then? Doesn't that cover it?"

"Your mother likes to *wallow*," said Russell, unexpectedly. "She likes everything talked into submission. I'm sure you've noticed."

Simmy laughed. "Poor Frances. Look what she's left me, Dad."

He barely glanced at the book. "I never felt I knew the woman very well," he said. "She was your mother's friend, not mine. She didn't really like me. They didn't like each other's husbands much at all. Perhaps that was a good thing — at least there was never any temptation to indulge in wife-swapping on all those infernal beach holidays." He chuckled happily. "Not like some people we knew, back in the bad old days."

"That's rubbish!" Angie snapped. "Total fantasy."

"Oh well, it doesn't matter. She's dead now. And that wretched husband of hers is having the last laugh." He gave his wife a very direct look. "I did hear you two, you know — bemoaning your witless menfolk. As if we were old dogs that couldn't remember the rules any more."

Simmy flinched at this attack. Where her mother had always prided herself on straight talking and facing facts squarely, her father had been open and honest, but far less confrontational. Now the roles were reversed, Angie had to be feeling the ground shift beneath her. Her skin was considerably thinner than most people realised — perhaps including her husband.

26

Angie seldom considered anybody's sensibilities, but her own were as vulnerable as anyone else's, when it came down to it.

And Frances? She was the spark that had set this in motion, the hovering ghost who needed to be exorcised. "She wrote me a letter," said Simmy again. "About the book. Do you want to see it?"

Angie took a steadying breath. "If you like." She took it and read it quickly. "No wonder the girls are upset. She always vowed she would treat them exactly the same as the boys — and now she's gone back on it."

"What do you mean?"

"When she adopted them — she made a great song and dance about them being completely the same as her biological children. So did Kit, in his way."

Simmy's head started to hum. "Adopted? Did you say *adopted*?" She tried to think back to those seaside holidays, the big noisy family, the three boys and the two smaller sisters. "How old was I then?"

"Six or seven. She had George when you were almost five, and wasn't willing to risk any more boys. So they adopted the two girls, sisters, fifteen months apart in age. Hannah was two and a half and Lynn just over a year. They were terribly sweet, with all that frizzy hair."

"But they look so like Kit. Everybody must assume they're his." She paused, trying to absorb the sudden revision of old assumptions. "So it was a secret? Is that why nobody ever told me?"

"They don't really look like him. And no, it was never a secret at all. You were too young to understand. And there was no sense in making an issue of it. You never asked, so we never bothered to explain. You were very incurious as a child, you know. Suddenly, from one year to the next, there were two new Hendersons, and you just took it as normal. We thought Christopher might talk to you about it, but apparently he never did."

"I don't remember," said Simmy, with a flash of desperation. "I should be able to, and I don't. As far as I'm concerned, the girls were always there. I must have thought that was how it was in families — babies just turned up, even though never in ours. I do remember wishing we could have one or two. I wanted to be a big sister."

"Don't start on that," warned Angie. "You got plenty of contact with other children. Not just the Hendersons, either. You were always having little friends coming to the house."

It was true. Other little girls had taken well to the way Simmy's mother welcomed them in with a casual goodwill. She fed them, gave them full rein in house and garden, and dismissed any phobias or allergies with robust scepticism. If they fell over, she swabbed the mud and grit off and set them back on their feet. Living in Worcestershire at the time, there were tamer patches of countryside to explore than out here in the wilder north-west. Simmy shuddered at the sudden image of small friends tumbling into rushing becks or getting irrevocably lost on the fells, if they had been living in Cumbria.

Angie went on, "And Frances always wished you were hers. She was madly jealous in the hospital, when

I got a girl and she got Christopher. She'd assumed all along hers was a girl, you see."

"I know." That much of the story at least was familiar. "Which must be why she's left me this," she summarised.

"And the flowers. You being a florist," said Angie drily. "And her girls being utterly unartistic, and liable to try to sell it."

"I won't do that." She gently stroked the page which lay open in front of her. "Look at this honeysuckle. She's made it seem really alive. I can almost smell it."

"It's not desperately *good*, though, is it? Not like those famous flower pictures you see on birthday cards and calendars and whatnot. I don't think Fran's mother was ever a proper artist."

"It's good enough for me," Simmy defended. "I'll always treasure it."

"Well, there you are, then," said Angie vaguely. "Everybody's happy."

"They're not, though. Kit wasn't terribly friendly, and the girls were almost hostile. It was all quite awkward. Christopher was the only one who was nice to me."

"You and he were always meant for each other, you know. We arranged it the day you were born. It was very perverse of you not to co-operate better than you did."

"Hush, woman!" said Russell from his warm chair. "You sound like an idiot, saying things like that."

Simmy merely smiled. It was an old joke, which she and Christopher had long since grown used to — although she had eventually realised how nearly it had prevented the two of them from developing a bond that went beyond the fraternal. They had known each other too well, so that when they had suspected themselves to be in love, confusion overwhelmed them. And then she had married Tony and Christopher had married Sophie. Simmy's marriage had outlasted Christopher's by several years, but both were over now.

"Christopher and Sophie!" Angie had mocked. "What a mouthful."

Sophie had been of mixed race, a loud and impatient woman, who had wasted no time after the divorce in finding a man more compliant with her wishes. She had three children in four years, and nobody really blamed her.

"I'm terribly hungry," Simmy realised. "The Hendersons didn't give me so much as a cup of tea."

"You always come here and take our food," said Russell. "What do you think we are?"

She looked at him, unsure as to his tone. "I think you're my parents," she said quietly.

"There's a bit of beef stew left over," said Angie. "Put it in the microwave. I'll be glad to get it finished. Your father doesn't eat as well as he used to. Miserable little helpings he has these days."

Simmy's concern about Russell had mutated some time ago into a mixture of acceptance and low-level impatience. She had to perpetually remind herself — and her mother — that he couldn't help the way he was, that there was nothing calculated or deliberate in the things he said. The shift in personality was mostly a matter of degree. He had always spoken his mind, just as his wife did, but his mind had generally been benign. He was a fount of knowledge when it came to local history, and a stickler for correct grammar. Now the sense that something was awry made him irritable and suspicious. He would flare into sudden panic, convinced that burglars or arsonists were out to get him. A good deal of this paranoia was rooted in actual events over the past year, where Simmy and he himself had found themselves under threat, and even direct attack.

"I don't get hungry any more," he said. "It's something I regret."

Simmy ate the stew quickly, and took her leave. There was a lot to think about, she concluded, as she drove up the hill to her home in Troutbeck.

CHAPTER
THREE

Bonnie arrived in the shop bright and early the next morning, despite the November gloom. Clouds sat heavily on the fells, shutting out the light, and damp dripped from the bare branches. There was no colour in the gardens on the road into Windermere. But the girl was like a beacon in a vivid outfit of red and blue. Pale-skinned and light-haired herself, she should have been swamped by the flamboyant clothes, but the force of her personality won through. Her eyes sparkled and she almost bounced with energy.

"What's come over you?" asked Simmy, feeling middle-aged and lethargic by comparison.

"Oh, nothing. Christmas. Ben. Spike. Everything seems so . . . *happy*." She sighed and then smiled. "Am I tempting fate, do you think?"

"Probably. But maybe not. It's nice to see such a cheery face on a day like this."

"Did I miss anything yesterday?"

"Not really. Hardly any customers."

"Well, here's one now, look. And it's only ten past nine."

Simmy did a double take at the man coming into the shop. It was almost a rerun of the previous afternoon, but not quite. This was a younger, chubbier version of Christopher Henderson. The middle brother, Eddie, who had never entirely come into focus for Simmy, being so much more ordinary than his siblings. She felt a strong inclination to take a step back, and if possible escape through the back room and into the little yard outside.

"Not exactly a customer, I fear," she murmured to Bonnie. Then, louder, "Hello, Eddie. What is it now?"

He managed to look reproachful and exasperated all at the same time. His large face and wide-spaced eyes were very much a likeness, as was the colourless hair, kept rather long. "That's not very welcoming," he said. "I gather I missed you yesterday."

"I thought you'd gone back to . . . wherever it is. If this is about that book —"

"It's not. My mother was free to leave anything she liked to anybody she wanted. None of us could be trusted with the thing, anyway. My kids would wreck it within minutes. George would just lose it, and the girls didn't even know it existed."

Which just leaves Christopher, thought Simmy. *And he's too unsettled to be saddled with something like that.*

"So?" she prompted.

He glanced at Bonnie, clearly wanting to speak privately. She stood her ground like a protective terrier. "I had a phone call from Dad last night. Everybody had gone off and left him on his own, and he was going over everything in his mind, the way he does. He's coped amazingly well with Mum dying, but the change to his life is a lot to get to grips with. I can't see him managing, to be honest."

So? she wanted to scream at him. *What does this have to do with me?* But she waited quietly for enlightenment.

"The thing is," he went on, clasping his hands together, almost wringing them in his embarrassment. "The thing is, I wondered whether your mother could keep an eye on him a bit more. I know she's got your dad to keep her busy, and the guesthouse and everything. But if she could drop in every few days for a chat about old times, I know he'd appreciate it."

"Why don't *you* ask her? Why me?"

"He's scared of her," said Bonnie, shamelessly getting involved. "Like most people."

"Not at all," he snapped at her. "But it seemed sensible to run it past Simmy first. And I wasn't sure what would be a good time — or how to go about it. Phone? In person?"

"Text. Email," added Bonnie with naked sarcasm.

He gave her a stern adult-to-child look, which made no impact on her at all. He was barely old enough to be her father, Simmy reflected. And he looked even younger than his thirty-six years.

"Quite honestly, I can't see it working," said Simmy. "She really does have her hands full already. And she's not a very good carer at the best of times."

"He doesn't need a *carer*, for the love of Mike. He just needs a bit of company, someone who's known him most of his life and could have a good chat with him."

34

"All the same, it really isn't her thing. As my father said, it was her and Fran who were the friends. The husbands were almost incidental." She thought again of the wife-swapping comment, and quelled a smile. "I did say I'd go and see him now and then — but I can't promise to do it regularly."

They fell quiet, apparently at an impasse. "Why do you need anybody, anyway?" Simmy said eventually. "The man has five children and any number of grandchildren."

"He prefers female company. And the grandchildren are all far too young to provide what he needs. He never was very keen on kids, if you remember. He wants a replacement for Mum, to put it baldly. He's always liked talking to women, about their houses and furnishings and that sort of stuff. He's worked in carpets all his life, don't forget. He knows about colours and curtains and how to hide the television cables."

Simmy inwardly rolled her eyes at the thought of chatting to Kit Henderson about interior design. Besides, she said to herself, that was almost certainly *not* what the man would choose as a topic of conversation. Eddie was naive to think so.

"I could go sometimes, if you like," said Bonnie, with a charming air of diffidence. "He sounds like a nice man."

Both the adults looked at her in astonishment. Simmy's first instinct was to veto the idea completely. Something about a lamb walking into a lion's den came to mind. Kit Henderson *was* a bit like a lion, she

35

realised. He had often been irritable and something of a tyrant in the seaside years. Any glitch in the arrangements, or bad weather, or childhood illness angered him. "I only get two weeks' holiday a year, and I won't let you lot spoil it," was a familiar cry. Without any discussion, his family and the three Straws had all colluded in making his holidays go smoothly. Now here was his son devoting time and effort to ensuring that he was cared for in his bereavement, in much the same pattern.

"He's not all that nice," said Simmy. "Sorry, Eddie, but you know it's true. You've all indulged him for most of his life, and now you're still doing it. I know he's prone to confusion and forgets things, like a lot of men his age, but he's not incompetent. He can go to clubs or groups and make friends for himself. He can get his own meals and go out for walks. And he should be made to appreciate his sons a bit more. Christopher lives only a few miles away . . ." She tailed off, suddenly aware that she too was trying to organise Kit's life for him.

"Christopher is nearly *twenty* miles away, and that auction house of his takes about eighty hours a week of his time — or so he says."

Bonnie squealed. "*Eighty hours!* That's nearly twelve hours a day, isn't it? Seven twelves are eighty-four. That can't be right. Doesn't he get a day off?"

Eddie emitted a spluttering little laugh. "You're right. Seven twelves *are* eighty-four, and no, he doesn't work that much. But he does sit there for six hours without any food or drink on a Saturday, doing his auctioneering act. And people are constantly asking him to value their silver teapots and chipped old plates. If he doesn't know, he has to look it up. I guess it's fairly full on."

"Sounds great," said Bonnie, a trifle wistfully. "Ben would love that."

"Ben loves everything," said Simmy, thinking that most people probably found auctions exciting and romantic. She even fancied going along one day herself to watch Christopher in action. She could go with her mother, perhaps, for at least part of an upcoming Saturday.

The arrival of a customer cut the dilatory discussion short, and Eddie went away, with a rueful expression. "At least you got your mum out of doing it," said Bonnie. "Where does his father live?"

"Glebe Road. It's a rather old-fashioned bungalow."

"What number?"

Simmy was watching the customer as she browsed amongst the buckets of cut flowers, trying to assess the potential sale. "I can't remember. I just know the house," she answered. Bonnie let the matter drop, and the customer made a substantial purchase. The day was well under way, and it was easy to forget all about the Henderson family. Approaches to local restaurants for special Christmas displays were the main task, and Simmy found herself with a modest list of commissions after a few phone calls. "Better than last year, anyhow," she said.

"That's great," Bonnie applauded. "And there's loads of places you still haven't tried."

"Not in Bowness and Windermere there aren't. And if I try to spread out to Staveley or Ambleside, I'll run up against the competition, and probably annoy them."

"Let the best man win, I say. If yours are better, that's fair enough. That's what competition is all about," she finished with a severe look.

Simmy smiled. "I'm sure you're right," she said. There were moments when Bonnie was obviously speaking for either Melanie Todd or Ben Harkness, both of whom felt that the florist could be making a much bigger success of things if only she would stop being so soft about everything.

As often happened, Ben himself put in an appearance at half past three. Bonnie had clearly been saving up news to tell him, and after their habitual fond kiss, which Simmy always found very endearing, the girl began to update him.

"You know that Henderson family — the wife died? She was Simmy's mum's best friend. The funeral was last week."

"Yes," he said with exaggerated patience. Ben never had any difficulty in keeping up with local people and their doings. "What about them?"

"One of the sons came in today, early, and wanted Sim to tell her mother to go and visit the old man, because he likes talking to women, and might get lonely."

The boy snorted. "Some chance!"

"That's what Simmy told him — didn't you?" She invited her employer into the conversation, with a

38

cheery look. "She said her mum was no good as a carer, and anyway the old dad isn't very nice."

Simmy winced. Had she really said that?

Ben nodded. "My mum knows him a bit — because of the carpets. He's a real expert. It's not actually architecture, obviously, but my mum gets asked sometimes. She's got him on her database."

Mrs Harkness was an architect at the peak of her powers, working mainly from home, while juggling five children and a husband. Ben was her second, and more of a challenge than the others all added together. The fact that Ben knew the contents of her database came as no surprise.

"I said I might go and visit him, but they didn't seem to think that was a good idea." Bonnie threw Simmy a look somewhat less fond than the first one.

"I could go with you," said Ben carelessly. "If you like. It's only a few minutes from my house, anyway."

"You know where he lives, then?"

"It's that big ugly bungalow in Glebe Road," he nodded. "He's there on his own now, then? None of his sons or daughters want to live with him, I guess."

"They've all got lives to get on with, and most of them have families already," said Simmy defensively. "They might ask him to move in with one of them, I suppose, but Eddie didn't say anything like that."

"So he tried to delegate it." He looked at his girlfriend. "It's not your problem, kid. It's not even *Simmy*'s problem. The world's full of old people on their own. You can't feel sorry for all of them."

Bonnie narrowed her eyes at him. "Logic, Ben. Watch the logic. You're arguing from the general to the particular. I never said I wanted to visit all of them — just this one."

"I can't see why you should," said Simmy. "He really isn't very interesting."

"Maybe not, but I get the feeling his son might be," said Bonnie slyly.

"Who? Eddie?" Simmy was bemused.

"Not Eddie — his big brother. Christopher. I saw you with him last week, when he came in about the funeral flowers." She giggled. "I've never seen you like that with a man before."

"I've literally known him all my life. How do you expect me to be with him?"

Bonnie said nothing more, and Ben knew better than to speak out of turn. A moment later the telephone rang about an order and the subject was dropped. Ben hung around for another ten minutes and then wandered out into the dark street, where evening had come even earlier than usual, thanks to the persistent cloud. "Meet you down there," he said over his shoulder to his girlfriend. Simmy fleetingly wondered how the arrangement had been made so swiftly and certainly. It sometimes seemed that the youngsters communicated by telepathy.

Bonnie left at five, with Simmy planning a further hour or so creating a display needed for the following morning. "See you tomorrow," she said absently. "Thanks, Bonnie." She was constructing a substantial piece for a local hotel to position in the foyer. It consisted mostly of evergreens and berries, with a group of hothouse gerberas in the centre. Their stalks were floppy and uncooperative, until she was forced to wire them from top to bottom — a fiddly and time-consuming task.

Her mobile warbled at her while she had her hands fully occupied, but she managed to reach it after a few seconds, stretching across to the shelf where she'd left it, still holding the flowers in place with the other hand.

"Simmy?" came Bonnie's little voice, sounding even more childlike and breathless than normal. "We're at Mr Henderson's house, and I think he must be dead. We can see him lying on the floor, in the living room. Ben's calling the police now. I thought you'd want to know right away. No, that's not really right. I wanted to hear your voice. It's really *scary*. We think he must be *dead*."

Carefully, Simmy released the drooping gerbera, and put her free hand over her stomach. "He must have had a heart attack or something," she said.

"No, I don't think so. There's a terrible lot of blood. Ben says somebody's killed him."

CHAPTER
FOUR

Simmy's immediate response, which lasted roughly five seconds, had been to assume that Bonnie was making a singularly insensitive joke. There had been a number of murders and criminal acts that had involved Simmy and Ben, over the past year, with Bonnie being drawn into the maelstrom as well, since becoming part of Persimmon Petals. Melanie Todd, who Bonnie had replaced in the shop, also counted herself as one of the little gang of amateur sleuths, but in reality she had generally been very much on the sidelines. One major exception had been that summer, when the girl had cradled a dead man's head in her lap on the edge of a lake. If there was now another murder, Melanie was going to find herself entirely out of the picture, and Simmy presumed that this would be just as she wanted it.

The entire distressing history flashed through Simmy's mind, even before Bonnie finished speaking. By then, Simmy had understood that the girl wasn't joking. And yet there was no conceivable reason why Kit Henderson should come to a violent end in his own living room. Unless . . . "It must be suicide," she said. "That must have been what Eddie was worried about this morning." She thought back over the conversation. "Although he never said anything about it, did he?"

Bonnie was still breathless, almost whispering. "He didn't do it to himself, Simmy. No way. It's much more horrible than that."

"Oh. Why are you phoning *me* about it?" This question burst from her with some force. "It has nothing whatsoever to do with me, does it?"

"Simmy —" Then she was cut off, with sounds of a car engine, doors slamming, male voices. "I'd better go."

At least I haven't just delivered any flowers to him, Simmy thought. There had been occasions where the very fact of a floral tribute had appeared to precipitate violence. Or at least it had drawn her into something she would otherwise have been oblivious to. Although, there *had* been Henderson flowers only a few days before, because there had been a funeral, and Frances had liked the idea of a lot of bright and scented wreaths on her coffin, and made sure everybody knew it. The day before she died, she had summoned all her children to the house, where she had seated herself in a deep armchair and given her instructions. Christopher had described the scene to Simmy and Angie after the funeral, making Angie almost starry-eyed with admiration. "She was always such a strong woman," she sighed. "What a wonderful way to go." The dying woman's refusal to enter into detailed discussions with Angie over her imminent fate had all been forgiven in that moment.

Simmy was still in the back room, the gerberas still refusing to stand up straight, the phone still in her hand. What ought she to do? She had been given the most unwelcome kind of information, and then left to deal with it as best she might. The loss of Kit was not a personal blow. Even Angie would admit as much. With Frances gone, taking with her nearly forty years' worth of friendship and shared memories, Kit had already become almost incidental. A bigger concern was Russell, who might extrapolate the man's murder to mean he himself was equally in danger. "I'm a husband, as well," he might say, with his recently loosening logic. "It might happen to me."

The obvious explanation had to be that an intruder had been caught by Kit, who had been overzealous in defending himself. Perhaps the old man had gone for the robber with a poker. Weren't burglars very often drugged-up and volatile, barely responsible for their actions? Some nasty little lowlife might have simply chosen the bungalow at random, for its shadowy position and unlocked door. Although, if that turned out to be the truth of it, there was even more reason to worry about Russell. Paranoia had been his prime symptom over the past several months, and this could only fuel it further.

Angrily, Simmy slammed the unoffending phone onto the bench, abandoned the flowers and went through to the shop. She turned off the lights and checked the locks on the street door. Then she went out of the back, into the small streets, where she had left her car that morning. But once in the driving seat, she could not decide where to go. Home to Troutbeck? Or down to Bowness? Or even leave the vehicle where it was, and walk the short distance to her parents' house?

Bonnie had done a wrong thing by phoning her when she did. An hour later would have been better: the police would have taken charge, filled in their initial fact sheets and chivvied the youngsters well clear of the scene. As it was, she had been dumped on, and she didn't like it. There was nobody she could think of who could provide a lap strong enough to receive the news in their turn. So Simmy was stuck with it, and that wasn't fair. If she ran to her mother and told her what had happened, that would only cause upset before it needed to be caused.

The loneliness of her situation hit her. She had nobody she could simply go home to, cuddle up with and let the world go its own wicked way without her having to worry about it. She felt exposed and friendless, on that dreary November evening. A man was dead for no good reason, found by two excitable young people who had each other to confide in. Ben would treat it as an intellectual puzzle, and Bonnie would shed the initial shock and fear in the process of assisting Ben.

She was saved by the phone ringing, as she went on sitting in the unmoving car. "Simmy," came Ben's welcome voice. "Where are you?"

She told him, adding, "I don't know what to do. It's none of my business, is it? Why did Bonnie have to phone me when she did? I've been in a real state ever since."

"She just wanted to hear your voice, I think. She was left out there when I went in the house, and then I called the cops. I didn't think about her at all," he admitted with a long palpable sigh. Simmy could almost feel the breath in her ear.

"She said there was a lot of blood."

"A fair amount, yeah. And it's no good you saying it's got nothing to do with you."

"Why? What do you mean?"

"The man was holding a piece of paper with your name on it, for one thing."

Simmy pressed back in her seat, instinctively trying to escape. Then reason kicked in. "That's only because of the will and my bequest. He was probably having another look at it when the intruder barged in and killed him."

"Bequest?" Ben repeated, as if the word were new to him. "What bequest?"

"Frances left me a book. I forgot to tell you. That's why I went there yesterday, after work. I've known the family literally all my life. She wanted me to have a little something. It's not a bit important."

"I expect it is. I *knew* there must be something like that. Bonnie said it was just that you'd gone to the funeral with your mum, and the Hendersons were practically the only people you knew in the area when you came to live here."

"You've been talking about me, have you?"

"For the past twenty minutes we have, yes. The police made us go away, but I'd seen the bit of paper, and the open door, and the mugs of cold tea. They should know by now that I'm not stupid."

"Everybody knows that, Ben," said Simmy wearily. "What open door?"

"When we got there, the front door was open — just a little bit, not wide. I thought it meant someone had forced it, and broken the catch, so it wouldn't shut properly, but that wasn't it. They'd just run off without pulling it shut behind them. Don't you think that's weird?"

"Not really. I imagine that a person might not be thinking very straight if they'd just committed murder. Maybe he did leave it wide open and it blew nearly shut after he'd gone."

"No. I think he — or she — was still there when Bonnie and I showed up. They'd been intending to make a quick getaway, so left it open while they were in the house. That's what I thought at first, but it doesn't really work. There might have been a change of plan and he — they — whoever — went out the back way. I heard the kitchen door bang. I was *right there*, Simmy. Practically in the house with a killer." He sounded proud, as if somehow due credit. "And I didn't panic. I walked all round to check, and noted how everything had been left."

"But you didn't see anything?"

"Sadly not. Nor did Bonnie."

"And Kit?"

"What about him?"

"Well — was he . . .? You know." She couldn't say, *Did he die in your arms? Did he say anything? Could you perhaps have saved him?*

"You mean, was he already dead. Yes, he was, just. The blood wasn't flowing. His eyes were glazed. He'd been stabbed about three times, in different places. The wounds were really obvious, with blood all round them. They did it with a pair of sharp scissors. They were on the floor beside him." He was barely coherent, pouring out every gruesome detail.

Simmy stopped him. "No, Ben," she said. "That's enough. Let me think for a minute. It's all so ghastly. I mean — *scissors*? Wouldn't that take an awful lot of force?" She didn't want to talk about it, to imagine it and wonder exactly what it had been like, but neither could she avoid it.

"They were open, I guess. So just one blade was used. I didn't touch them," he added quickly. "At least, I don't *think* I did. It's all a bit blurred now, what happened in the first minute or so. They weren't still sticking in him, anyway."

"Scissors," Simmy said again faintly. Everybody had a pair in their possession, which meant that everybody had the means to commit murder. The everydayness of it added to the horror. And Ben had said it was a repeated attack. In and out, in again — perhaps in "a frenzy", as the police might say. The pain must have been appalling. Pain, fear, shock, disbelief.

"Poor, *poor* Kit. What a terrible thing."

"Yes. It came from the front, right into his chest. It didn't look as if he fought back, either." He went silent for a moment, although Simmy could very nearly hear him thinking. "You know, there's a lot of absolute

48

nonsense talked about the dead. They are so . . . I don't know . . . inert. Passive . . ."

"Dead," she finished for him. "That's what dead *is*, Ben." She thought, for the hundred-thousandth time of her own dead baby, inert in her arms, and knew that she was fully conversant with the definition of death.

"And their faces go all loose and relaxed. Expressionless. Even if they died in terrible agony, it couldn't possibly leave any trace, once all the muscles let go. It's really very interesting," he concluded with an appalling lack of emotion.

"Somebody deliberately killed him," she said severely. "It's the worst thing a person can do. And you should not have been there. Nor should Bonnie. That was my fault."

"Come off it. You're not telling me you knew we'd coincide with a killer, are you? Because only if you purposely set it all up can you claim any kind of responsibility. That is, for me and Bonnie being there. There might be more mileage in having a look at this bequest thing. That sounds to me as if it could well be useful in the investigation. Are you going to call Moxo about it, or shall I?"

"Moxo" was Detective Inspector Nolan Moxon, well known to Simmy, Ben and all their friends and relations, having been comprehensively assisted by them in a number of previous murder cases. He and Simmy had developed a friendship increasingly enriched by mutual respect and understanding. He had patiently waited for her to like him, making no secret of how much *he* liked *her*. He was one of the few people

49

she allowed to see how alone and vulnerable she often felt. Beneath the respect and liking and understanding, there lay a solid stratum of trust, born of extreme danger at certain moments in the recent past.

"He's going to want to see you pretty soon, isn't he?" she said. "You being the one who found the body."

"Right. I'm there now, as it happens. He's due back within the hour, once he's done all the business at the house."

"So you tell him about my bequest. Be my guest. Tell him I'm going home now, and will be in bed by ten, so if he wants to ask me some questions, it'll have to wait until tomorrow." She looked at her watch. It was half past seven. "And don't let him keep you late. I bet you've got plenty of homework."

He made a sound that could only be termed a guffaw. "Don't worry about that. This is the best homework I could hope for. Actual real-life forensics. Real *death*, I mean." He laughed again. "All the lessons and books and films in the world can't make up for the thing itself."

"Stop it," she ordered. At any moment he was going to say how lucky he was to have been the first on the murder scene. And if he said that, there would be small flickers of suspicion in the mind of the police that it was possibly a little bit *too* lucky. And if there was that kind of thinking about Ben, could it not all too easily extend to Simmy as well?

Ben was following her thoughts. "They will be a bit discomposed by the coincidence," he realised. "After all, I didn't have a very good reason for being there, did I?"

"It was Bonnie's idea." That, too, was an unsettling thought. "And I went along with it. I *colluded*."

"Well, then," he said, as if there was no more reason to worry.

The conversation ended with Simmy feeling both better and worse. Better because she knew more of the story, worse because she could see no way of avoiding yet another involvement. She drove home, trying to construct a picture from the facts she knew. It wasn't long before she was asking herself — what of George and Eddie and Christopher and their sisters? This second major bereavement within a fortnight would knock them all sideways. There would be reproach and recrimination, with Eddie claiming to have known there was cause for concern, and the others wondering if there had been more they could have done.

Or — and the thought knocked the breath out of her — what if one of *them* had killed the old man, from some long-standing resentment or injustice? What if Hannah or George or Eddie or Lynn had done it? Even, unthinkably, the eldest and best of them — Christopher himself?

CHAPTER
FIVE

Wednesday morning dawned even more slowly and darkly than the previous day had done. The very word "dawn" was a joke. Night seemed to hold on, fighting off the feeble sun, until well into the official daytime hours. Outside Simmy's house there were cars passing, their headlights on, their drivers half asleep like hibernating animals prematurely woken. She made no attempt to hurry over breakfast — which comprised porridge and scrambled eggs, because lunch was always meagre or non-existent. She resisted thoughts about Kit Henderson lying dead on the floor, and Bonnie being upset at the sight of him. Instead, she approached the matter sideways, via the book Frances had left her. She took it down from the mantelpiece where she had placed it on Monday evening. Somehow she felt even less worthy of it than she had at the start. Frances had snubbed her own daughters, as well as a daughter-in-law. Eddie had a wife who might well have enjoyed it, and George was apparently in a relationship with a woman named Leonora, who had come with him to his mother's funeral.

The book had something over fifty pages, like a large photo album. It was handsomely bound, with marbled endpapers. Somebody had made a proper project of it, preserving the paintings it contained. The story she had so far was nowhere near complete, she realised. There was a lot more meaning than she had first appreciated. There were tissue leaves protecting every picture, the whole thing harking back to an earlier century where people took care over their handiwork. But how much had Frances herself loved it? Had she been as careless of her mother's treasured artwork as her own daughters seemed to be? Had her father perhaps arranged the professional binding as a gift to his wife? There ought to be a dedication or explanation somewhere, surely? All the first page said was "Flower Paintings by Clarissa Edwards" in flowing calligraphy.

Simmy knew absolutely nothing about this Clarissa Edwards. The grandmother had never joined the family on their beach holidays. Frances had never mentioned her, so far as she could recall, and neither had her children. She had presumably died long ago — possibly even before Simmy (and therefore Christopher) had been born.

The pictures really were very individualistic. As a florist, Simmy had paid attention to innumerable cards and prints depicting a wide variety of blooms. She was familiar with the lush work of Georgia O'Keeffe, the delicate botanical drawings of the eighteenth century, and the precision accuracy of many Victorian watercolourists. Clarissa Edwards was like none of these. For a start, she had been careless with colour, as well as proportion. Her flowers were huge, their leaves unnaturally tiny. There were some strangely pink bluebells, and even stranger orange buttercups. And yet there was a rightness and easy recognisability to them that made Simmy feel they were almost within her grasp. The artist had filled every sheet of paper almost to the very edge, bordering the blooms with interwoven leaves and stems that served to highlight the main element with considerable drama. The same effect was achieved on almost every page. Each picture must have occupied many hours. It was the sort of creation a Victorian lady of uncertain health might devote weeks and months to, for want of any other claim on her time. But in the 1950s, women were far from idle. They were expected to keep their houses spotlessly clean, their families in neat and well-pressed clothes, with all the buttons in place. They might read a book from time to time, or possibly even stitch a needlepoint picture in the evenings, but they didn't paint exuberant pictures of flowers unless there was money in it.

Or unless they happened to be in a state of uncertain health, perhaps, like their grandmothers so often were. Was Clarissa bedbound? Did she break her back in her twenties and spend the rest of her life on a sofa? How many children did she have? Where did she live and what did her husband do for a living?

Angie would know. Angie probably assumed that Simmy had absorbed the story simply by being amongst the Hendersons so much as a child. There were times when Simmy's mother took it for granted that her daughter knew everything that she knew herself, and remembered events in exactly the same detail. To some extent this was justified. As an only child, Simmy had listened more closely to her parents' stories than other children might. She knew quite a lot about her own grandparents on both sides. She knew all her cousins, down to the second and third sets, if not personally, then by name and location. She had known Christopher well, for their first sixteen years, instinctively aware of his strengths and weaknesses, interests and frustrations. When the families dubbed them "the twins" they did their best to live up to the label. But they never discussed relatives. They talked about TV programmes, books, rock pools and cliff climbs. They built hides and sandcastles, gathering materials obsessively. Thinking back on those years now, Simmy suddenly understood why Ben Harkness had felt so familiar when she first met him. In a few ways, he was Christopher Henderson reborn. But in other ways he was completely different, of course. They might both enjoy making things from sticks and leaves, but no way would Christopher ever take an interest in the minutiae of murder, as Ben so obsessively did.

She was late. Bonnie would be wondering where she was. With a strong reluctance, she put on her warm coat and found the key to her car. And then, as she forced herself to confront the likely course of the day, she tucked the flower book under her arm, and took it out to the car with her. At some point, somebody was sure to ask to see it. Most likely, that someone would be DI Nolan Moxon.

Bonnie arrived at the same moment as Simmy did — both of them ten minutes past the appointed hour.

55

Neither made reference to this, by silent mutual consent. There were good reasons, after all. "Grim weather," said Simmy. "Are you warm enough?" The girl was wearing a thin jersey under a leather jacket. As many times before, Simmy wondered at the consistently good quality of Bonnie's clothes. She had never got round to asking about it.

Bonnie said nothing, but shrugged off the jacket and stood waiting for instructions. There was a midweek delivery due at any moment, which meant a wholesale reorganising of stock. Tired blooms were thrown away and fresh displays arranged. It was this that made Wednesdays more interesting and enjoyable than most other days. "I don't want to talk about what happened yesterday," said Bonnie, after a few minutes. "If that's all right with you."

"It's probably very sensible," said Simmy. "At least for now. We can't avoid it for ever, of course. I dare say we'll get a call from the police before long."

"Mm," said Bonnie, clearly determined to maintain silence on the subject. Simmy was impressed, and only slightly concerned. There were other people to act as counsellor or debriefer or whatever. Bonnie would not be left alone with her traumatic experience. Rather stronger than the concern was a sneaking sense of disappointment, even rejection. She had, she realised, assumed that she was the first person Bonnie would confide in, rather than almost the last.

An hour later, the fun of arranging flowers was over and Simmy was thinking about coffee. Not a single customer had disturbed them. Normality was resuming

— if indeed it had ever really been lost. If Bonnie hadn't phoned her from the Bowness bungalow, she might never have known Kit Henderson was dead. And it was entirely possible that her parents still didn't know. When that thought struck her, she knew she would have to tell them. The police might extend their enquiries to Angie, in any case, as a close family friend. Angie would have a comprehensive knowledge of the relationships and tensions going back over the decades. Simmy wondered whether she ought to make this clear to Moxon, or leave him to find it out from some other source.

Ben would be at school — or college, as they called it once they reached his age. His ambitions demanded an unreasonable number of A-level passes, and every moment was filled with study, during the hours he spent there. Even at home he devoted himself to Latin translations, forensic researches and software development. Simmy had abandoned any attempt to keep up with him, but Bonnie cleverly got herself included in much of his work. She had even picked up a grounding in Latin, working through *Gwynne's Latin* with an astonishing diligence. Ben's admiration was all she needed to keep going, but the added thrill of recognising the origins of flower names, or working out the meaning of everyday phrases made the whole business remarkably satisfying. "They never told us *any* of this at school," she marvelled, having reached Chapter Seven, which explained about verbs and tenses. "How could they be so neglectful?"

Simmy herself had to think hard before she could define the first or third person, and was momentarily stumped when wondering what the second person must be. "Good question," she agreed, while privately thinking that ordinary life did not really require such information. She marvelled at Bonnie's dedication, and hoped it was stretching her mind and opening new opportunities for her. But she did not regret her own ignorance.

The familiar croak of the defective doorbell announced a customer at last. Somebody somewhere must want some flowers, surely, thought Simmy as she turned to see who it was.

Not somebody wanting flowers, regrettably. It was her mother, looking confrontational. Standing tall, shoulders back, she made a striking figure. People did not mess with Angie Straw. The guests in her B&B did as she told them, without question. Luckily for them — and for her business — she was very relaxed about what they could and could not do. Laissez-faire was the order of the day at Beck View. Dogs, cigarettes and muddy children were all welcomed. It suited Angie to let standards slip, and she made a virtue of it. No useless embroidered cushions cluttering the beds, or fiddly little cartons of synthetic milk.

"P'Simmon," she began. "What's this I hear about Kit Henderson? Why did I have to be told about it by the postman, of all people? The *postman*," she repeated. "What sort of a cliché is that?"

"I was going to tell you," said Simmy. "Bonnie and Ben found him last night. Eddie came here yesterday and said Kit would appreciate a visit now and then. He was lonely and sad. He actually wanted *you* to go, and I said you'd be too busy. Bonnie volunteered, and Ben went as well. And they got there right after somebody had killed him."

Angie looked from her daughter to the fair-haired girl-child at her side. Angie was still trying to get a proper impression of Bonnie, as were most people. After a troubled start, she had been fostered by a local woman, with troubles slowly falling away, via anorexia and almost total failure at schoolwork. The final rescue and rehabilitation had been accomplished by young Ben Harkness.

"Eddie wanted me to take his father on, as well as Russell and the business and the dog and —"

"I told him you wouldn't have time."

"Quite right. What an idea!" Indignation bristled from her. "The man's got *five children*, for goodness' sake. Not to mention old girlfriends and workmates and God knows what. With Frances dead, some woman would snap him up within weeks, anyway. They always do, don't they?" It was a sour point with Angie, the way any useless man was regarded as a trophy by a certain sort of woman.

"I doubt it, the way his wits were going," said Simmy.

"He wasn't so bad. Fran exaggerated it. Russell's much worse."

"Anyway, that's all I know about it. Bonnie doesn't want to go over the whole thing again, so we decided to leave it until the police come to question us. They might want you, I suppose," she added, with a hint of malice. Her mother's cool heart sometimes took things over a line.

"Me? What does it have to do with me?"

"Close family friend," said Simmy.

"Rubbish. I wasn't *his* friend. I kept away from him as much as I could."

"Did you?" Simmy frowned. "I never noticed."

"Well, you wouldn't, would you? It was nothing important — just that I can't be doing with the idea that couples can't operate as individuals. They had almost nothing in common anyway, apart from the kids."

"Oh well. I'm sorry if you think I should have told you about it last night. Bad news can wait, though. You know it can. And with Dad so fragile, I didn't want to upset him."

Angie's indignation mutated into exasperation, and then frustration as the door opened again and another person came in. "And now look who's here," she said. "Time for me to go." She glared at the newcomer, "And you know where to find me, if you want to," she snarled at the startled detective inspector.

CHAPTER
SIX

Simmy made coffee for herself and DI Moxon, and tea for Bonnie. "We're never going to sell any flowers today, at this rate," she sighed. "I'll go bust if it keeps on like this."

"There'll be another funeral soon," said Bonnie softly. "Probably quite a few, actually. Isn't November the month when everybody dies?"

"Not really," said Simmy and Moxon in unison, laughing at each other in the new-found comfort of their friendship. Simmy thought about what her mother always said concerning men as trophies, and knew it was far from being a universal truth. Moxon had a wife who took him for what he was, and appeared relatively contented with it.

"Mr Henderson," he said firmly. "Poor man."

"Yes," said Simmy.

"You knew him — is that right? All we've got so far is testimony from young Mr Harkness, and Mr Henderson junior."

"Which one?"

"The eldest. Christopher. The others are being interviewed today. I gather Mrs Henderson died very recently." He rubbed his cheek. "That feels as if it must be relevant."

"You mean, because it was known that Kit would be in the house by himself?"

"Possibly."

"That's not it, Simmy," Bonnie interrupted. "It's more to do with the *motive*. Something about inheritance, could be."

Simmy's heart lurched. She thought of the lovely book of paintings still on the passenger seat of her car. Had there been other bequests — precious objects left to all the wrong people, and causing murderous resentment as a result? "That's not very likely, is it?" she protested. "The family never had any money."

"Christopher told us about your inheritance," Moxon said. "Once we'd established that you were there on Monday evening, and that you and your parents" — he sighed softly — "have known the Hendersons for nearly forty years." It was a delicate reference to her age, she noticed.

"Thirty-eight years and two weeks, actually," she said. "As I expect he explained."

Bonnie's head seemed to rise from her shoulders like an alert meerkat. "What?" she demanded. "You never told me about any inheritance."

"I told Ben last night. I assumed he'd tell you." Another detail occurred to her, and she turned back to Moxon. "He said Kit was holding a piece of paper with my name on it. Is that right?"

Moxon closed his eyes briefly. "That boy sees a deal too much sometimes."

62

"Well — what was it?"

With a funny little sideways look, as if checking he was not being observed, the detective produced a sheet of paper from a folder he was carrying. "The simplest thing is just to show it to you," he said, and handed it over.

Simmy read it, as she had read the letter from Fran on Monday, with no idea what to expect.

At the top it said, "Instructions to my husband". Then came a list that covered barely half the page:

Think again about getting a dog. It would be wholesome company

Keep the car well maintained, or preferably buy a better one. Visit the children in it

Plant trees in the garden as reminders. Cherry, juniper, hazel and even rowan. I leave the last to your own discretion

Give Simmy Straw my mother's flower book, and the letter with it

Be a better grandfather than you were a father

Simmy looked up at Moxon. "Blimey!" she said. "Sounds as if she wanted what was best for him, even if the tone is a bit . . ."

"Chilly," he supplied.

"And this is what he was holding when he . . ." She looked at the paper again. It was a photocopy, but there were tell-tale smudges across it. "Is that blood?"

He smiled ruefully. "It is. Now, our question is — how did this get into his possession? It wasn't with Mrs

Henderson's will. So where was it, and how did he get hold of it?"

"Couldn't she simply have given it to him?" asked Simmy.

Moxon pursed his lips. "I don't think so. I mean — can you imagine it? It's not the sort of thing you want someone to read while you're alive. So she must have left it somewhere for him to find, or given it to someone to show him after she was dead. And that person might well be the same one who killed him. That's the way the evidence looks at the moment, anyway."

Bonnie had been listening with interest, to the extent of trying to read the list upside down, as she sidled closer to Simmy. Moxon put out a restraining hand. "Now, I wonder if I could talk to Mrs Brown in peace? Could you perhaps go out and get yourself a bit of lunch or something? Just for ten minutes."

Bonnie gave him a defiant look. "I'll go into the back and scrub plant pots," she announced. "I've already got some lunch in my bag."

They watched her go, like indulgent parents. "She got quite a nasty shock," murmured Simmy, once the door into the back room was closed. "Even through the window she could see too much."

"The wounds bled quite copiously," he nodded.

Simmy winced. "Are you sure you should be telling me?"

"I'm sure I shouldn't, but I will anyway. If I don't, your friend Ben will. It was a very violent business."

"Yes, I know. Ben told me already that it was done with a pair of scissors. That's the most horrible thing

64

I've ever heard. Much worse than anything that's happened before. And it makes me feel very sick. My stomach hasn't got any stronger over the past year, in spite of what you might think."

"There's nothing wrong with your stomach," he said. "It's your heart that's soft."

She huffed a quick laugh, part amused relief, part recognition that he was complimenting her. Earlier in the year, she would have taken it as flirtation, or something even stronger. Now she was beyond making that sort of mistake about him.

"So it was an intruder, then? A burglar," she said, "who grabbed the nearest thing that would work as a weapon, because he was disturbed."

Moxon shook his head. "I think not. The door was open and nothing was upset in the room."

"I don't see how any of that proves it wasn't an intruder. It's quite possible that Kit never locked his door, for a start. Someone could just have walked in."

Again the detective shook his head. "Intruders do everything they can to avoid violence. If Mr Henderson was sitting peacefully reading, the robber would tiptoe round the house gathering what he could, and make a quiet getaway."

"What if he wanted something from the room Kit was in?"

"Trust me, okay. It wasn't a total stranger. It was somebody known to the victim. There were two teacups on the table. It looks as if the whole thing began amicably, and developed into a raging fight."

"Who, then? Aren't his fingerprints on one of the cups?"

"Regrettably not. Nor on the murder weapon. It looks as if the killer wore gloves during the whole period he was in the house."

"Well, it is November," said Simmy foolishly.

Moxon did not dignify this with an answer, but simply cocked his head and smiled forbearingly.

"No. Right. Silly me. But don't you think you're wasting your time coming to talk to me? I don't know anything that could possibly be useful. I hate to say it, but you'd learn a lot more from my mother."

He gave an unhappy smile of acknowledgement. "I expect you're right," he said. "But the only significant fact I can get any purchase on so far is the recent death of *Mrs* Henderson. That obviously must have thrown up a whole lot of changes. The balance of power in the family shifts. There's a sudden hole, which lets people express feelings they've been hiding for years. And that list" — he indicated the paper that Simmy was still holding — "it seems to me it must be of central significance."

She looked at him. "Which is why you keep wanting to talk to *me* about it," she realised. "Because here I am, on it."

"There you are," he agreed.

"But what's all that about the balance of power?" She wanted to add, *that doesn't sound like you*. Since when, she wondered, had he learnt all this psychology?

He laughed, as if he'd heard her thought. "They sent me on a course," he admitted. "I only finished it last week. I had to read about early influences and family dynamics and games people play. It was all very big in the eighties, but I wasn't old enough at the time to take it on board."

"Isn't it all terribly out of favour now, though? I thought we were into cognitive behaviour therapy and looking to the future, not the past."

"It seems there's room for both. And I know from recent experience how bitterness can simmer under the surface for years, before it erupts."

She thought back to their shared adventures. "Well, yes, but more often it's people trying to keep somebody quiet, to cover up shameful secrets, and that sort of thing."

"Did Mr Henderson keep faithful to his wife, as far as you know?"

The question was stark, abrupt and shocking. "What?" He waited calmly, until she went on, "I never heard anything about an affair, if that's what you mean. What makes you ask that?"

"Nothing in particular. It just helps to know who the main players are, so to speak. We've got five offspring, three in-laws, an ex-wife and a new girlfriend. I think that's right." He scratched his upper lip, where a mole was beginning to make its presence felt. Simmy wondered how he managed to shave around it.

"I'm impressed. I've never been quite sure whether Hannah was actually married to her chap, but otherwise that's it. George's new girlfriend is the main talking point. I don't think anybody's seen Sophie for ages. I doubt if even Christopher knows where she is now. And Eddie's got the same wife he's always had. They must have been married for about twelve years. They've got two girls, I think. Frances was very fond of them."

"Eddie — the middle son. Yes, tell me more about him. Ben Harkness said it was down to him that he and Bonnie were in Glebe Road yesterday, in the first place."

"Yes. He came here and asked if my mother would be kind enough to visit Kit from time to time. I said I didn't think she'd be up for that, and Bonnie jumped in and said she'd do it."

"But Eddie lives practically on the doorstep, doesn't he? Why did he need your mother, when he's got a wife and daughters who could give the old man some company?"

Simmy tried to salvage some shreds of information, gleaned at the funeral and over the years from her mother. "I have a feeling they didn't get on," she managed, eventually. "The wife and Kit. She's always been a bit of a snob, and I think she looked down on him. It's only a vague impression. You'll have to ask my mother," she concluded again. "Sorry, but there's no dodging it. She's your main source of background material on this one. I'm starting to discover just how much I missed over the years. I never even knew that Hannah and Lynn were adopted."

"Really? I mean — were they?"

"You didn't know?"

"It's not the sort of thing that comes up, unless there's a clear reason for asking. Was it kept a secret?"

"Not at all. I just totally failed to notice. I was only about seven at the time, but apparently I was a singularly incurious child. Still am, I suppose."

He shook his head slowly. "No more than most. In any case, they seem to be a reasonably united family. All still living in the area, taking good care of their mother in her last weeks. She must have been a brave lady, tying up all the loose ends like that. Leaving you that book was just something she wanted to be taken care of, as far as I can see. Like the other things."

"I never thought of her as especially organised," Simmy mused. "I suppose if you know you're dying in a few weeks' time, it concentrates the mind. Bit late to start planting trees, though, at Kit's age."

"She was very specific." Again he indicated the paper. "Wanted a juniper and a cherry. I think they grow quite fast, don't they?"

"Cherries do, but I'm not sure about junipers. Let me think — conifers, often a bluey colour. Actually, I think they are quite fast-growing. And not very suitable for a small garden. Hazels and rowans are fairly sensible, though. But it won't be happening now, I suppose." Implications began to occur to her. "The bungalow will be sold, and the proceeds divided five ways. That's not a bad little inheritance, assuming the mortgage was paid off."

"I'm not going to comment."

"Just tell me I wasn't going to get a share as well," she joked awkwardly. "Because that would probably make me a suspect, in your eyes."

"Stranger things have happened, but as far as I'm aware, you're safe. Although I suppose I can tell you that we haven't found any sign of a will in Mr Henderson's name. Early days, obviously, but we know he didn't make one when his wife did. That's unusual, actually."

Simmy was put in mind of detective stories by Dorothy L. Sayers and Agatha Christie where the will was at the heart of the whole case. "Uh-oh," she said. "You'd better focus on that, then."

He ignored the impertinence, and paused to put his thoughts in order. "Could I see the book Mrs Henderson left you? Have you got it here?"

"It's in the car. And the car's in its usual place, a street or two from your house. Do I have to go and fetch it now?" She looked optimistically out into the murky street, wishing for a customer to appear and keep her pinned to the shop. "It can't possibly have anything to do with the murder."

"Hard to see how," he agreed. "But you never know. How about I meet you at your car after work? Five-thirty? Do you remember exactly where you left it?"

"I think so." She told him as closely as she could, and hoped she wouldn't forget the assignation. Five-thirty still seemed a long way ahead.

"Can I come out yet?" came Bonnie's voice. She had opened the door a crack and was peeping through into the shop. "It's been ages."

"Yes, yes. Sorry about that." Moxon rubbed his hands together, as if to announce the end of the interview, and drained the last of his coffee. "See you this evening, then." He nodded at them both and strode out into the street.

"What a funny man he is," said Bonnie. "I don't think he knows what he's doing, half the time."

"He's been on a course, and now he understands psychology a lot better."

"Hah!" scorned Bonnie. "I'll believe that when I see it."

"Maybe he'll surprise us for once. I think he's got a few theories, anyway. And I can't see him letting Ben get involved. He's still getting over last time — and so is Ben's poor mother."

"Too right. You should have heard her last night, when we went back to the house and told her what had happened. She went as white as snow with the shock. She knew the Henderson man, remember."

"So she did." Simmy paused. "Did she like him, then?"

"As far as I can gather, most women liked him. She said he had a special way with him. It sounded as if she might have had a bit of a thing for him, ages ago."

Simmy was stunned. "Surely not! He's nothing to look at. He's got almost no sense of humour. *Had* no sense of humour, I mean. He hardly played with his kids when we were on holiday. What could anyone possibly see in him?"

"Don't ask me. Maybe your mum could explain it to you."

"Let's not talk about it any more," said Simmy, as firmly as she could.

"I don't see why you don't want to. You've already said you didn't like him much. It doesn't affect you at all. So why not see if you can work out who did it? What's wrong with that?"

It was a familiar question, to which the answer was always feeble. "I just don't want to," she said.

And then at last there was a little run of customers. It almost amounted to a *surge*, given the quietness of the week so far. One after the other, three people came in search of flowers, to be wrapped and given a card. Two birthdays and an anniversary were all happening the following day, the bouquets to be kept secret and fresh overnight. "It's like a conspiracy," said Simmy, when the last one had gone. "As if they planned it."

"It's the lunch hour," Bonnie pointed out. "And every day is somebody's birthday."

"Hmm," said Simmy. "Well now we'll have to get some more carnations, roses and lilies from the back room. That chap with the anniversary's wiped them out, look."

"He did go a bit mad. Feeling guilty, I presume." It was a well-worn observation, no less true for that. Many such discoveries had marked Simmy's first weeks as a florist. Motives for buying flowers turned out to be a lot darker than she had ever imagined. It could even be an act of malice, in extreme circumstances.

Deftly, Bonnie refilled the buckets that held the stock, ranking them by shade and size in a fashion she had made her own, right from the start. Her flair for design was far beyond the ordinary, and she never ran out of ideas for the displays on the shop floor and in the

72

window. In November, there was almost nothing on the pavement outside, but during the summer she had extended her skills by arranging enticingly scented and coloured blooms where passers-by couldn't fail to notice them.

Lunch was eaten carelessly, standing in their little area beside the till, watching the computer screen for new orders. Time passed slowly, with no further intrusions, and Simmy's veto on discussing the Henderson affair holding good. "This is tedious," said Bonnie, at two o'clock. "Should we be making something happen? What about calling some of those hotels in Ambleside? Weren't we going to do that this week?"

"So we were. Why don't you make me a list, with the phone numbers? You can find them on the tourist website."

"Or TripAdvisor, or about ten other places," nodded Bonnie. "Do you want me to make a real list, with a pen?" She gazed with wide-eyed interest at her employer. "Like in the olden days."

"Yes, please. Just like Ben would tell you. Just like any sensible person would do."

They both giggled at the thought of their shared affection for the boy who possessed the skills and knowledge of every century since Roman times, as comfortable with Latin as he was with computer languages.

"He should be here in another hour or so," said Bonnie, as if every intervening minute would be a torment.

CHAPTER
SEVEN

Ben was late, and because things were so quiet, Simmy urged him and Bonnie to go home earlier than the usual five o'clock. "It's so dark and horrible," she said. "You'd be best off in a nice warm house." Which house was up to them. Bonnie lived with her foster mother, Corinne, and Ben was one of a big family in a big Bowness house. There was a distance of roughly half a mile between the two.

Her wish to see them go was partly born of her own appointment with DI Moxon. He hadn't phoned her to change the arrangement, so she assumed he would knock off at around five, despite the fact of an ongoing murder investigation. Or would he be making a special trip to the street where her car was sitting, only to go back to the police station afterwards? Again, she let the question drop, as being irrelevant. Simmy Brown was no control freak; she let people do whatever seemed best to them, without either enquiry or interference. Now and then she wondered whether this was a virtue, or a selfish lack of genuine interest in other people. Her father would cross-examine the B&B guests as to the route they had taken from their homes in Essex or Lincolnshire, correcting any perceived errors, and then issue minute instructions as to how to get to Grasmere or Kirkstone, including every landmark along the way.

"It's as if you don't trust them to live their own lives," his wife would accuse, from time to time.

The daylight was completely gone by five, the streets of Windermere monochrome and deserted. She could smell woodsmoke on the air, from the stoves that everybody was suddenly using, burning trees in their thousands, with no apparent disquiet. Ben could present a five-minute dissertation on the subject, with only the slightest provocation. Whilst having no personal antagonism to the practice, he nonetheless dwelt scornfully on the complete absence of logic. "People cannot abide too much reality," said Simmy. "Or whatever the quote is. They just like the look of a real flame burning."

"Yes, I know," he patiently replied. "And it's 'humankind cannot bear very much reality'. You were almost right," he applauded. "It's T. S. Eliot."

"I'm impressed by myself," she had laughed.

Thoughts of Ben were much too often at the front of her mind, she decided. His firm opinions, infinite stock of quotes and facts, and intense interest in the world — all made him impossible to ignore. She often reran conversations with him, savouring the intelligence that he must have been born with, and which he exploited to the full. Nobody doubted that once he became an undergraduate, he would be a star of *University Challenge* as well as the favourite of all the tutors.

She was at her car before she knew it. But Moxon was nowhere to be seen. Of course, he expected her to leave the shop twenty minutes later than she had actually done, which meant a chilly wait. What an idiot, she reproached herself. Somehow she had assumed he would know by telepathy that she was there, and would magically join her.

Which did very nearly happen, as it turned out. She only had time to get into the driving seat, turn on the radio, and lift Frances Henderson's book onto her lap, before there was a tap on the window beside her.

Two men stood there, both of them welcome faces in different ways. It was a surprise to see them together, and she looked from one to the other in confusion, before opening the car door.

"You're early," said Moxon. "I guessed you might be."

"And Christopher," she said. "Hello."

"So this is the famous flower book, is it?" The detective directed his gaze downwards. "Can I see?"

She handed it to him, saying, "It's what you're here for, isn't it? Don't drop it, will you? It's a bit heavy."

He took it awkwardly, finding no level surface on which to put it down and examine it in the poor light shed by a nearby street lamp. "Use the bonnet," said Christopher. "I'll hold it for you, to stop it sliding off."

"Thanks." Together the men solemnly turned the pages, while Simmy sat half in and half out of her car. There was something comical in the setting, and the intent interest in a book that could mean little or nothing to either of them. If Christopher had ever cared about his grandmother's artistic efforts, he would surely have persuaded his mother to let him have them.

A shade too late, Simmy remembered to say, "Oh, Christopher, I'm so terribly sorry about your father. Such a dreadful thing to happen."

He dipped his head to look at her. "It didn't just *happen*," he snapped. "Somebody deliberately killed him. You can't imagine what that feels like."

"No, I can't." She tried to, managing to glimpse the outrage and fear and sheer numbing shock. The inescapable sense of victimisation and helplessness. If someone was prepared to break the strongest of all the commandments, then there was little chance of defending against that person. Again, words from Ben Harkness came to mind, to the effect that it was only the bonds of convention and social pressure that prevented wholesale slaughter of one against another. Everyone had the means to kill, he pointed out, adding something about a man called Hobbes.

"Sorry, Simmy. I didn't mean to snap. I don't know what I'm doing today. I don't know why I'm here, either." He looked to Moxon for an answer. "What did you want to ask me?"

The inspector gave an uneasy glance towards Simmy. "Just whether you think it can have anything to do with your father's death."

"It?"

"The book. These pictures. Have they got some significance that I'm not seeing?" He looked again at Simmy, with an apologetic grimace. "It's only because of the letter Mr Henderson was holding, you see. As if it was an issue between him and the killer. Do you see?"

"You think somebody else expected to inherit it, and was so angry they stabbed him to death?" Christopher glared at Moxon. "That would be insane. Especially as it had nothing to do with my father — it was Mum who left it to Simmy, not Dad."

"I have to follow everything up," said the detective heavily. "However unlikely it might seem that it concerns the investigation."

"Well?" interjected Simmy. "What do you think now you've seen it?"

"It's very nice."

"It's not worth anything," said Christopher. "And I should know. If it was a hundred years older, it might be. Or if my gran had been famous. As it is, it's just a book of pretty flower pictures, with a good-quality binding."

"Well, I love it," said Simmy defensively.

"My mum must have known you would. So now everybody's happy."

It was entirely the wrong thing to say, twenty-four hours after the murder of one's father, and the dense silence that followed made this clear. "Oh, Lord," Christopher groaned. "What an idiotic remark."

"We know what you meant," said Simmy, looking to Moxon for support. He had not missed the *we*, it seemed, and was trying to convey tolerance and understanding, while still maintaining his role as a detective investigating a murder. People who said they were happy might be regarded as suspicious. Again, Simmy thought of her lifelong friend as a "person of interest", as the saying went. On a whim, she suddenly burst out, "Why don't you come back to Troutbeck with me, and we can have a good long chat? Where's your car?"

Christopher looked startled. Simmy concluded that it wasn't only her who often mislaid a vehicle. The blurred boundary between Windermere and Bowness meant it was quite usual to leave one's car in the former, where the streets were emptier, and walk down into the latter. "Around here somewhere," he said vaguely.

"Well, I must get moving," said Moxon, doing his hand-rubbing routine again. "I'll be in touch with you. Both of you," he added. Something in his eyes made Simmy wince self-consciously. A kind of superior knowingness, tinged with amusement and something a bit more acidic. She brushed it away as irrelevant and nodded a brief farewell.

"Let's go and look for your car, then," she said to Christopher. Already she had worked out that if she offered to take him in hers, he would then be stranded in Troutbeck for the night, and that way complications lay. Far too many complications to be countenanced, in fact.

They found his long silver-coloured estate quite quickly. "I need plenty of space for the job," he explained. "I'm always having to cart boxes of junk to and fro. I'm lucky they don't make me use a van."

"I must come and see you in action sometime," she said idly. "I've never been to an auction. My mum rather fancies it as well. She wants some new china."

"You'd be welcome," he said, without much enthusiasm. "And I must admit, I've almost never been to Troutbeck. Are you sure you want me invading you? What about supper?"

"I can do something quick for both of us, if you like. Sausage, egg and chips. That sort of thing."

"Fantastic," he sighed. "Just like old times."

It wouldn't be at all like old times, but she went along with the fantasy. It was dawning on her that this man was considerably changed from the boy she had known more than twenty years earlier. Their last joint holiday had been when they were sixteen, and there had been a disconcertingly sudden escalation in their feelings for each other. It all came rushing back to her, as she led the way up the steep road to her home. George had been twelve and three-quarters, intolerably sullen and withdrawn, except for the moments when he turned nasty, asking deliberately embarrassing questions of everyone around him, about their deepest feelings and beliefs. Eddie had been fourteen, anxious about his place in both the family and the wider world. He had developed mild asthma and was pale and thin. The weather had been fairly vile for most of the fortnight, too. Simmy had let it all pass her by, barely aware of anything but the alarming physical urges that her body was experiencing, entirely beyond her control. She remembered Angie saying, on the drive home, "That's the last time we do that. We've grown too far apart for it to work any longer." Somewhere Simmy had detected a subtext, but she made no effort to examine it. She was too distraught at the notion that she might never see Christopher again.

The cottage was chilly, and she hurried round turning up the heating and closing the curtains. The sausages she had in mind were a near-forgotten pack at the back of the fridge. Sitting Christopher down at the kitchen table, she admitted that the use-by date had passed. "But only by two days," she added.

"No problem. I've got a cast-iron stomach."

"I guess you would have, after all that travelling."

"What doesn't kill you makes you stronger."

"Mm."

"Simmy — you said on Monday that you'd always liked my dad. Was that true? How much have you seen of him since you came to live here?"

"Gosh! That was a bit sudden. To tell you the truth I haven't seen him at all since then. The last time must have been when I came here to visit, three years ago or thereabouts. My parents and yours were having a pub lunch together in Ambleside and I went along. And I did go to see Fran once or twice when she was ill, but Kit was out each time."

"And *did* you like him?"

"I don't know," she said. "I certainly didn't *dislike* him. He's always been perfectly nice to me, in a distant sort of way." She couldn't say all she was thinking — that Kit had obviously felt his intellectual differences from the Straws. Russell would quote poetry, or discuss plays and films that Kit knew nothing about. Angie reminisced about her wild youth in London, with protest marches a regular activity. She had been to Greenham Common, and waved CND placards. Kit Henderson neither understood nor approved of such antics.

"The two families were not natural allies, were they, when you think about it?"

He shook his head. "Of course they weren't. It was just the accident of the maternity ward that brought us together And my mum's insistence on never letting anybody go. She'd have their addresses off them within minutes, and write to them for the rest of their lives. You would not believe the number of letters she's kept. Loads from your mother, obviously. I think every moment of your childhood must be there, all written down for posterity."

She flinched. The notion of posterity was a painful one in the Straw family. Simmy was a childless only child. The line stopped with her. "My mum really did like Frances," she said. "Your mother had a special knack of making friends that mine really doesn't."

"I'm sorry if I sounded cross. I just don't like the way myths get created and then turned into facts carved in stone. The truth is much more messy and slippery than we let ourselves realise."

She was moving around the kitchen, collecting plates and pans and cooking oil for the makeshift supper. Christopher turned on his chair to follow her back and forth, not letting his eyes leave her face. It felt as if he wanted something from her that was not exactly sympathy or reassurance, but attention and serious consideration of what he was saying. "She told me your sisters are adopted," Simmy said without warning. "I had no idea until yesterday."

"You mean, Angie told you? Why? I mean — how did it arise?"

"With me wondering why one of them didn't get the flower book instead of me."

"Because there's no chance in the world that they'd appreciate it. Either of them. Which has nothing whatsoever to do with them being adopted. They're nice enough girls, but nobody would ever call them artistic. You're the obvious person to have it. And I suspect there was another reason, which is much more embarrassing."

They were sliding from one topic to another, adding to the already worrying image of an amorphous thing called Truth, slipping through their fingers like jelly. Now it was more like being on a fairground ride, where you were directed at random down tunnels and chutes that took you to somewhere unknown. The sausages engaged her for a minute or two, before she remembered she had also promised chips. There was a bag of frozen ones that were supposed to spend twenty minutes in the oven. "I've got this all out of sync," she muttered. "You're distracting me."

"I came here to talk to you, not eat. Leave the chips and just fry some bread or something."

She put down the spatula she'd been holding, and looked at him. "The trouble is, I'm starving hungry, even if you're not. Make yourself coffee or tea, and let me concentrate for a bit."

"Haven't you got any beer or wine?"

"Sadly not. I thought I'd hold off from solitary drinking until I'm over forty. Not long now." It was oddly soothing to know that he knew exactly how old she was. She had always felt that about him, ever since she could remember.

"Don't remind me," he begged. "And neither of us seems to have a lot to show for it. I haven't even got any parents now."

"I've got a shop, and you've got a brilliant job."

"Yeah, right. And we've both got our health, I suppose."

"You never wanted children — is that right?" Her own lost child had been the first thing to spring to mind at Christopher's harsh words about their lack of worldly success. "So it's no point complaining about that now."

"I didn't want them when Sophie wanted them. That was quite some years ago now. I'm a different person."

"So you *do* want them?"

"Do you?"

It stopped her heart, in mid beat. She could feel it suspended in shock, taking her breath with it. The words were like bullets, fired at her point-blank.

"I wish I had the one that died," she shot back. "I wish that about twenty times a day."

"Oh God." He looked at her, stricken. "I forgot."

The hot frying pan was right there, to hand. She could have picked it up and thrown it at him. She could have dashed boiling oil into his face. Who could have blamed her if she had? But she did no such thing. "Well, you won't forget again, will you?" she said.

84

"No. And you won't forget that my father was murdered. We gather these tragedies as we go through life, carrying them on our backs until the weight of them kills us."

She actually laughed at that. The pompous words hinted at self-pity as well as a retreat from the intensity of the moment. "Come off it," she said. "So what was that thing that's so embarrassing? Let's get back to that."

He put his face in his hands, shoulders slumped. "Do we have to do that now? I'm not sure I've got the strength. I didn't sleep for a moment last night, and it's catching up with me. I've got to drive back to Keswick somehow. And then down here again tomorrow, I shouldn't wonder. That police chap seems to keep coming up with more and more questions. And somebody's got to turn everything off in the bungalow and stop any more burglars getting in."

"You think it was a burglar?"

"I *hope* it was," he said, his voice muffled by his hands.

"Humankind cannot bear very much reality," murmured Simmy. "I think I got it right this time. Anyway, eat something, and then if you're too knackered to drive home, I suppose you can stay in my spare bed."

He looked up and smiled wanly. "I think I'll do just that," he said.

CHAPTER
EIGHT

Simmy slept very badly, acutely aware of Christopher in the next room. It had been six months or more since she had entertained an overnight visitor, and the habit of living alone had become deeply engrained. She had recently heard a woman on the radio saying "I like a man in my life, but not in my house" and the truth of it had made her laugh aloud. At the same time, she had worried that this was awful news for men, who generally seemed to want very much to share their home with a woman.

When she did drop off, there were dreams involving seaside and blood and two men fighting over something that looked like a burnt sausage.

They had made no plans for breakfast, but she assumed they would both be impatient to get to work. When she emerged from the bathroom, fully dressed and wondering whether Christopher liked porridge, there was no sound from his room. Should she wake him with a cup of tea, she asked herself. Then a sudden panicky thought hit her: what if he had died as well, during the night? These things went in threes, didn't they? Frances, Kit and then their son — was it so impossible? The irrational terror sent her straight to the closed door, which she knocked on loudly.

"What?" came an equally loud response.

"Sorry. I just wondered whether you'd like some porridge."

"Good God, Simmy. I thought the house was on fire. Are you always so loud in the morning?"

"I've got to get to work. So have you, apparently. Can I come in?"

"It's your house."

That was no kind of an answer, but she opened the door anyway. Christopher was standing by the window in boxer shorts and a T-shirt. "Sorry," she said. "I don't often have visitors."

"And I don't often stay in anyone's house. We need your mum to explain the rules to us."

"I think I should offer you a shower, make you tea in bed and then cook eggs, bacon and black pudding for you."

"Is that what Angie does for her B&B people?"

"More or less. More, actually. Cereal, toast, morning paper and real milk. She's very conscientious."

Christopher glanced down at his phone. "I haven't got time for anything. Harry's going to want to go over the schedule for the next few months, this morning. I'll be late whatever happens."

"Your father's just been murdered. I'm sure he'll make allowances."

He gave her a complicated look — defeat, pain, followed by a clenched-jaw resolve. "I *want* to go to work. You hear people say that, don't you — especially men. It always sounds as if they're trying to avoid the ghastly truth. That's most likely how it is with me, as well. I want life to go on as it was before. I *enjoy* going to work. I don't want Harry to find someone else to do my job."

"What sort of a man would do that?"

"A man whose business is too fragile for interruptions or mistakes. It all has to run like clockwork, and he needs me to see that it does. You have no idea how much there is to do behind the scenes."

"I'd really like to find out sometime."

He stopped obsessing and smiled. "Simmy — you really are an amazingly soothing influence. Did anyone ever tell you that?"

"Not that I can remember."

"Surely you do. When Hannah and George used to fight so savagely, you were always trying to make peace between them."

"Only because I was so scared. I wasn't used to anything like that."

"They're still just as bad, you know. Neither of them will ever miss a chance to upset the other. It must be something chemical."

"I still can't get over the girls being adopted. How come I never realised? My mother assumed you'd told me all about it."

"I didn't want to talk about it. It seemed so strange. There was our teacher explaining about how babies get made, and my parents just seemed to go out and collect a pair of girls with no biology involved at all. They gave us about two days' warning. George was beside himself with rage."

"Which must be why he hated Hannah so much, then."

"Partly, yes. And she was awfully provoking. But he didn't lose anything by their arrival. I never understood it."

"He lost his place as the youngest. Suddenly he was the middle one of five."

"True. But most people really hate being the youngest. I asked him once, when we were in our twenties. He said he couldn't explain it himself. It was just a sort of compulsion that became a habit."

"And she was every bit as bad, if I remember rightly."

"Worse, if anything. Listen — I really must go. Can we carry this on this evening, do you think? I could take you for a meal somewhere as a thank-you-for-having-me sort of thing, if you like."

Only then did Simmy realise that she had missed her usual Wednesday evening visit to her parents. This was now Thursday, and she would be a lot less welcome. On Thursdays beds were changed and freshened for the weekend guests, which outnumbered midweek ones by a considerable margin. Stocks of food were replenished and grill pans cleared of residual grease. Angie had never forbidden Simmy from dropping in, but the quality of her conversation was definitely poor on a Thursday.

"Okay, then," she said. "Thanks very much."

"Meet me in Bowness, then. Seven-thirty at the Chinese. How does that sound?"

"Lovely."

She forced a quick mug of coffee onto him before he drove off into the murky morning. Simmy watched him go from the front door of her cottage, thinking she had no phone number or address for him. The flowers he had commissioned for his mother's funeral had been paid for in cash — well over a hundred pounds for a handsome spray from all the siblings. Kit had used a different florist, somewhat to Christopher's embarrassment. "Typical," Angie had said, as the mourners filed past the pile of tributes at the crematorium. "That man has a perverse streak."

Simmy had been at her mother's side, taking half a day off from the shop and leaving Bonnie in charge. She had only dimly admitted to herself that she'd been motivated by curiosity as to how the Hendersons had turned out since their teenage years, even less that she badly wanted to see Christopher again. She had been to very few funerals in her life thus far, all of them obliterated by the dreadful business of burying her own baby daughter. Angie had been insistent, from a maternal wisdom that Simmy had been slow to notice. "You know — there's a lot that happens at a funeral. It brings back all kinds of stuff from the past, strengthens bonds between those still living. Makes you see how precious time is. I really like funerals," Angie finished. "They're much better than weddings."

And it *had* been a good experience on the whole. Angie's audible comments about the flowers had been awkward, since Lynn and Eddie had both been standing close by, doing their best to pretend they hadn't heard. There had been another instance, in the crematorium, concerning the vicar and his obvious ignorance of Frances Henderson's character. When he said, "A devoted mother and grandmother to her large family, and loving wife to Christopher," Angie had snorted. "Platitudes," she muttered. "And he can't even get the names right."

At the assembly afterwards, in a local hall, eating minimal refreshments, Simmy had relived moments from those seaside years, helped by brief conversations with some of the siblings. "George looks well," she'd said. "I heard he'd been having some problems."

"His liver's been playing up. Scared him into giving up the booze," Christopher had told her. "They think he'll get away with it, if he can keep dry. He'll be okay. He's not short of willpower."

"He's only thirty-five," she mused.

"I know. Three boys in less than four years. My poor mother!"

Rerunning this conversation now, Simmy found additional resonance to it in the light of her discovery about the two sisters who came after the trio of boys. Frances must have been superhuman to manage so many children all so close in age. And how had it never occurred to Simmy to wonder how come Hannah was only ten months younger than George? She knew when all the birthdays were, if she thought about it. She'd seen the two impossibly close siblings battle fiercely throughout their early years and not once looked more closely at the reasons for it.

"I have no natural curiosity," she thought to herself with a sigh. "Just as my mother said." The Hendersons could have provided a more observant child with a good deal of information about families, siblings, and the way they toughened each other up in preparation for the real world. Instead, Simmy had used Christopher as a shield from the turbulence of it all, begging him to take her off to distant rock pools, where Hannah's screams could not be heard.

The logical progression of these musings brought her to the fact of Kit Henderson's murder. It followed almost unsurprisingly from the memories of arguments and hair-pulling and wildly exaggerated threats. "I am *really* going to kill you," George had said repeatedly to his sister. And if Hannah had dismissed the words with a laugh, Simmy had more than once believed him. It all came back to her now, the vivid flashes of real terror she had felt at times, on the chilly Welsh beaches, where the adults mostly left them to entertain themselves.

By the time she had mentally re-enacted much of those summers, she had finished her porridge, as well as two thick slices of toast and marmalade, and was gathering bag and coat and car key. The drive down to Windermere was shrouded in November mist, the lake ahead of her entirely invisible. The twists in the road had engrained themselves on the part of her mind that controlled the car, but they could still bring surprises. A large vehicle coming the other way always made her brake excessively, so that objects flew off the seats behind and beside her. The unyielding stone walls on either side meant reversing to a wider section, or creeping past each other, with acute concern for wing mirrors. There were often sheep in the road, or dogs, and once even a collection of young pigs were cheerfully rooting in the verge, ignoring all traffic.

She arrived at the shop in an opaque and ill-defined mood. Kit Henderson had been violently killed by somebody who probably knew him and therefore must have passionately hated him. Christopher, his son, who might easily be high on the police list of suspects, had spent the night in her house. Kit's daughters had suddenly become something rather different from Simmy's lifelong assumptions. Adoption was not a subject Simmy had thought about in any depth. None of her friends or cousins had been adopted — as far as she knew. The word itself had a broken rhythm to it that reflected the dislocation of the child's life. Something heavy and mechanical gathered around it. Behind that, there was the mystery of who the original parents might have been, and what must have gone so cataclysmically wrong for them to part with their baby. Did the mother not suffer at least as desperately as Simmy herself had done, with her arms so agonisingly empty? In the case of Lynn and Hannah, biological sisters, both removed from their mother, had this been doubly distressing?

Violence, distress, rage, mystery — everything that Simmy avoided as much as she could. All she wanted was her flowers and her sweet young friends and a day or two of sunshine. Instead, she was scheduled to spend another evening with Christopher Henderson and his sadness. Why on earth had she agreed to his invitation? What on earth were they going to talk about? Their joint past felt like a dangerous topic to broach: what if they remembered it all quite differently from each other?

She and Bonnie went through the usual opening-up routine without saying much. A few pots were taken outside, the computer activated and consulted, a token swipe with a duster over the fronts of shelves and they were ready to face the day.

"Corinne says your mum must be in pieces over what happened to her friend's husband," said Bonnie. "So soon after the funeral and everything."

"I'd have thought she'd be more worried about its effect on *you*," said Simmy, feeling oddly defensive. "Surely my mother doesn't rank very highly in the list of people who'll be upset?"

"I'm just telling you what Corinne said. She usually knows about that sort of thing."

Simmy had a qualified respect for the woman who had steered Bonnie through a very rocky adolescence, despite having few obviously respectable characteristics. Purple hair, facial piercings and scant regard for the law had initially made Simmy very wary. But Corinne was a stalwart member of Windermere's community, as it turned out, effortlessly befriending DI Moxon, Ninian Tripp the potter and Simmy Brown's own mother. "There's not a malicious bone in her body," Ninian had said at one point. "A lot of very unhappy children have

94

been given exactly the sort of relaxed affection they needed," Moxon had told Simmy. "The woman should get an OBE."

And she probably would, one of these days, thought Simmy. But that didn't entitle her to pass comment on Angie Straw's emotional state, all the same. Where Corinne took life easily, retiring without apparent regret from the role of foster mother and turning to folk singing instead, Angie was showing increasing signs of exhausted frustration at the way her life was going. However hard she tried not to draw comparisons, Simmy could not deny that her mother made things worse for herself by being needlessly judgemental and critical of almost everyone she met. Only her B&B customers escaped censure, because in that department, Angie had only the lowest of expectations. She knew that people on holiday were demanding and messy, unpunctual and unrealistic. She was fully prepared for the worst, and when it didn't happen, she would become positively cheerful.

"She didn't really like Kit much," Simmy told Bonnie in the shop. "I can't imagine she's going to miss him."

"That's not it, though, is it? It's the awful thing of wondering if she knows who killed him. I mean — it could have been one of the family. Don't you think she might be thinking that, and getting upset about it? Them having always been such close friends, I mean."

Bonnie's wide blue gaze was impossible to take badly. Simmy smiled in spite of herself. "I suppose it's possible she's thinking that sort of thing. But it can't have been one of the Hendersons. Why would any of them kill their father? He wasn't perfect, but none of them had any reason to do that to him. How often does anybody kill their own father, anyway? It just doesn't happen."

"It's a taboo," Bonnie nodded sagely. "The worst sort of murder. In just about every society in the world."

"Right." Simmy gave this a few moments' thought. "But that's not likely to make much of an impression on the police, is it? They'll just focus on the evidence, wherever it leads them."

"Yeah. Ben says it's got to have something to do with that letter the man was holding."

"He's just guessing." Again Simmy felt a need to protect herself. After all, the page in question partly concerned her and the book of flower pictures. "Now, let's see what we need to order for the weekend."

"Ben never just guesses," said Bonnie calmly sticking to the subject. "He uses logic and observation."

"So he does. But I wonder sometimes . . ."

"What? Wonder what?"

"How come he always seems to be right there when something ghastly happens. How come you and he were *right there*, on Tuesday? It seems impossible that it was a coincidence."

Bonnie treated her to another clear-eyed stare. "No, of course it wasn't a coincidence. That man — Eddie is it? — he *knew* we'd be there, didn't he? Maybe he arranged the whole thing. Didn't that even occur to you?"

The patronising tone would have made her angry, if she wasn't already so horrified at the idea of Eddie Henderson as a killer.

CHAPTER
NINE

"That doesn't make the slightest bit of sense," Simmy argued loudly. "What reason could he have had to do that? Are you saying he wanted you to see his father being murdered? Or what?" Her mind seized up, refusing to pursue any of the multitude of implications there might be to Bonnie's suggestion.

"I'm only saying he knew we'd be there. He could have told somebody, maybe. Somebody who didn't want the old man to talk to someone like us."

"No — wait. Eddie didn't know *Ben* would be there — only you. You offered to go, but you never mentioned Ben, did you? You've got the order of events all wrong."

Bonnie slumped for a few seconds. "You're right. So this is about me — do you think?"

"Of course it isn't, Bonnie. Don't be ridiculous. You're not remotely connected to the Henderson family, are you? Neither is Ben, come to that."

"I'm not, but he is. His mum knew the old man."

"That doesn't count. Unless . . ." Simmy flushed at the outrageous thought that had occurred to her despite her efforts to maintain a wall against any wild notions. "No, it definitely doesn't count."

"Unless she had a fling with him. Is that what you were going to say?" Bonnie, too, had gone pink at the very idea. "I'm fairly sure she didn't. And I can hardly ask Ben, can I? Or her."

"We're being silly. Let's change the subject."

"A customer, look." Bonnie cocked her head at the door, which opened a second later. "A real live customer," she added in a whisper.

Simmy looked round with a smile. The newcomer responded with a matching grin. "Hiya!" she chirped. "What a lovely shop! I've never been in here before."

It was a woman in her early thirties, wearing a blue fleece jacket and muddy black boots. "Don't you just hate November," she went on. "I thought I should leave the pushchair outside — it's so bloody big it'll knock all your pots over."

They could see a large three-wheeled contraption on the pavement outside, with a miniature pair of boots like her mother's kicking against the footrest. "That's Cleo," said the woman. "I'll have to be quick, or she'll have the whole thing over. She's more like a baby elephant than a human being."

Bonnie and Simmy both laughed. "So what are you looking for?" asked Simmy.

"Have you got any roses? I need a whopping big bunch of them, with all the trimmings. Red, ideally, but pink would do."

"How many? A dozen?"

"At least. How many have you got?"

"Probably three dozen. There's a delivery due tomorrow morning. I'd have to mix the colours if you wanted as many as that."

"I'm tempted, but I'd never carry them, would I? The car's up by the church. Give me eighteen, nicely wrapped. Is that okay?"

"No problem," said Simmy, wondering what the story was. "I'll be three minutes." She disappeared into the back room for ribbon and foliage to add to the flowers.

"Is it somebody's birthday?" she heard Bonnie ask.

"I wish it was. That'd be much easier than what I've got to do. No — they're for my mother-in-law. A peace offering. I have a feeling it'll take more than this, but at least it's a start."

"What did you do?" Bonnie's voice was breathlessly amused.

"Told her to stop getting ghastly frilly dresses for the kid. Honestly — is that so terrible? But she took it really badly, and screamed at poor Steve, saying I was the most ungrateful creature since . . . some ancient Roman woman, or something. Said she'd never buy us another thing, and then we'd realise how much she'd done for us. That it was Cleo who'd suffer, and she hoped we'd understand one day how rotten we'd been."

"Ancient Roman woman? Who's that, then? I can't think of anybody especially ungrateful."

Simmy came back in time to see the customer's slack jaw at this unexpected remark. "It might have been Medea — is that right? She'll have got the whole thing back to front, anyway. She's totally ignorant. Just

100

wanted to intimidate me. I'm as ignorant as she is, to be honest."

"Medea was vengeful, not ungrateful," said Bonnie. "She killed her children, and some versions say she cooked them and fed them to her husband. That's not actually in the original, but it's how she's been known in recent times. She'd caught the husband being unfaithful and was extremely annoyed."

The customer was both fascinated and horrified. "My God! Then I hope Ma-in-law didn't know that was the story. If she does, that's telling me how much she really does hate me, isn't it?"

"You know — the same thing happened with a cousin of mine. I've got lots of cousins," Bonnie confided.

"What? They were cooked and served up to their father?"

All three of them laughed, this time with a hint of hysteria. "No," Bonnie spluttered. "Fell out with the mother-in-law because she kept buying terrible clothes for the kids. I think it happens in a lot of families."

"Steve says I should just have quietly put them away and not said anything."

"Are these okay?" asked Simmy, proffering a lavish bouquet of deep-red roses, surrounded by wispy fronds of maidenhair fern. "I'm afraid they're quite expensive."

"It'll be worth any money to smooth things over. We do need her on our side, especially when the next one arrives." She patted her abdomen, under the fleece, drawing attention to a large pregnant bump.

She departed, leaving behind an atmosphere of rueful female humour that Simmy realised she seldom experienced. "Wasn't she nice," she sighed. "I wonder where she lives."

"Out on a farm somewhere, to judge by the mud on her boots. The accent wasn't local. And they're not short of cash, if she can buy all those roses."

"Melanie would probably know them." Simmy still missed her original assistant, despite the way Bonnie had made herself so useful. Bonnie was still too much of a child for real intimacy; there had been nothing childlike about Melanie, despite her being only two years older than Bonnie.

"It makes you think if Kit Henderson had sent flowers to whoever was so upset with him, he might still be alive," said Bonnie.

Simmy never wanted to hear remarks like that. The power of flowers was something she felt uneasy about. "I don't think 'upset' quite covers it," she said. "If you want somebody dead, you're a lot more than upset."

"I know. But even so . . . I still think you can talk a person down if you try."

"Not always. But I see your point." She looked out into the street, where Cleo and her mother were disappearing in the direction of the church, their progress somewhat crooked, thanks to the difficulty of guiding a buggy holding an armful of roses. "I hope it works for that woman, anyway."

"Has Moxo seen you yet?" Bonnie asked in an abrupt change of subject. "About your legacy?"

"Last night," Simmy nodded. "He didn't find it very interesting." She was about to add the detail of Christopher spending the night in her house, when she swallowed back the words. Bonnie might be a lot less interested in Simmy's love life than Melanie had been, but she would still read more into it than was there. "It can't possibly have any connection to what happened to Kit."

"I still haven't seen it. Where is it now?"

"Still in the car. I forgot to take it back into the house."

"Why don't you go and get it? It sounds nice."

As always, Simmy wilted at the prospect of walking back through the chilly Windermere streets in search of her car. It would take barely ten minutes in total, but once inside the shop, she liked to stay there all day. Face it, she told herself, you're just a lazy slob. It was surprising that she remained so slim, given how little exercise she took.

"Go on," the girl urged her. "It might get nicked if you leave it out there."

There was very little danger of that, as Bonnie well knew. But it would be better to have it with her. She could show it to Ben when he came, as well as one or two interested customers, perhaps. It could be propped up somewhere, and used as a feature. "All right, then," she said. "But I'll need a plastic bag for it. It's raining, look."

There was the same fine drizzle there had been for the past few days, on and off. Classic November weather. And no more welcome for that. "Nasty," Bonnie agreed. "But at least it isn't cold."

For some reason, this made Simmy laugh. "You sound just like my father," she realised. "And you're both wrong — it's a lot colder than it looks. You can tell by the way people are all hunched up out there."

"What people?"

They both looked out of the big window on a scene that was almost devoid of life. One elderly woman was hurrying along on the opposite pavement, and a middle-aged man was about to meet her, going the other way. "I've been watching people in the street all morning," said Simmy. "They're *clemmed*, if that's the right word."

"Never heard it before."

"Surely you have? It's North Country, I'm sure. It's in *The Water Babies*. I think Mr Grimes says it."

"We can ask Ben," said Bonnie cheerfully. "He's sure to know. Now go and get that book."

Making a much bigger production of it than necessary, Simmy eventually did as suggested. The book did look abandoned, there on the back seat amongst an untidy assortment of debris. It was ungrateful of her to leave it like that. Frances Henderson would be sorry to see it treated so dismissively.

When she got back, Bonnie was pale and agitated. "What happened?" demanded Simmy. "I was only gone a few minutes."

"Ben called. He's got to go and answer more questions this afternoon. He won't have time to come in here first. He says I can't go with him. He sounded . . . well, *scared*."

"Why?" It would be an exaggeration to say that the boy was never afraid of anything, but it was certainly rare.

"You know we were saying it might not have been a coincidence that we were at the Henderson house just as he was being murdered? Well, it sounds as if Moxo's got the same idea. He went to Ben's house just now and talked to his mum, wanting to know exactly how well she knew the old man, and why she thought Ben was so eager to visit him, and stuff like that. Then he phoned Ben at college and said he needed to ask him about things all over again."

"But that's not scary. He usually *likes* being questioned by the police. It makes him feel important and useful."

"I know. But he doesn't like his mother being involved. And she's not happy about it, obviously. And Moxon was really heavy, apparently. Not like he usually is at all. And Ben doesn't know what to say to him."

"He told you all that in a couple of minutes?" Simmy hugged the flower book to her chest, thinking she must have been out longer than she realised.

"Yeah. And some more. He thinks maybe Moxo thinks *he* killed old Mr Henderson."

"No, Bonnie, he doesn't think that. There is no way in the world that can be right. He *knows* Ben. He likes him. He trusts him. For heaven's sake, that's just plain stupid."

"You don't have to tell me. But the thing is, it's all about the *evidence*, you see. And Ben thinks there might be some that looks bad for him. The way he left me outside, and got blood on his legs, and there not being any sign of anybody else. The police don't have any choice but to follow all that up. Nobody knows that better than Ben, and that's what's worrying him."

Simmy took a deep breath. "Which is why it's crazy. If he *was* ever going to kill anybody — and that's a ludicrous idea — he'd be incredibly careful not to leave any evidence. He'd make a brilliant criminal, because he knows so much about how the police work."

"Yes," said Bonnie impatiently, "but that won't count for anything, will it? Not if they think they've got *evidence*." She shouted the last word, and then turned away. Simmy thought she heard tears in the voice, and put a hand on the girl's delicate shoulder.

"Come on. Moxon's got far too much sense to go following a stupid trail like that, whatever it might seem to be suggesting."

"Ben says he won't have much choice," Bonnie insisted, her voice rising again.

"Calm down. If it really is looking that way, then it'll be because somebody deliberately arranged it. And Moxon will understand that."

"Eddie Henderson set us up? Yes! That must be it. We almost worked it out already, didn't we? Can I call Ben and tell him?"

"Better not. He'll be in a lesson, won't he? The break must be over by now."

Lesson. Break. She knew she was using words from her own schooldays that might well be obsolete, but their meaning was still clear. Bonnie nodded. There were strict rules about using phones during school hours. "I could text him, though," she said brightly.

"If you must," Simmy shrugged. "And then we're going to leave it for the rest of the day, and focus on work." She deliberately lowered her own voice, hoping for a note of authority. "Did you get me that list of hotels yet?"

"One or two."

"So get it up to six, and then we can start phoning them. Christmas will be here before we know it, and we'll have lost our chance. You can draw up some ideas for what we'll be offering them, as well. Table centrepieces and big displays in the foyer is as far as I've got."

"All right. Yes, you're right. I shouldn't be obsessing about stuff I can't do anything about. It's not productive."

The girl was clearly quoting her boyfriend, but Simmy couldn't fault the sentiment. "Quite right," she approved. Then, having got Bonnie focused on a specific task, she found herself quite unable to shake off thoughts of Ben in police custody, being charged with a murder because of some quite obviously ambiguous evidence. But would such evidence — so patently open to the wrong interpretation — carry any weight in court? Would the Public Prosecutor even accept that it comprised a reasonable case?

When her mobile rang, she felt as if somebody somewhere had heard her thoughts and was coming to the rescue. The little screen admitted it had no idea who was calling.

"Simmy? It's Christopher. Are you too busy to talk?"

"No, not at all."

"Good. It's about Lynn — would it be totally out of order if she joined us this evening? She's dreadfully upset about Dad, and Barry's being a prat about it all, apparently. I told her I've got plans, but she really needs to get out of the house. Is that okay, do you think?"

Simmy's instant reaction was disappointment, followed by surprise at her own feelings. "That's fine," she said heartily. "It'll be good to catch up with her a bit more. Same time and place as we decided this morning?"

"Actually, Lynn's not keen on Chinese. I can book a table at the Belsfield. Would that be okay with you? I'll pay."

She remembered how her father had always scorned hotel food, as being below his demanding standards. He was probably very out of date on the subject, and besides, Simmy Brown was no gourmet. "All right, then," she said.

Bonnie's inquisitive look was impossible to ignore. "That was Christopher," Simmy said. "He wants me to have a meal with him and one of his sisters this evening."

"Better tell Moxon, then," said Bonnie crossly.

"What? Why should I?" The idea was deeply irritating. "It's nothing to do with him."

"*Everything* has to do with him," said Bonnie. "He'll want to know what they say, and whether you think either of them could have killed their dad."

It was akin to the feeling a mother must have when she's just got her baby to sleep, and then some noisy intruder wakes it again. She had Bonnie nicely settled at a distracting task, when Christopher had to phone and stir things up again. Exasperation rose to the surface. "That's nonsense," she snapped. "And what makes you think you can listen in to my private calls?"

The big blue eyes filled with reproach. "I couldn't help it. You were standing right there. Am I supposed to pretend to be deaf? And *anyway*, I never asked you who it was. I didn't say a word. You told me of your own accord."

"I suppose I did. Sorry. I didn't even know he had my number. I try not to give it to anybody." She slammed the mobile down on a shelf. "I hate the damned thing most of the time."

Bonnie smiled her forgiveness. "It's a bit late for that. We're stuck with them now. You're just being stubborn, don't you think?"

"Like my mother," Simmy acknowledged. "What a thought!"

Two more customers gave them something to do — matching very particular shades of mauve and lilac with a patch of curtain material for one woman, and explaining in great detail how to keep poinsettias in good condition for the full twelve days of Christmas to another. Both women made Simmy want to scream — *Don't you know there's more to life than this?* And yet, how could she, when she was making a living from just such trivia? And how could she ever justify telling another person what was the right way to get through life? What made her think she knew which way was better than any other way?

She maintained a helpful, polite manner and was rewarded with genuine thanks. "You're amazing," said Bonnie admiringly.

"I was screaming inside," Simmy admitted.

"They're not all like that."

"No, thank goodness. Is it lunchtime yet?"

"Pretty much. I'll get the bagging, shall I?" *The bagging* had been a rural term for a packed meal taken by children to workers in the fields — in a bag. Ben had discovered it from an old man he'd met on one of his historical researches. He'd taken to referring to the constant supply of food he kept in his schoolbag as his bagging, leading to it being adopted by Bonnie and then Simmy.

Simmy laughed. "Cornish pasties and a bottle of cider today, is it?"

"Muesli bars and an apple for me. Don't know about you."

"I think I might still have a packet of crisps somewhere."

As they snacked at the back of the shop, Simmy had a thought that she couldn't resist expressing. "But Moxon can't have any grounds for suspecting Ben, because you can be a witness. You can swear the man was dead when you got there. They'd have to take that seriously."

110

"Mm," said Bonnie, avoiding her eye.

"What?"

"I didn't actually see him. I was still outside when Ben went in. He saw the door looked odd and made me wait."

"But you looked through the window. You told me on the phone."

"That was later. I might lie, though. I would, like a shot, but Ben isn't going to let me. He's going to make me tell the absolute truth, in every detail."

"Oh," said Simmy glumly. "That's a pity."

CHAPTER
TEN

Angie Straw broke with her usual practice by paying another visit to Persimmon Petals at half past four. "I want to see Bonnie," she announced, ignoring the elderly man who was trying to choose flowers for a lady friend.

"Well, here she is," said Simmy briefly, over the customer's stooped shoulder.

Bonnie went down to the front of the shop, standing meekly to attention. Simmy's mother was at least eight inches taller than the girl, and used it to her advantage. "I need to know just what happened on Tuesday," she said firmly. "Kit Henderson was a friend of mine, and if I understand things correctly, I might have been witness to his slaughter instead of you. That's if you hadn't offered to go and see him, when Eddie wanted it to be me. That's right, isn't it?"

"For heaven's sake, Mother," Simmy hissed. "Can't you do this somewhere else? I'm trying to help this gentleman with his flowers." The old man was sending nervous glances in all directions, obviously concerned for his own safety.

"Where do you suggest?" Angie demanded.

"Outside. Anywhere but here. Better still, wait until Bonnie's finished for the day and take her for a coffee or something."

"I haven't got time for that. I've been trying to get away all day, but the phone kept ringing, and some people arrived without any warning. Just showed up wanting two rooms. I'm going to have to put 'Reservations Only' on the sign at this rate. It's more than I can cope with."

Simmy had often wondered at the way her parents had handled out-of-the-blue guests. People would see the B&B sign as they drove by and decide to give it a try. It was a normal part of the business, but it put a lot of strain on a couple trying to live some sort of private life. "You can't do that," she told her mother. "You know you can't."

"Well, something's going to have to give, I can tell you that. Now, Bonnie — will you die of cold if we stand outside for a few minutes?"

"I don't expect so."

"Come on, then. I've got to have something sensible to tell Russell, and you're my best hope."

"He knows about it, does he? The murder?" Bonnie's question was asked as they left the shop, and Simmy never heard the reply. With an effort she attended to the dithery customer, who eventually spent ten pounds on a modest bunch of hothouse freesias, which did at least smell nice. She followed him outside, looking up and down the street for her mother and assistant.

It was no longer raining, but darkness had come already and there was a penetrating little wind funnelling down the high street. She found the pair against a wall twenty yards away, their backs turned to the chilling gusts. "So what's all this about?" she asked loudly, interrupting an obviously earnest conversation.

"None of your business," said her mother. "You're not involved. Go back to your precious customer."

"He's gone. And it *is* my business, much as I wish it wasn't. I saw Kit on Monday. Frances left me that book. I let Bonnie and Ben go down there on Tuesday. I'm a lot more involved than *you* are — that's for sure."

"She's worried about your dad," said Bonnie quietly. "She needs to explain to him that it's nothing for him to get upset about. But she can't just lie and hope he'll be reassured. He's too clever for that to work. You don't have to get cross about it," she finished.

"Worried, upset, cross — that's just about how I feel about all this mess. And you are, too, with Ben in trouble." She looked desperately up and down the street as if hoping for a saviour to materialise. "We're *all* in the same state, aren't we?" She sighed. "Sorry, Mum. I didn't mean to shout."

"Yes, well," said Angie, never one to apologise if she could avoid it.

"Anyway," said Bonnie. "Have I been any use, do you think?"

Angie included Simmy in her reply, which was her way of attempting to soothe ruffled feelings. "A bit. I was right that Eddie came here on Tuesday and asked you to ask me to visit his dad. But you, Bonnie, offered to go instead, and then Ben said he'd go with you. But Eddie wouldn't have known Ben would be going — just

114

you. And you left that quite vague, didn't you? No mention of an exact day or time for a visit."

"That's right. That's what I was just saying. I remembered all that about Christopher and the long hours he works, and then it all got a bit sidetracked, and Eddie went away without anything really being decided."

"Which isn't what we were saying this morning," Simmy realised. "And that's good, isn't it?" She gave Bonnie a glance that she hoped conveyed the message — *Don't say anything about all that in front of my mother*. Except it was quite likely to be too late, given Angie's determination to extract the whole story from Bonnie.

Bonnie merely shrugged, which suggested she'd understood. Then she shivered. "This wind isn't very nice," she muttered. "Can we go in?"

"Mum? Are you finished with Bonnie now? She's freezing, look."

Angie waved an arm in a gesture of *Do what you want*. Then she said, "It's not as if anybody really *liked* the blasted man. Nobody's going to be broken-hearted that he's dead. It's just a lot of trouble and suspicion for not very much."

Simmy cast an anxious look at Bonnie. Had the girl learnt yet that Angie Straw was prone to such remarks, and ought not to be taken seriously?

"He was *murdered*, don't forget. Nobody deserves that, however unlikeable they might have been. And Kit wasn't as bad as all that. No worse than most people. We never had any reason to dislike him, did we?"

"In a way, it's even worse, don't you think?" said Bonnie hesitantly. "It gives everybody a headache."

"What?" said Angie.

"She means the moral ambiguity of it," Simmy said. "If a good person murders a bad person, nobody knows what they're meant to think."

"They think: well done, you. Serves the swine right."

"They don't. You know they don't. We've said all this before. Some laws are absolute, with no excuses or mitigations. In theory, anyway," she finished, aware that she was coming close to contradicting herself.

"Except when moral ambiguity gives you a headache," said Angie sarcastically. "Well, never mind now. I've got what I came for. Thanks, Bonnie. I'm sure Ben's going to be back to normal in no time. Although it must have been pretty nasty for the poor boy."

Again Simmy attempted a silent message to the girl. *What have you told her??* Bonnie gave a little shake of her head in reply. "That's okay," she said to Angie. "I don't think Ben's too upset, actually. You know what he's like."

Simmy hurriedly added, "He loves the whole business. Doesn't he, Bonnie?" Too late, she realised she'd said the wrong thing. Instead of trying to divert her mother away from any dangerous ground, in which she might learn that Ben Harkness was under suspicion, she had only made it sound as if he had somehow engineered his presence at the bungalow at the crucial moment. And again, she wondered how such a coincidence could possibly be explained away.

Had Ben known something was likely to happen, when he offered to go with Bonnie?

"He'll get himself into trouble one of these days," said Angie.

This time Bonnie and Simmy were united in staring open-mouthed at the crass remark. Ben had been in the direst of trouble only a few months earlier. He had come close to death at the hands of criminals. His mother, Bonnie and Simmy had all been frantic, and Ben had become even more treasured by them as a result. "God, Mum. Listen to yourself," said Simmy.

"All right. I know I'm being insensitive. I'll go. Shall I give your love to your father?"

"Of course," said Simmy tiredly. "And I'll see you at the weekend. Saturday lunchtime, if that's all right."

Again, Angie merely waved, and went rapidly down the street towards her home in Lake Road.

"She's quite something, isn't she," said Bonnie.

"She's a disgrace. What did she want to know all that for, anyway? She's not usually bothered to know the gory details."

"She knew the family. They've been friends forever. She definitely is bothered. Actually . . ."

"What?"

"She seemed *more* than bothered. She seemed to be scared of something. As if she might have an idea who did it, and wanted me to tell her something that would prove her wrong."

"Which you couldn't do."

"No," said Bonnie with regret.

"Because if you could, that would get Ben out of trouble at the same time."

"Right."

Simmy became thoughtful, trying to remember everything she'd ever known and experienced of Kit Henderson. The fragmented picture that resulted was inconsistent with the scrappy comments she had heard in the past few days. The stereotype of a family man surrounded by children, twinkly and smiling and smudged by sticky fingers, was nowhere near the reality. He had been critical of them much of the time, complaining when they cost him money and leaving almost all their care to his wife. There had been moments when Simmy suspected he could not remember who she was. He had almost never spoken directly to her until she'd been about thirteen, when he began to show more interest. And then, at her wedding, he had insisted on dancing with her. "I'm your surrogate father," he'd declared. "I've known you from the first day of your life." He had been drunk, and had held her too close. But so had two or three other middle-aged men. It seemed to be part of the whole wedding experience.

And yet he had danced very well, twirling her round and remaining very nimble on his feet despite the drink. She had laughed, and realised she was actually rather enjoying it. Tony, her new husband, was a useless dancer. He had agonised about that first ritual waltz they were required to do, practising for weeks. And still he trod on her toes three times.

118

It was terrible that Kit was dead. This realisation hit her without warning. Not just dead, but murdered, only two or three weeks after his wife had died. Perhaps the tragedy of Frances's dying had partly obliterated the horror of her husband's. Perhaps two premature deaths were too many to process properly. By current standards, sixty and seventy were both too young to die.

"Poor old Kit," she sighed.

"Yeah," Bonnie agreed, though with less than total conviction. "Yeah," she said again, more firmly. "Nobody should be murdered. That's a definite."

The evening engagement with Christopher and Lynn absorbed all Simmy's attention from five o'clock onwards. She went home and changed, finding it strange not to be preparing a meal for herself. Even stranger to be driving down to Bowness again barely an hour later. The Belsfield was the biggest hotel in town, facing the lake on a rising slope, solid and old-fashioned. Nobody could accuse it of being "boutique" or "niche". It was where the better-heeled stayed, enjoying the large rooms and handsome gardens. But it was not unduly expensive, and despite Russell Straw's prejudices, it offered a perfectly good menu.

It also provided a big car park at the rear. As Simmy found a place under a tree, she saw Christopher and Lynn standing beside the entrance, evidently waiting for her. They appeared to be arguing, Lynn making

119

jerky motions with one arm as if chopping hunks off a loaf of bread with the side of her hand.

Getting closer, Simmy could see clear signs of weeping. Lynn's eyes were red and sunken, her cheeks rough under the yellow overhead light. "I am so sorry about Kit," Simmy offered. "It was such a dreadful shock."

The young woman merely sniffed and nodded.

"Come on, then," said Christopher. "I've booked the table. We've got time for a gin or something first."

Simmy calculated the chances of a gin, plus a glass of wine, being enough to activate a breathalyser if she was stopped on the way home. The season of Christmas staff dinners had not yet started, which meant the police were unlikely to be unduly zealous for another few weeks. "Gin sounds just the thing," she said. Then she asked Lynn, "Have you driven here on your own?"

"No. Christopher brought me. I'm staying at his place tonight. Barry can take a day off tomorrow and see to the kids."

Simmy had to think hard before she recalled that Lynn had two small girls, the same as Eddie had. They had been the only children at Fran's funeral, kept close by a man Simmy assumed to be their father, while Lynn did her duty in the kitchen. She had heard mutterings about the unsuitability of taking children to such an event.

Suddenly it struck her as odd that Lynn should impose herself on this dinner, to the extent of altering the venue to a much more upmarket occasion. Christopher's explanation looked thinner on closer inspection. There was a subtext pushing itself forward — the abandonment of Barry and the children, the obvious argument that had been aborted abruptly when Simmy arrived — it felt potentially awkward, and even perhaps antagonistic.

Christopher was ushering them through to the bar, a hand on each woman's back. He and Simmy were both tall, while Lynn was a mere five foot two. It made for a lopsided threesome. None of them spoke until they were settled at a low table with their drinks. Then Christopher raised his glass with a grimace and said, "To Dad, poor old chap."

Neither Simmy nor Lynn responded. There was something almost crassly inadequate in the gesture. But he meant well, presumably. Then Simmy remembered that Ben Harkness had been summoned to a police interview, and Eddie Henderson could have had sinister reasons for suggesting Kit be visited, and nothing was as it seemed. Or might not be.

"Chris said you were going to the Chinese, but I preferred to come here. I've been here before once or twice. It's really good food."

"I've never eaten here," said Simmy. In fact, the last time she had been inside the hotel had been nearly a year ago, in circumstances of considerable danger and difficulty. Looking around now, she recognised details — carpet, curtains and big picture windows all came into focus at once. "But I have been in that room over there." She pointed.

"I come here quite a lot," said Christopher. "They do antique fairs now and then."

Lynn was looking from face to face with an intensity that Simmy found irritating. Finally, she met the look square on, and held the other woman's gaze long enough to alter the tone of the conversation. "You haven't changed at all since you were about ten," she said. "I would still have recognised you." It was true — the frizzy light-brown hair and the deep-set eyes were just as they'd always been. "I remember you were always up to mischief."

"Was I? What sort of mischief?"

"Oh — teasing the boys. Telling tales to Frances. Making a lot of fuss about every little thing."

"That wasn't mischief," said Christopher. "That was bloody-mindedness. She was a horrible little beast. So was Hannah, of course, only more so."

It occurred to Simmy for the first time that the family patterns of the Hendersons and the Harknesses were almost identical. Older boys, followed by little sisters, five children in each case. It made her wonder if that had provided a point of contact between Kit and Helen Harkness. Had they discussed the trials and pleasures of a large family? Surely they must have done. You couldn't talk about carpets without referring to the rigours they would endure at the hands and feet of several children.

A waiter came to tell them their table was ready and they spent a few minutes ordering food and drink. There was a briskness to it that suggested the purpose of the evening was considerably more serious than simply eating a good meal. They were close to a window, looking out on to the dark waters of

Windermere below them, bordered only patchily by lights.

"So," began Lynn portentously. "Are we going to talk about who killed our father?"

CHAPTER
ELEVEN

Only then did Simmy grasp that *she* was the interloper, and not Lynn at all. Christopher must have insisted that he could not break his engagement with her, and that if Lynn wanted to spend the evening with him, she'd have to agree to Simmy being there as well. They had an obvious need to talk about their father's death; a need which was liable to be frustrated by the presence of a somewhat distant friend. Simmy could have nothing to contribute. She almost stood up there and then and made her excuses.

But Christopher seemed to feel differently. "Good question," he told his sister. "And something I'm sure Simmy can help us with."

"Me?" She blinked at him.

"An objective eye. With some experience of criminal behaviour, I gather."

She flushed. "That sounds bad. But yes, I have got unpleasantly close to some nasty people."

"And so has your young friend Ben. Isn't that right?"

She looked into his brown eyes, trying to understand the purpose of his questions. The eyes were disturbingly familiar, taking her back twenty years and more, to when she and he had been soulmates, on that final

124

family holiday. She had loved him then, and wanted to spend every moment with him. They had mutated almost overnight from friends to lovers. Or rather, not quite lovers in the usual sense. They had not had sex or even kissed. But they had lain on the sandy beach, gazing into each other's eyes and talking sporadically. Her body had throbbed with a frightening will of its own that lay entirely outside her control.

And then they had gone separate ways, with exams and jobs and grown-up lives, and she had actually forgotten how intense it had been, until now.

"Um," she said. "Sorry. What are you asking me?"

"Ignore him," said Lynn, with a little laugh. "He didn't mean to sound so accusing. He's been the same with all of us — trying to make us confess."

"That's rubbish, and you know it," Christopher shot back at her. "I know it wasn't *Simmy*."

"And it wasn't me or Hannah or Eddie or George, either. It's just as likely to have been *you* as any of us. We all resented him in our various ways."

"Did you?" said Simmy in bewilderment. "Why?"

"Have you got all night?" Lynn flashed back. "Because that's what it would take to tell you."

"Come on," begged Christopher. "That's going much too far."

"It's not, though, is it? You can say what you like, the truth is going to come out now he's dead. It always does. All those horrible secrets he kept the lid on — they'll be common knowledge in no time flat."

Her brother gulped, and cast an alarmed look around the huge dining room. Nobody was close enough to be listening, for which he looked very relieved. "I don't know any horrible secrets," he hissed. "I don't know what you're talking about." He looked at Simmy. "Do you?"

"No idea," she said, with perfect honesty. "But I can't believe there's anything bad enough to kill him for. Although, as I said, I barely knew him. I don't think I should even be here." Again, she was inclined to simply get up and leave. But the waiter was bringing their starters, and had opened a bottle of expensive red wine, and it would be an act of considerable courage to interrupt the proceedings at that point. Courage or aggression? Disapproval, or plain cowardice? The motives were opaque, and therefore wide open to interpretation. Besides, she was enjoying the proximity of her one-time beloved. Again, she looked into his eyes, trying to read the extent of his own recollections, as well as understanding what it was he wanted of her now.

"Isn't it strange," he said softly. "Here we are, almost forty, and it feels as if we were sixteen again."

"Oh — you two!" Lynn burst out. "Haven't you grown out of all that long since? No wonder you never noticed what my father was up to, Simmy. You only had eyes for Chris, and here you go again."

"Do you all call him 'Chris' now?" Simmy asked, choosing obtuseness as the least difficult response. She could simply ignore the implications of what Lynn had said, or so she hoped. "Nobody ever did when we were young."

"I don't know." Lynn frowned. "It might just be me."

"Never mind that," said Christopher, with a sympathetic glance at Simmy. "You've got to stop making these vague slurs on Dad's character. I know he had a few girlfriends, over the years, and that was hard on Mum — but it was never anything serious. No more than most men get up to, I'm sorry to say."

"Not my dad," said Simmy, with some force. The idea of universal male misbehaviour was one she had never accepted as true. It might have been common in a bygone generation, when men felt they could get away with it because their wives were hopelessly dependent on them financially, but since then they'd learnt that the risks associated with adultery were seldom worth the effort. A scorned wife was not just furious these days, but capable of very painful revenge. "He's got more sense."

"Your mum would probably castrate him," smiled Christopher. "Mine wasn't half so ferocious. And she didn't really care that much what he did, as far as I could tell."

"She told me she wished he would just go off with some floozy and leave her in peace," said Lynn. "But she could never get up the nerve to throw him out."

"He wouldn't have gone. He liked the bungalow too much."

"She could have gone herself, of course. That never seemed to cross her mind."

Again, Simmy felt uncomfortably intrusive. She ate her mackerel pâté and said nothing. The others were getting into deeper waters, reminiscing about their parents and correcting each other's assumptions. It was all part of grieving, Simmy supposed. A compulsion to talk through what had happened and what had been lost. It was also increasingly apparent that Christopher and Lynn, the eldest and youngest of the family, knew each other less well than Simmy had expected. Their memories did not match, as they began to recount events from the past. Lynn's vague accusations against her father were overlaid by softer stories of his amusing ways. "He would always stop and talk to dogs in the street, but never let us have one of our own. Said he couldn't stand the smell of them indoors."

Christopher raised his eyebrows. "I never heard him say that."

"Well, he did. It was all to do with the smelly carpets he had to deal with in people's houses."

The main course was almost finished, with Simmy ahead by a wide margin, due to her near silence. She had drunk more than a glass of wine, as well, with Christopher topping her up two or three times. The drive home would be semi-automatic, the car almost knowing the way by itself — but the twists and turns in the narrow lanes could be treacherous on a winter's night, and she resisted the urge to take another mouthful.

"We can't possibly work out who might have killed him, all the same," said Christopher flatly. "We could go through every detail of his life and find a hundred people he'd annoyed, and get nowhere. Everybody makes enemies, after all. It's human nature."

"Speak for yourself," said Lynn, which was exactly what Simmy was thinking. "I never made an enemy — did you?" Lynn asked Simmy.

"Not that I can think of. Even Tony isn't my enemy." She sighed. Her ex-husband was becoming a remote and slightly embarrassing figure from her past; a failure in so many ways. She never heard from him, and was not even sure where he was living.

"I thought George was your enemy," said Christopher to his sister.

"No, you didn't. That's Hannah, not me. He never bothered much with me. It was those two who fought all the time."

And they were off again on their anecdotes and disagreements as to just what happened when Lynn was a mulish teenager and her brothers were taking off on their various careers. Simmy listened, aware that Ben Harkness was going to want a detailed report of all that was said, as soon as he could get to her. "What do they all *want*?" he would ask. And "Who had the most to gain from the old man's death?"

Answers were impossible to glean from the conversation between the siblings. She tried to catch Christopher's eye again, almost unconsciously. The realisation that there was still some connecting thread between them was bubbling somewhere inside her, warm and auspicious. She was content to sit there across the table from him, recapturing the past, which had seldom been sunny, but had definitely been enjoyable. He looked at her every few seconds, making an obvious effort to include her, and draw her out of her silence. He made apologetic faces, smiling and widening his eyes. He interrupted his sister to say,

129

"Simmy — are you having a pudding? What about coffee?"

The meal was nearly done. It was nine o'clock. "Coffee, yes," she said. "I should be going soon."

"Good God, look at the time!" shrilled Lynn, having glanced at her watch. "I said I'd phone to see if the girls went to bed properly."

"Properly?" Christopher echoed.

Lynn flapped a tipsy hand at him. "You haven't got kids — you don't understand about the rituals. Barry's pretty good, but he sometimes forgets something. Christa isn't talking yet — she's really behind, actually. She just squawls if one of her toys isn't right. And Ginnie won't always explain, if she's in a bolshy mood."

The world of motherhood and bedtimes and favourite toys was as alien to Simmy as it evidently was to Christopher. "Sounds like a nightmare," he said. "When I was in the Pacific, people just let their kids fall asleep when they were tired, with none of all that routine baloney."

"And I know an American woman who records every single second of her child's day — sleep, food, nappies — the whole thing documented on an app."

"She's mad," said Christopher shortly. "They should have the kid adopted by normal people."

"Like Mum and Dad did with me and Hannah? Right," said Lynn, with an expression close to pain.

"Yes, actually. Do you doubt it?"

"I certainly don't subscribe to the idea that we should feel everlasting gratitude, or loyalty. They did it because they wanted to. They wanted two girls, and

130

that's what they got. They were perfectly ordinary parents, nothing special. You boys weren't done any favours by it, and we were never totally integrated with you. Maybe natural-born girls wouldn't have been, either. I'm not saying it was a disaster, but I'm not starry-eyed about it. I just get sick of all the mushy stuff about the whole business."

Well, thought Simmy. *That's telling it how it is, sure enough*.

"Does Hannah feel like that, as well?" Christopher asked.

"Probably. We don't discuss it. Once we'd agreed there's no point in trying to track down our original parents, there wasn't much more to be said. She had the worst of it, of course."

Before they could get back to how George had persecuted his new sister from the outset, Simmy raised a hand. "Okay," she said. "I think I should go. Won't you let me pay at least something towards the meal?"

Christopher shook his head. "Definitely not. Look — why don't you come to the auction on Saturday? It goes on all day — come for the afternoon, at least. It's quieter then, and easier to park."

"No, I can't. I said I'd go and see my parents. Another time, okay?" Again their eyes met, and she found herself in a panic at the thought of not seeing him again.

"The next one's not for three weeks." She thought she could detect a matching panic in his voice. "They're always on a Saturday in Keswick. You'd be hooked in no time," he promised her. "We always have plenty of quality china — vases for your shop. Mostly they go very cheap."

"I'll definitely come along one day. It sounds great."

"Load of old junk," said Lynn sourly. "You would not believe the rubbish people put in for sale."

"And somebody always buys it," Christopher flashed back. "Every item has somebody looking for it. My job is to bring them together."

"All those dishonest dealers, stitching the whole thing up," Lynn went on. "Ordinary people don't stand a chance."

"That's rubbish. It's equal chances for everybody. A bid is a bid. And we know who the shysters are. We've got ways of dealing with them."

"Shysters," repeated Simmy, "what a wonderful word." She was still standing at the table, not trying very hard to tear herself away. "Well, I'm really going now. Thanks again for the meal." And she really went, slowly winding between the tables, and out through the back entrance to the car park. It was well lit, but she still felt nervous in the shadows under the trees. Experience had taught her caution, forcing her to accept that people would use violence to protect themselves from discovery, once they had committed a crime. And somebody had certainly done that, just a little way down the hill from the hotel, in Bowness.

It was only a little after nine. She would have an hour at home, wondering whether to go to bed early or watch some television, or catch up with some overdue housework. None of those options appealed to her, so she fished her phone out of her bag and turned it on.

132

The possibility of an interesting text was remote, but not out of the question. Other people *always* seemed to have messages or tweets or Facebook comments to divert them at any hour of the day or night. There was, apparently, a whole huge world of connection out there, where exchanges of news and views went on constantly. Somehow, Simmy had failed to immerse herself in this extraordinary plane of existence.

There was nothing waiting for her. But remembering where she was, she took the initiative and keyed in the number of Ben Harkness's phone.

He answered immediately. "Simmy. Where are you?" He always asked that. It was a source of frustration to him that his technology told him the identity of the caller but not the location. It wouldn't be long, he insisted, before that was another automatic feature.

"About one minute away from your house. The car park of the Belsfield. Are you busy? Can I come for a little chat, do you think?"

"Um . . . well . . . why don't I come to meet you? We could go somewhere."

"Where? I don't want any more to drink, and it's cold out."

"Right. Okay. Come here, then. But my mother's going to want to talk to you as well if you do. She's in a bit of a state."

"Poor Helen. I imagine she is, if what Bonnie told me today is true. I do want to hear all about what happened. I expect you want to tell me, don't you?"

He sighed gustily. "I'm not sure I do, actually. It's been a hellish day. Nobody really *listens*. Maybe you'd

133

be different. You can't stay long, though. I'm knackered." Not for Ben the late nights that most teenagers saw as a matter of necessity for the maintenance of a cool image. He made no secret of the fact that he liked going to bed at ten, and getting up at a sensible time. Although he did stay up if he had a project to complete, crouched over the desk in his room, reading or working on his laptop.

"Surely Bonnie listens to you?"

"Oh, yes, of course *she* does. It's everyone else, I mean."

"It *is* a bit late," she acknowledged. "I should just go home." She could hear herself, a woman old enough to be his mother, wistfully wishing she could end the day in his company. It was pathetic.

"Up to you."

"What're you doing tomorrow?"

"The usual. College till about two, and then I'll come and see you and Bon. I've got loads to do over the weekend. I've got behind with the Latin somehow. And there's a whole lot of online research I need to catch up with." He sounded young and stressed and at odds with the world. All very unusual for him. "It's been a hell of a day," he said again. "Mostly thanks to my mother."

"I want to hear all of it."

"You'll be on her side. Even Bonnie thinks she's got a point."

"Why? What's she saying?"

"I can't tell you now. She'll hear me. If she had the power, she'd keep me locked up here until the whole

134

Henderson thing is settled. She's scared I'll be the next victim — can you believe it? She's got Moxo thinking along the same lines, which is totally stupid. Oh, she's coming upstairs with Wilf. I'll have to go. She told me not to use the phone any more tonight."

"Tell her I called you. It's not your fault."

"No. I'll see you tomorrow. There's not really much to tell you. Nothing that won't wait, anyway."

"Okay. Night, night, then. I hope you sleep well."

"You too," he said with another loud sigh.

CHAPTER
TWELVE

She woke long before sunrise on Friday, thanks to the early night she opted for as the least dreary choice, when she got home from Bowness. Seven o'clock on a November morning was uninviting in every way, but she got up all the same. There was a restless feeling that something was going to happen. The whole week had been a succession of shocks and surprises, revelations and suspicions. It was all scattered amongst Ben, Christopher, Bonnie and other more remote people, and nothing seemed to be connected to anything else. The pleasure she'd felt at inheriting the book of pictures had been overlaid almost immediately by Kit's death. The book had been forgotten, yet again, the previous afternoon. It was just sitting there in the shop, unprotected. She hoped Christopher was right when he said it had no commercial value. However improbable a break-in at a florist shop might be, it was still conceivable, and to have the book stolen would be awful.

She had a number of tasks piling up at the shop, after a week of distraction. It needed more than a casual dusting and maintenance of stock. Bonnie's list of hotels to call was a high priority, as was a need to make changes to the general appearance of the place, to reflect the onset of Christmas. So she ate a swift breakfast and left the house shortly after eight. The day would be one of decisive action, she promised herself.

The high street was quiet in the grey light. Everything was still, with a pall of dankness making pavements and other surfaces greasy-looking. The handle of the shop door slipped out of her grasp and she noted that she was leaving wet marks on the floor as she went in. Just the setting for unpleasant surprises — electricity failure or disastrous road accidents — she thought. The world felt unreliable and uncaring. Anyone out on the fells this morning would be chilled and scared. Fires wouldn't light, and maps would go limp and blurry. Simmy quite often imagined the inhospitable heights, only a few miles beyond the small towns around Windermere, and how easy it would be to perish out there, as a puny scrap of life in the vast wilderness.

She turned on all the lights, activated the computer and tuned the radio in the back room to some cheerful Radio Two music. A consignment of flowers from the previous day had still to be distributed around the shop, as well as turned into two birthday tributes, for delivery that day. Both were very local, and she was tempted to let Bonnie take them. But Bonnie didn't drive, and it might not look good for a delicate girl like her to be seen walking through town on such an errand. People would pass comment, probably critically, to the effect that Persimmon Brown was exploiting her poor young assistant.

She caught herself up, wondering how she'd come to be so sensitive to criticism. Was she afraid of being blamed for everything that went wrong, because she did feel responsible for her father's decline? She had been carelessly trusting in situations that called for vigilance; naively unprepared for the wicked things that people could do.

And when, for heaven's sake, was she ever going to find friends of her own age, instead of devoting so much time and attention to teenagers who could be her children?

Bonnie interrupted these gloomy self-examinings, bursting into the shop with a quick grin as if all was right with the world. "Hiya!" she chirped. "What a horrible day!"

"You seem very cheerful."

"Oh, well — you can't let it get you down, can you? Weekend tomorrow. Christmas not too far away. Corinne's got a gig she's been wanting for ages, and Spike's foot is all better. And I get paid today," she finished.

"All that and no mention of Ben? I spoke to him last night." She bit back the next remark, which might have dampened Bonnie's mood.

"Yeah, he said." She waved her mobile. "Just finished talking to him. He'll be round here this afternoon, to bring you up to date."

The afternoon felt rather distant to Simmy. If she maintained her determination to be active and focused all day, there would be a dwindling interest in Ben and

138

his difficulties with the police. "Okay," she mumbled. "Now — there's a whole lot to do this morning."

"Yes, but — don't you want to hear at least a bit about what happened to Ben yesterday? I mean, when we closed up, he was still thinking they thought he might have done the murder."

"I never really worried about that. I'm sure he managed to talk DI Moxon out of that idea."

"Well, yes, he did."

"So that's all right, isn't it? Listen, can you do something to freshen this whole place up? You know you want to. Christmas is coming. We might as well make the most of it."

"I need a whole lot of decorations for that — glass baubles, silver ribbons, sparkly snowflakes. I'll have to go to Poundland or somewhere, and it's still too soon, Simmy. We can't do it before the end of the month."

Simmy sighed. "I suppose you're right. But you can sketch out some ideas, and make a list of what you'll need. It's only another two and a bit weeks. I've got to do two birthday bunches of flowers, and get them delivered. You're in charge this morning, okay?"

"All morning?" Bonnie looked alarmed. "It can get busy on a Friday, you know."

"Half an hour to get them done and a bit more than that to take them to the people. So no — not the whole morning. I'll probably be back by half past ten."

"Good. I don't like it when there's a queue."

"Trust me, that won't happen." Simmy quickly gathered the wherewithal for the two orders, and had them assembled in well under the predicted thirty minutes. Her fingers worked automatically, as her eye kept a close check on colour and symmetry. The arranging of flowers was not a subject she had formally studied, other than browsing a number of books and websites for tips. The technicalities of maintaining shape, involving hidden wires and the indispensable oasis, had been picked up as she went along, on the age-old method of trial and error. She did not believe that an appreciation of colour could be taught, in any case. Experiment was the thing here, and a degree of risk-taking.

The finished items were distinctive in both cases. One mixed shades of purple and pale pink, with a splash of red, and greyish foliage. The other was a palette of orange, yellow and bright green. "Did the people specify the colours?" Bonnie asked, when she saw them.

"Not at all. They said I could use my initiative. I'm not even sure which should go to which customer. They're both in the same price range."

"Who are they?"

"A woman in a flat, a little way down the road from my parents, who is sixty today, and a younger one in the same street as Melanie's family. The flowers are from husband and children."

"Orange for the sixty-year-old and purple for the young mum, then," said Bonnie firmly.

Simmy laughed. "I won't ask why." She attached the cards accordingly, and went out to the van, which lived behind the shop.

140

The deliveries went well. Both women were clearly anticipating some kind of tribute, with relief as apparent as pleasure in their responses. Both expressed admiration for the way the blooms had been arranged, and were suitably effusive in their thanks. Simmy drove back to the shop shortly after ten, thinking the day was going every bit as well as she'd wanted it to.

There was a man talking to Bonnie. It took a few seconds to identify him as Eddie Henderson, given that she could only see him from the back. Her instant reaction was of resistance and impatience. *Not again*, she thought. This man was the source of much of the trouble there'd been all week. Then she reproached herself for the unfairness of her thought, and overcompensated with a warm greeting. "Eddie! How are you doing? I am so *terribly* sorry about your dad. It must be ghastly for you."

He turned round, revealing an expression of anger. "Ghastly is right, yes," he snarled. "And I want to find the swine who did it, and make sure he gets what's coming to him."

"Of course you do. We all do." She looked around him at Bonnie, who was unusually pink. "Are you all right?" she asked.

"Um . . ." said the girl, with an accusing glance at Eddie. "I suppose so. He was shouting at me."

"I was not! I was just wanting some answers. The police won't tell me anything, and I can't get hold of that boyfriend of yours. I phoned the house, but his mother refused to let me speak to him. I remember his

141

mother," he added, slightly less angrily. "Helen Harkness — she had her whole house recarpeted, about twelve years ago. Spent thousands on it."

Simmy was still looking at Bonnie, but she processed this information carefully. "How did you know? You weren't living at home then, were you?"

"It was all he talked about for weeks. And there was some trouble about it with my mother."

The implication was impossible to ignore. "Surely not? I mean — Helen and Kit? Is that what you're saying?"

Eddie rolled his eyes. Bonnie made a sudden yelp, part amusement, part horror. But Simmy had a feeling this idea was not entirely new — that there had been hints along similar lines earlier in the week.

"I'm saying she knew him for a short time, several years ago, and I would expect her to show more concern over the fact that he's been murdered."

"She's only shielding Ben, like a good mother should," Bonnie burst out. "He had a very nasty experience only a few months ago, and she thought she'd lost him. She can't face going through anything like that again."

"Nobody says she has to. I only want to *talk* to him. He might have seen something on Tuesday, without realising it."

Bonnie gave a superior little smile. "That isn't very likely," she said. "If there was anything there to see, he'll have told the police exactly what it was."

Simmy was still thinking about Helen. "How long does it take to carpet a house? A week? Probably less. I

142

don't see how that could provide the basis of a lasting relationship."

"It didn't," Eddie said tiredly. "But he met Cheryl through Mrs Harkness, and when he got some bonus money because of the big carpet job, he spent most of it on her, and that's when my mother got mad. Okay?"

Simmy was reminded of Frances Henderson's funeral, only a week before. There had been a small group of women sitting around a table at the gathering afterwards. Simmy had joined them. They'd introduced themselves rapidly, and the only name that stuck in Simmy's memory was "Cheryl" pronounced with the hard English *ch*, rather than the American "Sheryl", which Simmy thought much nicer.

"She was at the funeral," she said.

"Right. Along with half her family." He made a disgusted expression. "Can't think why they bothered. Hannah was pretty sore about it, I can tell you. Said it was offensive to Dad."

They were getting well away from the main subject, but Simmy could see that this suited Bonnie so well that she was happy to keep it going. Idle chat about distant friends and old histories was surely better than veiled implications as to Ben's probity, or lack of it.

"Offensive? How?"

"It's a long story. One of many, to be honest with you. I don't imagine it's a secret any more, the way my father carried on. It got worse after I left home, and the girls both took it badly. They kept on trying to force him to mend his ways, for Mum's sake."

"Can't have been very dignified for her," said Simmy, trying to imagine her own mother in the same situation. "But she had friends to confide in, didn't she? My mum, for a start. They probably laughed about it," she added.

"Wouldn't surprise me," he admitted. "I know I'm never going to understand the ways women react to anything to do with their relationships. They confound me every time." He sighed, and Simmy detected some marital dysfunction of his own.

"I guess consistency isn't always our strong point," she said.

"That's not it at all," Bonnie interrupted, but before she could elaborate further, the doorbell gave its usual cough and a customer came in.

It was a man in his early fifties, with a jaunty smile. Simmy knew she'd seen him before, but couldn't place him until several minutes into their conversation. He glanced at Eddie and gave a nod of recognition. "Came to put in an order for flowers for your dad," he said awkwardly. "Don't expect there's a date for the funeral yet, but didn't want to miss the chance. Is there a way that can be done?"

"Malcolm. That's good of you. We've not begun to think about it yet. The girls might decide we should limit the flowers, but I never like to do that. Especially this time of year. Brightens things up a bit."

Malcolm swept the scene with a diffident expression. "I don't suppose . . . ? I mean, what's happening behind the scenes, so to speak? The police and so forth. Any progress on catching the blighter who did it?"

Eddie shrugged uncooperatively. "No good asking me, mate. I'm not privy to any of that. If they talk to anybody, it's our Christopher. Eldest son and all that."

"I had a little chat with George last week. He seemed very cut up about your mum. Could hardly get a word out of him."

"You were at the funeral!" said Simmy, at last. "I knew I'd seen you somewhere. You were talking to my mother. You took my seat." She laughed to dispel any hint of accusation.

The others all gave her looks of patient forbearance, as if she was stating the blindingly obvious.

"George hasn't been well," said Eddie. "Depression, mostly, and some trouble with his liver. We don't see much of him these days."

"Poor fellow." Malcolm turned to Simmy. "Now — about the flowers. Would it be possible to put in an order and pay you now, and you keep it on hold until there's a funeral date? I'm not sure where I'll be, you see. The wife's booked us onto one of those winter cruises, and there's no way she'd agree to cancel it. I mean — Kit was a mate, I know, but not as close as all that."

Simmy gave assurances that such an arrangement was perfectly feasible, while privately wondering how she could make certain of remembering the transaction. Kit's funeral could be a month or more away, if the police investigation was protracted and the coroner declined to release the body.

The man went away, leaving Simmy, Bonnie and Eddie unsure of where they'd got to before his arrival.

There had been something about Kit Henderson's dalliances with other women, Simmy remembered, hoping they would not revert to that unsavoury subject. The man was dead — let his secrets die with him.

"That was Cheryl's husband," said Eddie. "As I suppose you worked out. Fancy her wanting a cruise, though. She was always such an ordinary little thing when she worked with Dad. Ran around after him without a word of complaint. Really fallen on her feet now, by the look of it. Married an older man who dotes on her, and takes her off to the sun." He shook his head at the unpredictability of life.

"Was she a friend of the family as well? I mean — why did she go to Fran's funeral?"

"We all knew her," said Eddie vaguely. "She always knew where Dad was, if we ever needed to talk to him. My mum would joke about the way she kept tabs on him — like a devoted sheepdog with her master."

"Sounds quite nice," said Bonnie comfortably.

"I should go," said Eddie, to Simmy's relief. "I hope I haven't upset you, either of you." He smiled at Bonnie. "You're a brave girl, I can see that. It must have been awful for you on Tuesday. And it was all my doing, I know. Sorry if I shouted at you. I'd got the idea in my head that the only hope was if you and your boyfriend saw something, you see. It was a desperate clutching at straws, I can see now."

"That's okay," Bonnie mumbled.

He left awkwardly, clearly aware that he had behaved badly and given the women a superior edge.

They waited a few moments before exhaling exaggeratedly. "Well, he's a one, isn't he," said Simmy.

"Do you think it might all have been a bluff?" Bonnie said slowly. "What if *he* killed his dad, and was here to check whether Ben or I saw anything that pointed to him? That's what people do, you know," she added seriously. "It's like when they go back to the scene of the murder to check they didn't leave any clues. It's a compulsion."

"I don't think Eddie killed his father."

"Okay, but we keep coming back to him, don't we? He might be much cleverer than he looks. He might have set it all up."

"No, Bonnie. We've already decided that's impossible."

"Oh, yes. All the same, I don't trust him. Why does he keep coming here? Surely he's got better things to do."

"I don't know," said Simmy. "But I expect we'll find out eventually."

Her premonition that the day would be a decisive one was starting to look rather shaky by the end of the morning. True, there had been the visitation from Eddie Henderson, but nothing else had happened to resolve the central question as to who killed Kit. It had been foolish to suppose it would, she told herself. The police would be conducting interviews and forensic examinations, and following up people from all aspects of the Hendersons' life. That would lead to an arrest and prosecution, she was sure.

The alarm of the previous day over Ben Harkness's role in the crime seemed to have evaporated, as Simmy had known it would. If there were any grounds for continuing alarm, they centred on Helen, and not her son. Helen's name had come up repeatedly in association with that of Kit Henderson, and yet she had not gone to Frances's funeral. And that suggested that she had not been particularly close to the family.

Another customer put in an appearance, making a regular Friday request for flowers to adorn the house over the weekend. Simmy had put some effort into this practice, making a special feature of the way this could give added significance to family life. She had created a leaflet to this effect, giving it out with all the orders, deliveries and purchases. "Give your weekends an added dimension, with a display of fresh flowers" it suggested. She offered discount rates for regular orders, and the whole thing had been a modest success.

As she left, the customer was confronted with another arrival, necessitating a little dance in the shop doorway.

Simmy looked up to see her old friend DI Nolan Moxon standing there. The very fact of his presence revived all her premonitions; the expression on his face confirmed them.

CHAPTER
THIRTEEN

"What's the matter?" she asked him quickly.

Bonnie had been tinkering with a display near the back of the shop, and only now noticed his presence. "Is it Ben?" she demanded, her voice high with panic.

"Nothing to worry about," he said, unconvincingly. "Going over everything one more time, that's all."

"So what's with the grim face?" Bonnie asked rudely. "You scared us."

"It's a grim business. And I didn't anticipate much of a welcome after yesterday."

"You told Ben he was a suspect. He was really worried. So was his mum."

"I did not say he was a suspect. Nor anything like that. He ran away with it, all by himself."

"He said there might be evidence that pointed to him, because he was in the room just as the man died, and I didn't see anything much, so couldn't be a proper witness. He said evidence is the thing that matters, and everything else gets pushed aside." Bonnie's fears were flooding out of her, her eyes shining with tears. "It was horrible," she finished.

"I know," he said gently. "And I think your young man might have learnt quite a lot from it. In a good many ways, I might add." Then he looked to Simmy, who was waiting passively for his attention. "That book," he said. "We keep coming back to it. Can we go through it again, do you think?"

"If you like. It's here somewhere. I keep forgetting to put it away safe." She spotted the book propped beside the computer, half covered with cellophane. She had pushed it aside when wrapping the weekend flowers for the latest customer. "But it seems rather ridiculous to expect it to solve a murder, doesn't it?"

Bonnie gave a smothered laugh, and Moxon looked pained. "That is not at all what I mean," he said. "Although, I *do* think there might be some significance to it. Mr Henderson died holding a list of instructions from his wife. It seems reasonable to wonder whether there was a disagreement over that list between him and the person who killed him. Wouldn't you agree?"

"I suppose so."

"And this book was *on* the list. Do you see?"

"So were plenty of other things."

"I know. Mrs Henderson made her wishes very plain."

"Sounds really bossy," said Bonnie. "It's what Ben calls power beyond the grave. People think they can go on controlling their family after they're dead."

"It's a natural desire, I suppose," said Moxon. "Nobody wants to be forgotten."

Neither female had a reply to that. The detective went on, "Your book was the only legacy that was listed individually. That makes it look important."

"But it's not," Simmy insisted. "It was only that Frances wanted it to go to someone with a feeling for flowers. It was an obvious choice, when you think about it. It wasn't worth selling it. I don't imagine it would fetch more than twenty pounds in Christopher's auction rooms. It's just a nice thing, with sentimental associations."

"We showed the list to everyone in the family. None of them had any comment to make." Moxon sighed.

"Why should they?" said Simmy. "It was directed at Kit, not them. *He's* got to get a dog and plant some trees, not them."

"True. So why did he die with it in his hand? He must have seen it before, and it's not too difficult to memorise everything in it. So why would it be at the centre of a fight that led to murder?"

Simmy was feeling increasingly uneasy. "Should you be telling us all this? I mean *why* are you?"

Bonnie gave him no chance to reply. "He's just brainstorming, hoping you'll come up with something he hasn't thought of."

Moxon closed his eyes. "You get more like Ben Harkness every day," he groaned.

"I can't come up with any helpful suggestions," said Simmy. "Except that it seems quite unremarkable to me that Kit should keep the letter — list — whatever you call it, close by. It was a direct message from his wife of forty years, who'd just died. It would feel like a connection to her. He might even have wanted to make amends to her by following the instructions in every detail. People keep saying it wasn't a great marriage,

151

don't they? Well, didn't your psychology course tell you that those are the ones where the surviving partner feels more acute grief? If it's been a close and loving couple, it's easier to cope when one of them dies."

"Is it?" He shook his head. "Sounds like an oversimplification to me."

Simmy let it drop, with more urgent concerns in mind. "Something makes me think you've got one of the Hendersons in mind as the killer. And that's absolutely horrible."

"No worse than thinking it was Ben," muttered Bonnie. "Following where the evidence leads, right?"

He sighed again. "That's more or less it, yes. But there's a lot more, not connected with the family at all. He fell out with his workmates more than once. He was completely estranged from his parents and siblings for most of his life. Nobody will say anything too harsh against him, but we're not getting a sense that he was especially liked."

"He was all right," Simmy automatically defended. "Women liked him."

"Probably for the wrong reasons," said Moxon dourly. "And there could be a bit of a money question, too."

"Money!" Bonnie cried. "That's the most common motive for murder, Ben says."

"Ben's wrong, then. The most common motive is loss of control, usually under the influence of drink, and a sudden flash of rage."

Bonnie waved a hand. "Those don't count. I mean *premeditated* murder."

152

"They didn't have any money," said Simmy. "That's why they never had any foreign holidays, and lived in a shabby bungalow, and always needed a better car."

"We had a quick look at the background. All part of a routine investigation. Mrs Henderson's mother — the one who did these pictures in your book — was something of a hoarder. She collected old things. We found a very elderly neighbour who remembers her very well. She only died ten years ago. Her things were all sold off in a house sale, but the neighbour says there was some sort of trouble over items of jewellery. They went missing. The family fell out over it."

Simmy and Bonnie exchanged a long silent look, both minds working hard.

"So — you think Frances had her mother's jewels tucked away, and when she died she left them to Kit, and one of their children killed him and took them?" Simmy was unusually brusque in her summary of a theory that struck her as ludicrous.

Moxon drew back, raising his chin as he did so, as if about to deliver a robust defence. His nostrils flared and his eyes grew more prominent. "That was unworthy of you," he said, visibly fighting for self-control. "Oversimplifications are never wise. What I *said* was that there could just possibly be a connection with some valuable items that have been unaccounted for, perhaps. We are doing our best to track these items, which is no easy task. We have no supporting evidence that any valuable jewellery even existed. There are people who can help us, of course. Ten years is not unduly long."

153

Simmy deflated rapidly. "Sorry," she said. "I don't know why that made me so cross."

"I do," said Bonnie. "You thought it might look bad for Christopher, and you didn't like the idea of that."

Simmy frowned. "You haven't even *met* him properly," she accused. "What makes you think you know what I think of him?"

Moxon was watching them both closely, nodding slightly to himself. "You knew him as a child, didn't you?" he said.

"What does that have to do with anything? We've been through all that. It's the whole reason why our families know each other in the first place."

"So he's like a brother to you? Is that it? And the others? Are you just as close to them as well?"

"I haven't been close to any of them for about twenty years. I did some of the flowers for Frances's funeral, and then I went to it for my mother's sake, that's all. And when Frances left me this book, I met the family again. On Monday. I've seen them all in the past week. So what?" She almost shouted the final words.

"Why did you tell us about the jewellery?" Bonnie asked. She had been quietly thinking ever since the information had been revealed. "If you don't think there might be something to it, that is. You must have a reason."

Again, respect and admiration were clear in his eyes. Again, he said, "You really are learning a lot from Ben, aren't you?"

"He makes everything seem so obvious," the girl smiled. "There are rules, you see. People generally have

154

some reason for saying things, even if they don't seem relevant. People like you, anyhow. You don't just waffle on about stuff that's not important. So there's something about these jewels that you think Simmy or I might know, or find out, or suggest. Isn't there?"

"Why not just get to the point?" demanded Simmy. "This is giving me a very bad headache."

"There really is no exact point. But I have to admit, I thought it might be worth running past you. Listen —" He looked cautiously towards the street door, checking that nobody was about to come into the shop, and went on to speak in a slow, formal tone: "This is not part of the main investigation. I'm happy to admit that there is no direct evidence pointing to valuables being stolen, or anything of that sort. And yet, it is a lead, and we have no choice but to take notice of it. Given that we've had a lot of useful assistance from you and your young friends in the past, it occurred to me that there could be some more help in a less than official capacity. Christopher Henderson runs an auction house near Keswick, as I understand it. This raises a number of ideas — theories, even. It gives him all kinds of opportunities. Now, don't get excited." He raised a hand to forestall the protest that Simmy was about to make. "We have no reason to think there's anything going on there — other than the inevitable minor scams and deceptions. But if the police show up, asking questions and poking around, that would be totally counterproductive. Plus, we haven't enough manpower to send anyone up there for the best part of

155

a day. So you . . ." He spread his hands in a wordless appeal.

"You want me to go as a spy for the police? How in the world do you think I could even *begin* to recognise a scam even if it was happening right under my nose? I don't know the first thing about what happens at an auction." But she remembered that Christopher had invited her to go, and she was already more than half hooked on the idea.

"Take Ben with you," said Bonnie. "He'd find the whole thing absolutely thrilling."

Moxon gave her another beam of approval.

"Just what I was thinking," he said.

Simmy made no promises. Instead, she raised objections about having to close the shop, not knowing what Ben's commitments might be, worrying that she might feel conspicuous or even bid for something accidentally.

"It doesn't start until ten," Moxon told her. "And goes on until about five. You could close an hour or so early, and be there by noon. The sale would still have hours to go."

Simmy pouted mulishly at the idea of the shop only being open for a couple of hours. Then she sighed, and said, "Well, given how quiet it is these days, I suppose it wouldn't matter."

"Christopher's not going to be selling his grandmother's jewellery, is he?" Bonnie said. "He wouldn't be such a fool."

"Not this weekend, anyway," said Moxon. "I believe items have to be delivered at least ten days before the sale date." He huffed a brief laugh. "Although I imagine he can break his own rules if he chooses to."

"You said you didn't actually think that was what had happened," Simmy reminded him.

"I said there was insufficient evidence for any firm theory," he corrected her. "I'd just be happy for you to go along and get a sense of how it all works. You never know — it might be the start of a whole new interest for you."

Bonnie giggled. "I know she doesn't want me to say it, but I think Simmy already has a new interest, and it's called Christopher," she said. "And don't shout at me again," she warned Simmy. "I can tell by your face — every time anybody says his name, you go pink."

"Which makes it all the more unlikely that I'll spy on him as you want me to." She had abandoned any attempt to deny the involuntary flushes that came with discussion of her old friend. At some point in the past twenty-four hours, she had indeed reverted to her adolescent feelings for him. Deny them as she might, these feelings were simmering warmly inside her, and no way would she ever manage to persuade Bonnie otherwise. At least it wasn't Melanie, her previous assistant, who had made it a personal mission to find Simmy a mate. Bonnie might be interested, but it was far from being an obsession.

"I *could* send a detective constable, I suppose," said Moxon. "If you really won't do it for me."

"I really don't see why I should act as an unpaid secret agent for the police," she said.

"You might think of it as a public service, in the interests of society at large."

"Ben would love it, if you took him with you," Bonnie commented. "I wish I could go as well, but Corinne's got me lined up for some shopping in the afternoon. And I've got to take Spike for a run. He's getting fat."

Despite herself, Simmy was growing increasingly excited at the prospect of a new experience. Never inclined to watch the legions of television programmes about antiques and salerooms, she nonetheless carried a notion of their romance. Unrecognised treasures, fierce competition to acquire an item, the sheer beauty of well-made old objects, whether teapots or candlesticks — it all carried a special appeal.

"All right, then," she said.

Ben came into the shop at three o'clock, much more hesitantly than usual. One glance at his face sent Simmy into a tizzy. He was pale, drawn and tousled. "Gosh, you look terrible," she cried, without thinking.

Bonnie flew to his side, and lifted one of his arms over her shoulders, huddling against him. If anything, the result was to make him look even worse. "I didn't sleep," he said, with a lopsided smile.

"Don't give me that," said Simmy. "Since when has one wakeful night made a person your age look like death? Something else is going on."

"Nothing you don't know about. Just stuff going round my head. My mum's not helping. And it was grim yesterday. Taught me more than I needed to know about how the police work."

"Moxo was here this morning," said Bonnie. "He thinks you and Simmy should go to Keswick tomorrow."

"What? No, I can't. I've got so much *work*." His head seemed to hang like a great weight on his neck, pulling his shoulders into a downward curve. "It's all a bit much."

"It's the auction. Christopher Henderson's place. Moxon wants us to do some spying for him."

"I can't," he insisted.

Simmy gave him a long look, calculating her anxiety levels. She was not his mother. He wasn't going to die. But there had been damage done to him a few months earlier, as much psychological as physical, and nobody was quite sure how vulnerable he had become as a result. This was combined with a heavy burden of schoolwork, and a sudden growth spurt, so that his former energy was sadly depleted, and had been for a while. "I'm not sure I'm brave enough to go on my own," she said.

"Brave? Why do you have to be brave?"

She felt foolish and pathetic, having to explain. But new situations frightened her, and always had. The prospect of walking into a crowded auction room where she understood nothing of the procedures, and was very unlikely to see a familiar face other than

Christopher's, was too daunting for comfort. "I won't know what to do," she said weakly.

"Neither would I. Why does that matter? Are you planning to buy something?"

"Not at all. So — what? Do I just stand there doing nothing? Won't that seem conspicuous?"

"Not as much as if you started waving at your friend the auctioneer," chuckled Bonnie. "Then you might accidentally spend a thousand quid on a garden statue or something."

"I'm not *that* stupid."

"Good. Why not take your mum? I bet she'd think it was a big treat. Has she ever been to an auction?"

"Not as far as I know. She did say she wants some new china, and an auction would be a good place to get it. But she could never get away at such short notice. She'll be much too busy. *Everybody's* too busy, aren't they? Even me. It makes you wonder who's got time to go and bid for antiques on a Saturday morning, in the first place."

"Well, you've got to go," Bonnie said flatly. "You told Moxo you would."

"I didn't say for definite. He wouldn't expect me to go on my own." Without it ever having been openly stated, she knew that the detective knew where she stood on the matter of unfamiliar places and people.

"Anyway — I want to tell you about yesterday," Ben burst out. At the same time, he slid down onto the only seat in the shop. His usual practice was to half perch on a corner of the table that served as the shop counter. "I haven't told either of you what happened."

Bonnie leant against him like a loving dog. "Go on, then," she prompted.

"I thought I knew all about how the police work. I thought I could just give them some pointers and timings and so forth, and it would be like the other times. Ambleside, Coniston — where they *listened* to me. Or I thought they did," he finished miserably.

"They did, Ben. That dossier you constructed over the Ambleside business was really useful. Moxon wasn't just pretending to humour you."

"Right. But I didn't *see* anything then, did I? It was all theoretical."

"You saw more than enough in Windermere," she reminded him.

"That's the thing," he nodded, as if they'd finally got to a central point. "My mum says it must be PTSD, going right back to that. She wants me to go and see a psych person about it."

Bonnie squeezed herself even closer, rubbing his shoulder soothingly. He patted her hand like an old man.

"Maybe you shouldn't tell us about yesterday, then," said Simmy. "Not if it's going to dredge things up for you, and upset you."

He shook his head. "Too late to worry about that. The problem was — it was some woman who interviewed me, and not Moxon. She's another DI, brought in from Yorkshire or somewhere, for a few months. I don't really understand why. They hadn't briefed her at all about who I was, so she jumped right in, wanting to know exactly what I was doing in the bungalow, and whether I knew Mr Henderson, and how I could explain my fingerprints being all over the room, and why I'd waited so long before calling for help. Then she wouldn't let me explain about Bonnie being outside, and me needing to keep her away. As it was, she saw more than I wanted her to. But the *smell*, and the *look* of him. She didn't get that. Thank goodness."

Simmy smiled at this old-fashioned male protectiveness, while thinking that Bonnie would very likely have been much more able to deal with it than Ben had turned out to be. Simmy knew from experience that women coped with the realities of death — and birth — rather better than men did.

Bonnie kept stroking him, almost purring. No shrill feminist objections from her to being protected by her young man. *Wise girl*, thought Simmy. There were plenty of other ways to skin the same cat. Meanwhile, Ben clearly needed all the reassurance and affirmation he could get. "It's a huge thing," she said, "when somebody dies. Even if they're ninety-nine and just pass away in their sleep — it still leaves a gap. When a person's murdered, it's much worse."

"I know," he said. "I've seen dead people before."

"It's not just *seeing* them, is it? It's understanding what's happened. And last time, you were distracted away from all that. You probably just pushed it all down and never went back to it." She found herself remembering elements from her own experience. "So now that there's been another death, all your buried feelings about the earlier ones have come flooding out, and you're having to cope with a double or triple dose. The point seems to be that you can't dodge it for ever. I think a counsellor of some sort would be really helpful. All that would happen is that you could sort out your own reactions and get them under control."

The boy grimaced, and shook his head. "I get the theory of all that, but what does it mean on a practical level? Am I going to be useless as a forensic archaeologist, after all? What if I can't face the reality of the business? I mean — in *Bones* they have to deal with the most revolting gory stuff, and they never even flinch. What if I don't manage it?"

Ben's ambitions had been conceived through a combination of obsessive watching of the American TV series, an encounter with sudden death on his seventeenth birthday, and a genius-level showing in academic studies, which virtually ensured that he could walk into any course of study he chose. Until this moment, the stark physical reality of murder had somehow failed to impinge on him.

"They'll expect that. It's bound to be a big part of the training."

"I feel a total mess," he said.

"Join the club," said Bonnie. "It doesn't last, though. You've just had too much going on all at once — like Simmy says. College work, all that business in Hawkshead, your mum having a meltdown and now this with the Henderson man. It would flatten an elephant." She gave Simmy a straight look. "And then you wanting him to go to Keswick — there's no way that'll happen. Why don't you take your father?" she finished, on a sudden flash of inspiration. "I bet he'd love it."

Simmy's first reaction was strong resistance, before she caught herself up. What was she thinking, to dismiss Russell as no longer a feasible partner in any new venture? Had his recent lapse into anxiety and self-absorption been so great that it justified such a view? "You know — that might be a really good idea," she said. "We've been tiptoeing round him, coming close to writing him off as a demented old fool, when he's actually not nearly as bad as we think."

"You've probably been making him worse," said Bonnie. "I've been thinking that for a while now."

"How?" The automatic defensive response was half-hearted. Simmy already had a suspicion she knew the answer to her own question.

"You said it yourself. Not letting him carry on as usual. He's not really *old*, is he? He might live another twenty years. Do you want him to be a burden on your mum and you for all that time?"

"My mother would kill him, long before that." It was only partly a joke. Angie's patience quotient was famously low at the best of times.

"So take him with you tomorrow. Don't open the shop at all — it won't matter much this time of year. Be there at the start, and just watch how it all works. It'll be *fun*, Simmy. And you'll see Christopher again, won't you."

"And there was me thinking I would be the decisive one today," said Simmy with a rueful little laugh.

164

CHAPTER
FOURTEEN

Simmy was on her parents' doorstep at five-forty, exactly simultaneously with a family of four expecting bed and breakfast services. The coincidence was unfortunate in one sense, because her mother would be engaged with the routine settling in and explanations that happened numerous times each week. On the other hand, her father might be available for a quiet conversation without the interventions that would inevitably come from Angie. On a sudden whim, Simmy had tucked the inherited flower book under her arm before leaving the shop, and was carrying it now. It might help her to provide a reason for going to Christopher's auction house in the first place, although the logic remained very shaky. Moxon's hunches about family valuables felt decidedly tenuous, and a long way from anything Simmy had ever known about the Hendersons.

Russell was not in his usual place beside the Rayburn. Neither was his dog. Before she could ask Angie where they were, the whole party of new arrivals were being escorted upstairs, and Simmy had no chance of gaining any attention. So she went in search of her father, starting with the family sitting room, access to which was forbidden to the guests. It was empty, so she tried the dining room, where four tables were already laid for breakfast. While there were only three rooms used for visitors, Angie had made a point of offering a separate table for children, especially after their parents had spent a whole night in the same room with them. The family room was at the furthest end of the house, since midnight arguments and fruitless attempts at discipline could be disturbing for other guests.

The dining room was as empty as the sitting room had been. That left only the big downstairs room where people could play games, read, talk or otherwise escape. Either that or the bedroom that her parents shared upstairs must harbour Simmy's father, and probably his dog.

He was doing a jigsaw in one corner of the room. Bertie, the Lakeland terrier, was lying across his feet. "Hey, Dad," said Simmy. "I couldn't find you."

"Well, now you have," he said with a smile. "You can help me with this, if you like."

She looked over his shoulder at the picture. It was a chaotic depiction of a domestic scene in which all the characters were cats. It was about three-quarters done. "How long has it taken you?" she asked.

"Oh, I didn't start it. There was a man here for a few days with his boy. The weather kept them in rather a lot, so they embarked on this foolish thing. They left without finishing it, and I couldn't bring myself to put it all away until I'd done it. It's much harder than it looks."

"It looks pretty hard."

He laughed. "You never were very fond of jigsaws, were you?"

"Not really. But I can see how they might appeal on a chilly winter evening. Except it's not very warm in here, is it?"

"It's all right. Did you want to talk to me? It'll be supper time soon. People have arrived. Why in the world they choose to come here in November passes my understanding. They'll have to go out again and find something to eat. But it's dry tomorrow, lucky for them."

"I did have something to suggest to you, actually. How would you fancy an expedition to Keswick tomorrow?"

"Expedition? On camel back, or snowshoes?"

She laughed. "Neither. In my car. I've been asked to go to an auction, and I'm too shy to do it by myself."

"Auction? What sort? Flowers? Old farm implements? A country house sale?" His eyes sparkled. "That would be interesting. I might find some fancy pots for the garden. Or a piece of old trellis. I decided I'd put up a trellis in the spring."

"It's mostly antiques, I think."

"Who asked you to go?"

"Christopher Henderson. He's the auctioneer — or one of them. I said it sounded interesting, and he told me to come and see for myself. I'd like to, wouldn't you? Mum says you need new plates and bowls and things — we could bid if there's anything we like."

"Tomorrow's Saturday. What about your shop?"

She pulled a face. "I thought I'd give myself a weekend off. Awful of me, I know, but nobody's wanting flowers at this time of year, so I'm risking it."

"Good for you. Wish we'd done the same. Fancy coming here on holiday in November," he repeated, with a shake of his head. "Some people are off their chumps, if you ask me."

"Off their chumps? Did you make that up?"

"I don't think so," he frowned. "Or did I? It sounds odd, now you mention it." He gave it some thought, before giving up the attempt. "But listen. I was thinking about words, just now. Have you ever thought about 'nounce' and what it means?"

"I can safely say I have not. Why?"

"Because there are so many prefixes to it. Pronounce. Denounce. Announce. Renounce. I think there might even be enounce, although I'm not sure about that. They all mean something a bit different. Didn't any of your teachers draw your attention to that at school?"

"Not that I remember, Dad. It's a while ago now."

"Hm."

"But Ben would agree with you that it's really interesting. Must be Latin, presumably."

"Must be," Russell nodded. He greatly approved of Ben's Latin studies, while regretting his own deficiency in the subject. Already, when Russell was at school in the 1950s, Latin had ceased to be a universally taught subject. He had done it for a year or two, remembering almost nothing apart from "*amo, amas, amat*".

"So what about the auction?"

"Auction? Oh, yes." He slotted another jigsaw piece into place, causing Simmy to fear that he had lost the thread of the conversation. But then he looked up at her. "I don't mind if I do. I've been cooped up indoors all week, and I could fancy a little outing. If your mother doesn't object, that is."

"She won't. She'll be glad to get you out of the way."

A flicker of pain crossed his face, and she instantly regretted her words. Where six months earlier, Russell would have laughingly agreed with her, now such a comment was liable to fuel his worries about security and nameless dangers. One peculiar effect of his condition was that he mistrusted sarcasm and irony. He had lost the ability to distinguish them from literal meaning, which often led to unhappy misunderstandings.

"Joke, Dad," said Simmy quickly. "She doesn't really think you're in her way. She'll just be glad for you to have a change of scene. She'd come herself, I expect, if she didn't have so much to do here."

"Kit and Frances are both dead," Russell said, with startling abruptness. "Our friends from the day you were born. I find that a terrible thing to absorb. Quite terrible. Someone killed Kit, in his own home. And you have been trying to keep it from me. You and your mother, of course."

"Yes, we have."

"I know why — of course I do. I might do the same thing myself in your place. But it makes me doubt you. Do you see that? It makes me think there are secrets everywhere, and nothing is what it seems. It makes my worries even larger."

"It's hard to know what to do for the best. You've changed so much over the past months." She choked on her own guilt and concern. "It's a natural instinct not to want to upset you any more."

He pulled himself to his feet, and stood face-to-face with her. "P'simmon Straw, listen to me. I am fully aware of how I've changed. I don't like it any more than you do. I'm even prepared to accept that something chemical in my brain is responsible for some of it. But there are hard facts of the matter, as well. A number of people close to you — and me, now — have been deliberately killed. I am aware that there have been sound reasons for this, which have no direct connection to our family, and that there is very little reason to think we will ever become murder victims ourselves. But that would have been Kit's belief as well. That's where all efforts at reassurance fall apart, do you see? Nobody can give me a guarantee, and without that, I can't seem to get around my so-called neurosis. But hiding things from me is definitely not the right approach." He reached for her shoulders and gave her a gentle shake. "Do you see?"

"Of course I do, Dad. And I know it's been my doing, even if unintentionally. I moved up here, disturbed your peace and dragged you into a lot of horrible happenings. It's the flowers. I never dreamt how flowers can be at the heart of intense feelings, nasty as well as nice. But that's how it is. They're so engrained in the big moments, that's the trouble." She

170

paused, wondering whether he was hearing her. Each one was urgently trying to convey something of major importance to the other. Simmy could feel her father's hands shaking on her shoulders, and knew that she was quivering in turn. It was a rare moment of shared revelation, digging down to the lower levels, where hardly anybody ever went.

"Well, that's what you get when someone promises you a rose garden," he smiled. "You know — like that lovely song. But rose gardens have lots of thorns and stinging things as well. That's the way life goes, I guess."

"So are you coming to the auction with me? I haven't been entirely honest about the reasons for going," she admitted. "There's a bit more to it than what I said just now."

"Come on, then. Let's go into the kitchen and start all over again."

Which they did, and Simmy carefully filled in the gaps in what Russell knew so far about Kit's death. It turned out to be very little fresh information, as they quickly realised. "And there was me getting so paranoid," he laughed. "Thinking I'd been excluded from all sorts of secrets. And you hardly know anything." He rubbed his brow. "Although I don't see how going to an auction is even remotely relevant."

"Nor do I," she said. "I could easily get a bit paranoid myself, wondering about it. Who am I meant to be spying on, and who for?"

"For whom," he corrected her mildly. "I'm tempted to think it's a conspiracy to give you a weekend off, and

nothing to do with the police investigations. After all —
when did you last have a free Saturday?"

"I left Melanie in charge a few times, back in the
spring. But not at all since Bonnie started. It didn't
even occur to me." She frowned. "But Moxon wouldn't
know that. And I can't imagine who he would be
conspiring with."

"Christopher, presumably."

"But Christopher has to be under suspicion for the
murder. The whole family must be, surely?"

"Not if he's got a proper alibi. Where does he say he
was on Tuesday afternoon?"

"I have no idea. I rely on Ben to find out that sort of
thing, if the question arises. But Ben's taking it all
rather hard. He looks awful."

"Poor boy," said Russell absently. "I wonder why it's
worse this time?"

"He says he hadn't got so close to a dead body
before and it was more upsetting than he realised."

Her father appeared to find this puzzling. "That
surprises me," he said. "Bodies are generally a lot *less*
upsetting in reality than people expect them to be. And
the lad's seen them before."

"I know. But there's definitely something the matter
with him."

"Didn't someone say his mother knew Kit and Fran?
Where did I hear that?"

"Mum, I expect. Although Helen didn't go to Fran's
funeral. I think it was ages ago, and never much of a
friendship."

172

"Hm," said Russell, so much like the father that Simmy had always known that she almost threw her arms round him in relief.

"What does that mean?"

"If Ben's in a state, it might have more to do with things at home, and not so much what he saw at the Hendersons'."

She thought about it for a minute. "Helen's certainly worried about him being hurt, after that business in Hawkshead. She's trying to stop him getting involved again — which is hopeless, of course. He was interviewed by the police yesterday — quite a heavy business, I gather. Bonnie was scared that they suspected that Ben was the killer." She smiled. "Can you imagine that? On the face of it, there was apparently some evidence that threw suspicion onto him. Silly, as it turned out."

"I always liked Christopher, you know." The abrupt change of subject threw her. Was Russell sliding back into the addle-headed state he'd often been in recently? "There was always something fearless about him that I admired."

"I know. He was very good company."

"He did you a lot of good. You were a timid little thing in those early years."

"I still am, Dad. That's why I need you to go with me to the auction. I'm far too wimpy to go by myself."

"Can we really buy something? Do they have good china? We need new serving dishes for the breakfasts so we can change the system we use now. We should put the bacon and sausages out on the sideboard, so people can take what they want. It's less wasteful that way."

"Is it? Aren't you just as likely to do too much, and have it left over?"

"Possibly. But if it hasn't been on someone's plate it can be warmed up again for the next day. Tricks of the trade," he grinned, tapping the side of his nose.

"But it won't work for eggs."

"True. The thing is, people have a habit of leaving meat, more than anything else. I don't understand why. I remember my mother always telling us to eat the meat, even if we left other things. I could never abandon a sausage halfway through."

"I still don't quite follow the logic of the serving dishes, but they probably have lots of china," she said. "And it'll be more interesting if we try to bid for something."

"How does it work? I wonder. I really have no idea at all."

"Nor me. I expect someone will explain it to us. They'll be happy to have new buyers, after all."

Angie Straw found them sitting close together at the kitchen table, like conspirators. "What's all this?" she demanded.

"We're going out tomorrow morning. We might be some time," said Russell.

"I see," said his wife. "And what happened to those potatoes I asked you to peel? There won't be any supper for us tonight at this rate."

CHAPTER
FIFTEEN

Simmy collected her father at eight-thirty the next morning, callously leaving Angie with most of the breakfast work. All the guests had been served, so the worst was over. Angie was clearly unsure about how to react. Pleased to have Russell out of her way, but sorry to be missing the fun, was roughly how it went. "Have a nice time," she said. "Don't be too late back. There's that American couple arriving at five. You know how you like chatting to Americans."

"I do," said Russell. "They're such fun to tease."

Teasing had been in short supply for a while, thought Simmy. Perhaps it had all been a temporary aberration, and her father would return to his old self, after all.

The plan had been to take the drive slowly, savouring the numerous beauty spots and landmarks along the way. Simmy would encourage her father to expatiate on all the many snippets of history he had acquired since living in Cumbria.

It worked better than she had dared to hope. Even as they followed the one-way system through Ambleside, he was noting how full Stock Ghyll was, and making a resolution to go and look at the waterfall before winter set in. "It's sure to be spectacular," he said. Then, as

175

they passed through Rydal, he waved a hand to the left, where the land rose mistily. "That's Loughrigg," he informed her. "And Elterwater's over there. Poor little lake — nobody ever remembers its existence."

"Same as Esthwaite," said Simmy, with a nervous laugh. Bad things had happened not long ago on the edge of Esthwaite Water.

"Not to mention Wastwater, Ennerdale, Haweswater and Bassenthwaite," he listed. "People are very unadventurous, you know. They think of Derwentwater, Windermere and Coniston, and leave all the others out."

"I suppose they all have their champions. They just haven't established the same levels of fame. I must admit I've never seen Haweswater or Bassenthwaite."

"You should be ashamed," he said kindly. "Although I blame myself. I ought to have forced you to come on an excursion with me. Several excursions, in fact."

"We'll do it next spring. First chance we get," she promised him.

"And we'll be passing Thirlmere in a minute. Perhaps we could stop for a bit and see how it's behaving."

"That's not it, is it?" She ducked her chin at a stretch of water to their left.

"No, silly. That's Rydalmere, as they used to call it. Another lovely little lake — or mere, as I should be calling them. You'd better not look while you're driving, but it's quite delightful. Very small, and rather an odd shape."

Traffic was irritatingly heavy, and proceeding too fast for Simmy to be able to crawl past all the sights as Russell pointed them out. She knew nobody else who could name almost every peak and valley, often with a snippet of history to go with it. "Poetry country," he murmured. "You can see why, can't you?"

"So much water," she noted. "There'll be floods again if it goes on raining." In fact, they had chosen a singularly dry day for their outing. The clouds had thinned after weeks of drizzle, but the light was still far from bright.

"Nothing we haven't all seen before," he said cheerfully, ignoring the repeated influxes of water in Cockermouth, Keswick and Carlisle which had caused considerable distress and loss. "In the olden days, the farmers were forever losing vital crops because of the weather. I suppose they might be still — but nobody worries about them any more."

"So *that* must be Thirlmere," Simmy said, five minutes later.

"No, you numbskull. That's Grasmere. How could you not know that?"

"I do, really. I thought we were further on, that's all."

"Fibber," he said. "You've got no idea. Those woods we've just passed are called White Moss Common. They're lovely for walking from one mere to the other. I can't think why we haven't done it together. Your mother and I came here about a dozen times in our first year."

"We've all been hopelessly busy."

"Well, more fools us. And there's the way into Dove Cottage, look."

She realised how blinkered she generally was when driving around the region. Admittedly, she seldom had to deliver flowers any further north than Ambleside, but there had been a few times when she'd been sent to Rydal, and even Grasmere once or twice. The profusion of small lakes, filling every hollow on every side, was undeniably confusing, but she had not even taken the trouble to give them a long look. Given that they were still slightly early for the Keswick auction, she would make a point of stopping beside Thirlmere as Russell had requested, and let him savour it as long as he liked.

"Young Ben's doing a project on Wordsworth, isn't he?"

"He was. I don't know if he's kept it going. It was all to do with Hawkshead and Ann Tyson. I think it lapsed after everything that happened."

"He should come up here. The great man lived in any number of different properties in and around Grasmere. He's buried here, of course."

The village of Grasmere was similar to Hawkshead to the extent that it existed almost exclusively for the delectation of tourists. The main road ran close by in a similar fashion, but traffic was not as discouraged here as it was in Hawkshead. And Grasmere's road was very much busier than the little meandering example further south. The A591 was a serious highway, with all the noise and danger and modern bustle that went with it.

"It's getting more and more mountainous," she observed. "Just look at them!"

178

"Helm Crag," he nodded. "And Silver Howe. Not sure what the others are. Don't the woods look wonderful!" The trees were still hanging onto the last of their autumn leaves, giving a mottled colour scheme of browns and greys, at the foot of the great fells. "Soon be bare branches and dead bracken on all sides."

And then, at last, the water on their left really was Thirlmere. "And that's Helvellyn himself," Russell pointed out, on the other side of the road. "You can walk to the top from here."

Simmy pulled off the road and turned off the engine. "Which is way up in the clouds," she observed. "Let's sit here for a bit. Tell me some history."

"Well, you know, I hope, that this is more of a reservoir than a natural lake. There's a dam just up there, at the northern end. It was constructed to supply the city of Manchester with water, in the early 1880s. There was passionate opposition to it, mainly because the little original lake had beautiful steep cliffs running down into it, and they've been submerged now."

"I did not know that," she confessed. "I had no idea."

The water rippled placidly not far below the point where they were parked. No other vehicles were in the small off-road area, and they could sit admiring the crags on the western side of the mere, with the faintest of reflections in the ripples. The peace was palpable, despite traffic passing at their backs. Simmy could see a dozen places where a person might hide away from the world, even building a tiny shelter for themselves. Overhanging branches on the edge of woods,

179

crumbling stone walls covered in moss, rocky outcrops — they could all offer sanctuary from the wicked world.

"It's so different from Windermere and Bowness," she sighed. "Don't you wish you lived out here instead?"

"Oh no." He was decisive. "I'd hate having to drive everywhere, for a start. Forty years ago, I might have tried it, but not now. This is no land for old men, as the saying goes."

"Just sheep, then?"

"Even they get taken down to softer levels in the worst of the winter."

They covered the last five or six miles without much additional comment, beyond the identification of Bassenthwaite in the distance like a sheet of lead. "So many of them," Simmy sighed, knowing how unoriginal she was being. "And most of us who live here just take them all for granted."

"There's nothing intrinsically special about a lake," said Russell. "The geology is far from mysterious. A wet climate, combined with exceptionally uneven ground, forms collections of water as a matter of course. Rivers feed them, and rocky foundations prevent them draining away as they would do in chalk land. All significance has been applied by humankind, and its confounded imagination."

"Don't give me that," said Simmy. "You absolutely love every inch of it."

They found the auction house with only a little difficulty. It stood close to a housing estate, with scant

180

provision for cars. Circling the cluttered parking area in vain, they were forced to go into a residential road and leave the car there.

"Bad planning," Russell remarked.

"Victims of their own success, probably," said Simmy. "All those television programmes about antiques have got everybody doing it. Come on — there probably won't be anywhere to sit, either, at this rate. People obviously get here really early."

Inside the main entrance was an office with people clustered around it. Simmy and Russell watched them, trying to grasp the process that was under way. It was quarter to ten. "We have to buy a catalogue," Simmy concluded. "See — everybody's got one."

"Shouldn't we have come to a preview, to see what's for sale? Once they start bidding, we won't be able to wander round looking at things."

"I expect we should, ideally. But we didn't, so we'll just have to catch up." She peered through a set of double doors into a large room containing rows of chairs with people on them, many settled comfortably, looking as if they'd been there for hours. Shelves and stacks of objects were densely arranged around all four walls. There were pictures hanging up, big pieces of furniture projecting into the room, rugs and carpets draped over a rail fixed halfway up one wall, and a few cabinets she assumed must contain the most valuable items. On a wall above a table was a large screen; below it was a bank of laptop computers and telephones.

"Blimey!" she said. "It all looks ever so efficient."

"Do you need a buyer's number?" asked the woman in the office, when they got to the front of the queue.

"Oh yes," said Russell eagerly.

"Have you bought here before?"

"First time."

"We'll need you to complete this form, then. The sale starts in ten minutes," she warned. "You'll be lucky to get seats."

They were given a boldly printed number on a card, and directed into the big saleroom. There were no empty chairs, but people were resting against the furniture around the walls, so Simmy and Russell gingerly perched on the arm of a big leather chesterfield, half expecting to be told to move.

"What a load of riff-raff," whispered Russell. "Look at them!"

It was true that there were numerous men with sharp eyes and two-day stubble. One had a docile toddler perched on his shoulders. There were women only marginally better groomed. Long grey hair was common, framing lean, wrinkled faces. But there were also some sleekly prosperous individuals scattered around, amongst the majority of quite normal-looking people.

The screen was showing the lots, changing every few seconds — a compelling parade of figures, collectables, toys, ornaments, and all sorts of other objects. Simmy was watching it in delight, when it went blank and a crackle came over a public address system.

And there was Christopher, somehow unobserved until that moment. He was sitting on a raised rostrum, flanked by two women at a lower level, each with a laptop. Another woman hovered close by. With little fanfare, Christopher launched into an introductory spiel about commission rates, procedures for paying, estimated length of the auction and warning about parking in restricted areas. He seemed relaxed, comfortable in his situation. He was also unmistakably charismatic. Perhaps it was the way everything was set up — all eyes on him, including the team of subservient women, his easy manner and ready smile. And *should* he be smiling like that, less than a week after the death of his father, Simmy wondered. Wasn't it rather heartless? She watched him with complete absorption, the rest of the room a vague sea of faces and antiques that mattered nothing to her.

"Hello! There's that man from Fran's funeral," said Russell into her ear. Unlike his daughter, he had been scanning the room with interest, curious to know who came to such sales, and impatient for the real action to get started.

"What?" Simmy blinked at him. "What man?"

"There. See." He pointed unselfconsciously at a row of chairs in the middle of the room. "Grey coat."

"Oh, yes. He came into the shop yesterday. I can't seem to get away from him." She watched the man with a woman she quickly realised was Hannah, trying to judge the relationship between them. It all appeared to be focused on the sale catalogue, and their heads remained a respectable six inches apart as they showed each other items of interest.

"Malcolm Wetherton," said Russell confidently. "And isn't that one of the Henderson girls next to him?"

"Yes, it's Hannah. Fancy that! Now shush. It's starting, look."

The lots were visible both in reality and on the screen above Christopher's head. The first was a mink coat from the 1930s, held aloft by one of the women workers. On the screen it looked oddly different. Bidding was slow to start, with Christopher urging, "Fifty pounds? No? Forty, then. Come on, someone start me at forty. Okay, how about thirty?" It should have sounded pleading, the figures dropping so rapidly, but it was all done with a twinkle, and once a bidder raised a hand at twenty, there was a sudden brisk exchange, during which the final bid reached fifty-five pounds.

"Out of fashion, fur," said Russell. "Probably cost ten times that when it was new."

And so the pattern was set for the next fascinating hour and a quarter. Simmy barely glanced at the people in the room, except to try and work out who was bidding, now and then. And every few minutes she glanced at Hannah and the Wetherton man, their presence oddly discomforting. At eleven-fifteen, Russell demanded coffee from the cafeteria attached to the building. They made their way around the edge of the saleroom, Simmy reluctant to miss any of the proceedings. "We should be quick," she urged. "We'll have lost our place."

"Never mind. We can find others." Her father was obviously enjoying himself enormously, despite showing no sign yet of bidding for anything. Simmy herself was starting to find the whole procedure somewhat repetitive. The same few people seemed to be buying almost every lot, with whole rows ignoring the business in front of them and chatting rather loudly amongst themselves. She was glad for the break, holding the coffee mug with both hands and wondering what provision there might be for lunch, in another hour or so's time.

The coffee was insipid, and Russell was obviously eager to go back for another session. "I'm going to mark the prices things fetch," he said. "I'm sure we've got a few pieces just as good at home. For a start, what's happened to suitcases? I've seen three battered old objects go for thirty or forty pounds each."

Simmy could offer no explanation. "You're not thinking of selling anything, are you?"

"There's a lot of clutter around the house," he said thoughtfully.

"This is not going to be the start of a new interest, Dad. You'd end up buying a whole lot more than you sell."

"I could learn the ropes, and make sure that doesn't happen."

She ought to be pleased that he was enjoying himself so much, she told herself. The purpose for their being there was growing fainter as time went on, and the boredom level increased. Christopher was wholly immersed in his work, and had barely nodded her way once. He had to constantly scan the room for bidders, listen to what the women with the computers were

185

telling him, remember where the numbers had got to, and generally maintain concentration. His voice rose and fell, sometimes gabbling so fast the words ran together, and other times pausing for reluctant bidders to yield to temptation. It took Simmy a long time to grasp the rhythms of the process, and to understand when he was addressing someone directly through Skype or whatever system was on the computer. One thing that did surprise her was the blatancy of the bidding. She had expected small gestures — scratching a nose or flicking a finger — but people waved their catalogues or hands quite openly in order to attract attention. Then, once they were under the eye of the auctioneer, everything grew more subtle. A small nod signified an ongoing intention to buy. The traditional fall of the hammer was never omitted, and at that signal, one of the flanking women moved the image on the screen to the next lot to be sold. It was a hypnotic mixture of modern technology and age-old business practice.

At some point after midday, Simmy ceased to be bored. The miscellaneous section had all been sold and attention turned to china and porcelain. Familiar and unfamiliar names came and went. Royal Worcester, Staffordshire, Belleek, Poole — so much high-quality stuff was here for the taking, and some of the prices seemed to her surprisingly low. Lovely jugs, tea sets, ornaments were being bought for the price of a dozen roses. Then she felt a movement at her side, and before she knew it, her father was waving his rolled-up catalogue in a frenzy. He ignored her alarmed whisper of "Dad!" and before she knew it, had secured a gilt-edged dish, with a rosebud pattern in the centre, for twenty-five pounds.

"Number?" said the auctioneer, with some impatience.

Russell looked blank.

"You have to show your buyer's number," Simmy told him. "Where have you put it?"

The whole room seemed to focus on him as he searched for the card. Sighs and rustles could be heard. At last he extracted it from a pocket and held it up. "Sorry," he called cheerfully.

Christopher smiled tightly and moved briskly on.

Then, seemingly for the first time, Malcolm Wetherton caught sight of Simmy and recognised her. He had turned to see the cause of the delay, along with sixty other people, and seen her and her father. She watched him nudge Hannah and say something to her. She too craned her neck for a look, and smiled when she caught Simmy's eye. A smile that held absolutely nothing of friendliness or even fellowship. Just one of those smiles people gave instinctively when they met another person's eye. Simmy gave a little wave, and then quickly lowered her hand in case the gesture be mistaken for a bid.

"When can I have my lovely dish?" asked Russell, obliviously.

"Good question. We'll have to go and ask. You know you've got to pay another fifteen per cent on top of what you bid, don't you? Or even more. I forget what he said."

"Outrageous," laughed Russell.

"You were very rash," she chided. "For all you know, it's got a great big chip or crack in it."

"Oh, pooh. They wouldn't sell it if it was damaged. That woman wanted it as well, you know. I was determined to outbid her."

"Hannah and the Wetherton man have finally seen us. I've been watching them on and off all day. She doesn't look very pleased about us being here." She had forgotten that DI Moxon had asked her to come, and that she was apparently supposed to assess the likelihood of Henderson heirlooms being sold by Christopher, now his parents were both dead. If that *was* what he'd wanted from her. It had been very far from clear. In any case, she was sure she'd failed. All she'd done was learn a tiny fraction of the auction-room procedures and allow her father to make a reckless purchase.

"What are we doing now?" asked Russell, like a child. "Is it time for lunch?"

"Very much so. And then we're going home. It'll all be finished before five o'clock. I hope you've had fun?"

"Lovely," he sighed. "Best day I've had for ages."

They went to the office to pay for the dish, but before they could begin the transaction, Simmy felt a hand on her shoulder.

"Have you got time for a little talk?" asked Hannah. "I think we should."

"My dad as well?"

"Um . . . preferably not. Let him collect his dish and go and wait in the car or something."

"We're having lunch. You could join us."

"All right, then. That'll be better than nothing."

Simmy waited, thinking that perhaps here at last was a chance to do what Moxon wanted. She recalled Eddie Henderson's remark about Hannah's sourness over something Kit had done. Some tawdry piece of philandering that demeaned Frances. Christopher and Lynn had both talked about Hannah and George being very antagonistic for most of their childhood. There were aspects of Hannah that could well repay deeper enquiry. Ben Harkness would certainly think so.

They left Russell to fathom the procedure required of him before he could lay hands on his purchase, and went to the cafeteria. Simmy bought random items of food enough for two, and let Hannah hustle her to a table and embark on an urgent harangue.

"I hear you had dinner with Lynn and Chris on Thursday," she said accusingly. "And you've seen Eddie a time or two as well. You seem to be trying to insinuate yourself back into our family, for some reason. All because of that book my mother left you, I suppose. Well, I don't know what you think you'll get out of it. They're both dead — those people who adopted me, and then blackmailed me into never trying to find my natural parents. I can't help feeling I've been short-changed. How do you think it is for me, seeing you get that book? I'm their eldest daughter. It should have come to me."

"Do you really want it? It's not worth anything." Simmy was too startled by the attack to address the more central accusation, which was so outrageous as to be impossible to confront directly.

"I don't want the actual *thing*. But I don't want my mother — the only mother I've ever known — to favour you over me."

"She hasn't. She didn't. She never did that."

"Oh no? Pushing you at Chris the way she did, giving you all your favourite sweets, making such a production over how nicely you speak compared to me and Lynn. It was sickening sometimes."

"Twenty years ago, Hannah. I've hardly even seen her since then."

"Maybe not, but she kept on thinking about you. She saw you as some sort of paragon. I always felt her comparing us to you, to your advantage. And then there was your father, always so loyal and helpful, making us laugh, never mean with money like ours was. It made him look like Scrooge."

Simmy felt more proud than annoyed, and made no attempt to argue. "Well, I'm sorry," she said weakly. "I don't know what I could have done about it."

"Stay away from us now. Don't go making eyes at Christopher. Lynn told me what you were like at the Belsfield. Following him up here, just so you could sit there all dreamy, watching him for hours on end. Sickening," she said again.

Then Russell found them, proudly brandishing his piece of china. "Look at it!" he crowed. "It's even more lovely than I thought. It's going to look perfect on the sideboard." He laughed. "God save the child who knocks it off and breaks it."

Simmy and Hannah both froze for a few moments, and then silently agreed to shelve the acrimony in the presence of this cheerful old man. "Well done, Dad," Simmy smiled. "It's good to have a souvenir of the day."

"I should get back," said Hannah. "There's some glass I've got my eye on. It'll be up before long."

"That's Malcolm Wetherton you're with, isn't it?" said Simmy.

"What if it is? He does a bit of dealing here and there. Has a stall in the antique market down in Barrow, once a month. He's got an excellent eye for a bargain. Cheryl usually comes with us as well, so don't you go making anything of it. Jack and I are perfectly happy, and so are the Wethertons."

"But it's a bit of a coincidence, isn't it?"

"In what way?"

"Well, with Christopher being an auctioneer . . ." Simmy's mind was slowly forming dark notions about corruption and malpractice in the auction room. But that would involve Christopher in shady dealings, which felt all wrong. For one thing, he would not be such a fool. And for another, he was *decent*. All her life, she had held him somewhere inside her as a beacon of decency and fairness. His clear gaze could not conceivably conceal guilty secrets and dishonest deals.

"That's not what —" Again she stopped herself. Russell was looking from one face to the other, in confusion. "I got you some pie, Dad," she said. "It's meant to be hot, so you'd better eat it quick. They're not very nice when they go cold."

"Are you married, my dear?" Russell asked Hannah. "Forgive my forgetfulness. I do remember you very clearly as a little thing on the beach. You and your sister were always so *lively*."

"Yes, married with a little boy. He's five. Lynn and I were not so much lively as trying to get away from our brothers," said Hannah. "Screaming our heads off in panic, and you grown-ups all thinking it was harmless play." Her brow darkened. "I was in terror for a lot of the time."

"Surely not," said Russell mildly.

"Oh, yes. Sheer stark terror. I really thought George would kill me one day." She paused, and put a hand to the back of her neck, as if in pain. "And now somebody's killed our dad."

"Well, it can't have been George," said Russell with a laugh.

"Can't it?" said Hannah. "I'm not so sure."

CHAPTER
SIXTEEN

Driving back to Windermere, Russell cradling his precious dish on his lap, Simmy rehearsed what she would say to Moxon when he inevitably caught up with her. George had been the shadowy figure in the whole Henderson business from the start. He had attended his mother's funeral, sitting stiffly in the front pew with his siblings and girlfriend, and then disappeared before the tea and cakes afterwards. Tales of his behaviour towards his sisters had erupted in the following days, leaving Simmy wondering how she could have been so unobservant. And how Christopher could have removed himself so irresponsibly from the fray. As the oldest brother, he surely had a duty to maintain some sort of peace and harmony amongst the others. Instead, he and Simmy had gone off together, fostering both mothers' fantasies of a permanent bond beyond that of pretend twins.

She also wanted to debate the matter of Hannah's resentment at having been adopted and then abandoned by Fran, albeit involuntarily. The woman seemed to feel that a kind of natural justice had been flouted; that if she had at least made herself known to her birth mother, she would have a parent to fall back on, so to speak. Of course, she could still begin the quest for that original mother, who might well turn out to be only in her fifties, and somebody worth knowing.

Then her phone trilled somewhere behind her. "Dad — can you reach my bag and answer the phone?" she asked.

"Not really. I might drop the dish," he demurred. "It's probably nothing important."

"I suppose so. I don't know why I switched the silly thing on, when I'm driving." She knew quite well, in fact, that she had assumed she could delegate answering it to Russell. Putting it on the back seat had been the main mistake.

The noise stopped and Simmy kept driving. But it niggled at her for the next five miles. Who would call her on a Saturday afternoon? Moxon was the most likely, but she had a few other ideas. Perhaps Christopher had finished selling all the lots at the auction, and wanted to speak to her. Perhaps her mother was wanting to know how they were doing. Perhaps Bonnie, Ben, Melanie or even Ninian had called. Ninian Tripp had been abandoned as a lost cause, only a few weeks earlier, after a tepid romance that left Simmy profoundly unsatisfied. She felt, perhaps unfairly, that he owed her a sort of apology. And she would really enjoy a long catch-up call from Melanie, her former assistant in the shop.

"I hope they left a message," she worried.

"Who?"

"Whoever it was phoning me."

194

"They will if it's important. Isn't this a lovely road," he sighed. "Isn't it fabulous up here? We're so lucky to live here permanently. I never get tired of it. You know — I'm planning to ride up and down here on the bus when I get too decrepit to drive."

She laughed. "You'd get a better view that way. You could see the top of Helvellyn, on a nice day."

They had a pretty good vista as it was. Lakes, fells, almost-bare trees and clusters of blurry sheep lay on all sides. It was a waste to obsess about who was calling her. Her father was right — the person would try again if it was important.

They wound their way down through Ambleside and on to the very familiar road into Windermere. The lake on their right was gently lapping its banks, birds bobbing on the water and not a single sailboat venturing out onto the chilly November mere. It was three o'clock and the light was dimming. There was no sign of the sun. "It does have a certain charm at this time of year," Simmy agreed. "You can see why people still want to come and use the B&B even now."

Russell heaved a noisy sigh. "Despite one's secret wish that they wouldn't."

She took him home, where Angie was clearly refreshed by the peaceful day she'd had. "Have a good time?" she asked them, as if she really wanted to know.

"Very interesting," said Russell. "All those *things* being sold. It was quite a revelation, I can tell you."

"What did you buy?"

He fetched the dish, and proudly presented it. "Not a chip or a crack anywhere," he assured her.

Angie took it from him and gave it a careful examination. "It's lovely," she said, as if surprised. "How much was it?"

"Well, the bidding price was twenty-five pounds, but then there's another twenty per cent on top of that. And they take fifteen per cent off what they give the seller, so they do very well out of it. It sounds like a swindle, when you stop to think about it, but I suppose they have to pay all those overheads and salaries and such. And there's all the added drama and serendipity and chance of getting something for a tenth of its value. I think we can cheerfully donate a further two pounds forty, for the experience."

Angie laughed, after a mildly horrified moment on hearing the price of the purchase, and Simmy felt as if she had personally achieved a distinct improvement in the atmosphere at Beck View. "I'll be going now," she said. "I'm sure I'll be seeing you again before long. Somebody phoned me, and I want to see if they left a message."

Sitting in the car, she extracted her phone from the bag and tried to discover who had called her.

It quickly became apparent that the person in question was Helen Harkness. There was a voicemail message from her, saying "Simmy? Can you give me a call when you get this, please?"

So Simmy did as requested.

"Hi. Thanks for getting back so quickly. I was wondering whether you'd have time to pop round here for a bit? Are you at home? I did try your landline, but there was no reply."

"I'm in New Road, sitting in the car. I can be there in about three minutes."

"Oh, thank you." Relief was so strong in Helen's voice that Simmy suspected the onset of tears. "I really don't know who else I can talk to."

It was actually slightly less than three minutes later that Simmy pulled up outside the Harkness house in Helm Road. It was only a short way down the hill into the northern reaches of Bowness. She found herself worrying about Ben as she rang the doorbell, as well as wondering what was at the centre of the problem.

"Oh, that was quick! Come in. I'm sorry to interrupt your day. What were you intending to do, instead of coming here?"

"Nothing much. Go home, I think. It's nearly dark already."

"Ghastly, isn't it. Makes you afraid that summer will never come again."

Helen waved Simmy into the front room, which was strangely empty. For a family of seven all to be scattered around the house, in kitchen and bedrooms, was highly unusual. It was impossible to miss the implication that Helen had banished them all.

"Is Ben okay now?" Simmy asked. "He wasn't his usual self at all yesterday."

"That's what I wanted to talk about. I can't get him to open up to me at all. I suppose I've overdone the protective mother act, after what happened to him in Hawkshead. But I don't see why that should stop him from talking to me about Kit Henderson."

"Have you tried asking Bonnie?"

"She's just as bad. He must have warned her to stay quiet. But I can see she wants to tell me what the matter is. I heard her trying to persuade him to tell me something. He really snapped at her, poor little thing."

They were still standing in the middle of the room, Helen too wrought up for social niceties.

Simmy could not think of anything to say. Her own faint suspicions were coming into clearer focus, offering an explanation for Ben's silence. She moved towards the sofa in the middle of the room and slowly sat down. "Oh dear," she said.

"Never mind 'Oh dear'. I want something better than that. You know how his mind works, at least as well as I do. His father is being useless. I can't really blame him. He hasn't got a moment to himself these days. That job's going to kill him, the way it's going. I keep telling him to take early retirement, but he won't."

"He's a teacher, isn't he?" Ben's father had successfully remained detached from all her dealings with the family thus far. Simmy did not even know his first name.

"Head of languages. It's a nightmare most of the time."

They were well off the main subject. While this might be seen as a waste of time, Simmy was actually rather glad. If forced to reveal to Helen the direction her thoughts were taking, there was likely to be considerable embarrassment as a result. And she could not be sure how Ben would react if Simmy were to speak for him. She might have it completely wrong. But from what she had seen of him the day before, she was convinced that some sort of intervention was required.

"So — Ben," said Helen, with solid determination. "What's the matter with him?"

"I honestly don't know for sure, but I think it's a few things all wrapped up together. For one, he's afraid for Bonnie."

"Rubbish! That girl's as tough as the proverbial old boots. She bounces back every time. I've never known such a resilient creature. Compared to her, my girls are all as fragile as glass." Helen had three daughters, as well as Ben and his brother, Wilf. "I can see I'm not a patch on Corinne for mothering skills."

"Well, maybe it's not about Bonnie so much. I think, actually, it's to do with the fact that you knew Kit Henderson years ago."

Helen sank into an armchair, having been walking round the room up to then. "What?"

"I might have it totally wrong. He hasn't said anything directly, but I got the impression that he's worried about it. Kit had a reputation, apparently, as a ladies' man. A few people have made comments along those lines, some of it bordering on some rather nasty implications. And I rather think he — Ben, that is — has put two and two together, and come up with an idea that he can't talk about to you. Do you see?"

"I'm not at all sure that I do. You're telling me that my son thinks I had some sort of *affair* with the man who laid our carpets, twelve or fifteen years ago? God help us — I was pregnant with twins at the time."

Simmy grimaced. "Really? That does make it rather unlikely, I suppose." She paused to think, ignoring Helen's spluttering protest. "But you did other business with him, didn't you? Later on? Recommending him to your clients, or something?"

"Who told you that?"

"I don't remember. It can only have been my mother, I suppose. I hardly ever saw Kit or Frances, once I was grown up, but I heard about them on and off. They've always been family friends of ours. Frances and my mum were pretty close."

"Let's go back a step. Even if Ben does think there was something between me and Kit, that doesn't explain the way he's been these past couple of days. It's *more* than that. It started after he'd been interviewed by the police on Wednesday. They must have said something to upset him."

"Bonnie said he thought they'd got some evidence to incriminate him. She really thought he might be accused of killing Kit himself. They were both pretty scared about it on Thursday morning."

"They can be such children at times," Helen murmured, with a sorrowful expression. "Just when you think your work is done and they can stand on their own two feet, they regress. Even Wilf still has his moments." She shook her head slowly. "I do remember talking to Kit about it one day. We'd bumped into each other at a client's house, and started chatting. My twins must have been about two, and were driving me absolutely mad. He was rather comforting, talking about his girls and the way one of them was always

200

fighting with one of the boys. Like a little tiger cat, he said. I do remember that."

"Hannah," nodded Simmy. "I saw her yesterday. She did fight a lot with George, although I think he started it, and she was just defending herself."

"It was Ben and Tanya in my case. They've never really liked each other. And there was Kit, a sympathetic voice of experience, having gone through the same sort of thing twenty years ahead of me. He kept saying everything always turned out right in the end."

"It didn't, though, did it? Not for him, anyway."

"That's got nothing to do with what I'm talking about. His children are all doing okay, aren't they?"

"More or less, I suppose. Funny how similar your two families are. That might have occurred to Ben, as well."

"We're still not getting anywhere, are we? I still think there's one big element in all this that's reduced him to a wreck. I've never seen him like this. It's unnerving."

"Well, I can only think of one other explanation," said Simmy carefully. "It's a really wild idea, but I can just about see how it might have felt like a logical deduction. For Ben, anyway — since logical deductions are what he does."

"Go on."

"Well, assuming he does think you and Kit were . . . you know . . . then he might also think that Kit was making some sort of threat against you. Blackmail, maybe. Threatening to tell your husband. Or even making fresh overtures once his wife had died. I am only guessing," she emphasised. "Just trying to think the way he would."

Helen was certainly not slow on the uptake. She got the message instantly. "And so, rather than let my life be ruined by a casual fling years ago, I killed the wretched man. Is that what my beloved son thinks of me?"

Simmy could see the woman was torn between horror and amusement, as well as a growing anger. "It would explain why he's so upset," she said faintly.

Helen made a visible effort to treat the matter seriously. "And it would fit what he's been like with me since Tuesday. Veiled accusations. All sorts of incomprehensible questions. I should have worked it out for myself," she sighed.

"I don't see how you could have done," Simmy reassured her. "And I think he feels that the adults are all swimming in much deeper water than he is. He feels young and ignorant, and vulnerable."

"And he thinks his own mother is a murderer," said Helen breathlessly. "Well, that's certainly a new one on me."

Simmy left ten minutes later, having had no offer of tea or other refreshment. Helen thanked her, in a choked sort of way, and they parted awkwardly. "I'm probably completely wrong," Simmy insisted.

"If you are that must mean that *you're* the one with the overactive imagination," the woman snapped. "Which would be good in one way, I suppose, but might make me wary of getting close to you in the future."

On her drive back up to Troutbeck, these words rang painfully in her head. She had tried to do as Helen had asked, and in the process might well have made a lot of things very much worse. She should have simply professed ignorance of Ben's thought processes and forced Helen to go back and get what she could out of the boy himself. She had not explained her ideas very well, she supposed. If she'd put more stress on the worries on Thursday morning, that might have helped with the logic of the whole matter. Ben could have been alerted to the fact that the police would follow evidence wherever it led — and therefore if there were events or relationships from the past that suggested reasons for Helen wanting Kit Henderson dead, that would have to be investigated. And if Helen had secrets, her clever son might well feel obliged to ferret them out, however scary and painful that might turn out to be.

But, of course, Helen hadn't killed Kit. *Of course* she hadn't. Moxon had implied that the killer must have been a man. But he had been wrong about that before. And Kit had evidently known his killer; they had been looking at that famous list together and drinking tea.

She could not resist reviewing the list of possible attackers. It must be a compulsion that gripped everyone involved, from Christopher to Angie Straw. And everyone's list would be different, depending on who knew what about Kit's life. She imagined the police asking that unavoidable question: do you know of anyone who might have had a reason for wanting Mr

Henderson dead? Did he have enemies? Was he in any sort of trouble, financially or emotionally? Questions bred questions, delving into the darker side of the man's activities and relationships.

It was relentlessly unpleasant. It was having a bad effect on Ben and therefore Bonnie too. And it was distracting Simmy from something that promised to be very much sweeter. She still had the image of Christopher in his role as auctioneer, scanning the room, efficiently rapping his hammer at the end of every lot. He had been the charismatic centre of the proceedings, all eyes and ears on him, and he had acted up to it beautifully. Finally, he had found his vocation, and it fitted him to perfection. The scope for learning, specialising, profiting was clearly enough to hold his attention, after a life spent in restless pursuit of just such satisfaction. His work was varied, exciting and sociable. At any moment a stranger could walk in off the street with a cameo or a postage stamp or a tiny ivory figure that would sell for a million pounds. This alone must give the work a perpetual thrill.

But Christopher himself must be distracted by the violent death of his father, so soon after his mother's demise. His performance at the auction had perhaps been slightly *too* good, given the recent traumas. She niggled at this thought for the last mile. Did it mean he was cold and callous? Or a good actor? Or just a typical British man, eager to bury painful feelings and get on with normal life? She recalled how normal he'd been at the auction, and even earlier. On Wednesday he had shown much less emotion than might have been expected. Ben would probably see that as suspicious — as if he was really not so surprised at what had happened. But — terrible thought — if *he* had been the killer, then would there not be that gnawing sense of guilt distorting his features, a look that was so often mistaken for grief?

Her little house was in darkness, and not quite warm enough to be welcoming. The heating didn't come on until four, which meant it had only had half an hour to take effect. "This is no way to live," she muttered crossly to herself. She always seemed to get home thirsty and hungry and in a dour mood. Evenings were long and boring and she spent far too many of them thinking about work.

She had retrieved Frances's flower book from her car, feeling foolishly guilty towards the thing. It had remained in her car since she had shown it to her parents. The problem was, she didn't know what to do with it. There was a depressing inevitability to its fate — tucked away in a cupboard upstairs and forgotten, most likely. She had shown it to all the people who might find it interesting, as well as inspecting every page of it herself. What more could be expected? It was one of those objects that had no real use or value, other than aesthetic, but unlike a picture or ornament, it could not be properly displayed.

Thoughts of pictures and ornaments took her straight back to Christopher, and that was regrettable. None of the images and notions going through her head were going to lead anywhere. She would be better employed in watching the news channel while sewing a button back onto one of her shirts. She had kept it safe for months, since it came off, and now seemed a good moment to deal with it. The news was going through a bland phase, with no terrorist outrages or natural disasters to agonise about. She put a Fray Bentos pie in the oven, as a treat for herself. Only when it was ready did she experience a powerful pang of nostalgia for times past. When first married, she and Tony had mutually confessed to a passion for the things and had them at least once a week.

She had not given her former husband a thought for weeks; had not heard from him or about him for at least a year. The divorce was over and done with, a clean break, with no reason to stay in touch. Memories involving him were imbued with a sense of failure, and a degree of bewilderment. His grief over the loss of their baby girl had taken such a strange course that she had been forced to accept that the tragedy had driven them apart. She barely recognised him, two months after Edith had died.

But she ate the pie all the same, enjoying it all the more for being so hungry. They were uniquely delicious, especially the steak and kidney version. No way was she going to let Tony spoil them for her.

She had not quite finished when somebody knocked on the door. Setting the tray down on a side table, she went to investigate. With a caution that she partly deplored in herself, she called, "Who is it?" loudly through the closed door.

"Christopher," came a faint answer. It was a sturdy door, close to being soundproof.

"Good Lord, what are you doing here again?" she said in disbelief, before the door was fully open. He pushed in, slammed the door behind himself, and then stood there in the hall, staring at a point above Simmy's head.

"Sorry," he said. "I couldn't help it. I thought you'd wait for the end of the sale and then we could talk. But you went. I never thought you'd do that."

"And I never imagined you expected us to stay. I did talk to Hannah for a bit." As if that was any consolation, she thought grimly.

"I'm sorry," he said again. "I don't seem to be functioning so well now. I held it together while I was doing the auction — and then I just sort of collapsed. It was awful."

She could think of nothing to say to him. Two contrasting impulses were battling inside her. One urged her to grab him in a long hug and tell him everything would be all right. The other was to push him straight out again while ordering him to find someone else to cry on. There were so many associations with another man in mourning; she doubted she was ready to deal with a new one yet. And besides, it was never actually going to be all right. Fran and Kit would stay dead, whatever happened. Unfinished arguments, failed apologies, misunderstandings — they would all persist in the survivors for a long time. It had not been like that, of course, when Edith died before she had ever even lived, but Simmy had glimpsed these frustrations in her customers. They would say things like "I never told him . . ." or "I wish I'd said what I really thought when she was alive" as they tried to compose the message on the card that went with the flowers. She could well believe that not one of Kit Henderson's children had ever achieved a meaningful conversation with him. He wasn't that sort of man.

"It had to hit you eventually," she murmured. "You couldn't hold it off for ever."

"I thought I could. I was feeling rather pleased with myself, rationalising it all so it would be bearable. Thinking how my dad would never have wanted to live on his own. That he'd been saved a miserable old age. Stupid stuff like that." He was very red in the face, his eyes blurry. He still avoided her gaze, as if ashamed to look at her.

"You thought the murderer was doing him a favour?" She could not stop herself from challenging this grotesque notion.

"No, not really. Obviously not. But being dead, you see. That's the real point. And I was trying to make it less ghastly, just for my own sake."

"Come and sit down. I was just finishing my supper. Do you want a drink or something?"

"I shouldn't have come. It was wrong of me, driving all the way over here, just to see you again. I don't know what's come over me."

"And now you can't look at me," she noted. "What's that about, Chris?"

It might have been the very first time she'd used the shorter name. It had not escaped her notice that both his sisters were doing it now, which they had not done as children. Frances had been so emphatic that his whole name must always be applied that everyone had automatically obeyed. *Chris* felt daringly intimate, marking a definite change between them.

"Simmy — it's so strange seeing you again now. It feels as if we're both about ninety-nine years old, and we've lived through all kinds of hell since we knew each other as kids. You're different and the same. I know you, but I don't. It's been haunting me ever since my mum's funeral, how close we were on those family holidays, and then we just seemed to forget each other. How did that happen? Shouldn't we have stayed together?"

"Sit down," she said again, her heart thumping wildly. "I'm not sure I can cope with all this." She picked up the round tin containing the remnants of her pie, and wondered whether she could swallow the final segment. Regretfully, she decided not. "You've put me off my pie," she said.

He stared right at her, then, unblinking. "Have I?"

She made a sad little *huff* of laughter, and put the tin down again. "I've got some red wine. I think that might help," she said.

The next hour saw the bottle finished, and remarkably little conversation pursued. Simmy sat across the room from him, and tried to maintain control of her thoughts. Any expressions of feeling from him would

209

have to be treated with scepticism, given the state he was in. She was afraid to encourage him into any disclosures concerning her, and tried instead to keep the focus on his family. "The main thing for now is your father, and who killed him," she insisted.

"Well, yes. But I have no idea whatsoever. Isn't it for the police to find that out? And . . . this might sound weird . . . I'm not in too much hurry for that to happen. I mean, I'm going to hate that person, aren't I? Really detest and loathe his guts. I don't want to carry that around all the time. It's unhealthy."

She smiled. Here was a more familiar Christopher, a latter-day hippy full of old-fashioned peace and love. "You sound like my mother," she said. Although Angie hadn't been quite such a love child herself in recent times.

"That's probably where I got it from. She was always so full of stories about London in the sixties. She made it sound like a whole other world."

"She romanticised it. She didn't even get to London until 1969. She missed most of the excitement."

"I don't believe you. I think she was right in the heart of it. Don't spoil my illusions."

"You're right. I guess the sixties lasted quite a way into the seventies as well. It was more of a culture than a calendar-based thing. And it did sound rather wonderful," she sighed. "Pity it didn't last. Just look at us now."

"What do you mean? You sell flowers. How sixties is that?"

"And you could easily have a stall in the Portobello Road."

"I could. So that's all right, isn't it."

They finished the wine in silence. It was getting late and very obviously Christopher was not going to drive back to Keswick. That went without saying. But a very big question was beginning to loom: which bed was he going to be sleeping in?

CHAPTER
SEVENTEEN

Simmy woke from a dream in the middle of the night, to find a man's arm across her middle. She lay there enjoying his snug embrace, quite content not to move. But her thoughts were almost frantic. The dream had been an irrational mixture of past and present, where she was sixteen, but Christopher was thirty-eight. All his siblings were there, and both sets of parents, in a pandemonium of packing, or catching the tide, or both. They were all together in a huge unfurnished house that had stacks of lovely antiques piled on the front lawn.

She remembered it in every detail, trying to untangle anything from it that was a real memory, or a meaningful message for the present. That last year had been at Prestatyn. Although a favourite, it had not been their destination every year. They had tried Rhos-on-Sea, Colwyn Bay and Aberystwyth over the years. Prestatyn was fine if the weather was good; otherwise it was a disaster. A small Roman bathhouse took ten minutes to inspect, and the even smaller ruined castle took less time still. There were shops and an amusement arcade, which the Straws regarded as tawdry. Simmy was strongly discouraged from going there, and the Henderson children never had enough money to make it worth bothering. The presence of the Pontins holiday camp caused Angie in particular a degree of angst. When the company was sold up in the mid 1990s, she hoped it would all go away. Instead, the camp at Prestatyn was one of the few that survived to be modernised and embellished. But the lure of the huge beach, its rock pools and muddy swamps kept them going back. They found it quite easy to ignore the crowds on their package holidays, and find their own private areas.

Simmy recalled all this now, in the small dark hours of the night. How they had set up camp against the sea wall and repelled all invaders. Russell and Kit would have their own special chairs, which they carried back and forth every day. Everyone else would be loaded with towels, buckets, sandwiches, drinks, books and sometimes a radio.

An image from her dream came back to her. Fran, her face close to Angie's, speaking in a low relentless monologue of complaint. Angie had been embarrassed, worried that the words were audible to others in the party. "He had his hand right down her front," Simmy heard. "And she can't be more than twenty. Don't you think I ought to do something?"

Angie had merely shaken her head, and flapped a hand. "We'll talk about it later," she said.

"What was all that about?" Simmy asked Christopher, as they retreated to a handy sand dune.

"Just my dad at his old games again. Take no notice."

But Simmy had watched Kit more closely for the next day or two, seeing him brush against girls in bikinis when they went up to the town for ice cream, or make some flirtatious remark to a waitress over their evening meal. She remembered how she had been amazed at her own blindness to his behaviour until that moment. And the acute distress she felt on Fran's behalf. But she never said anything more about it — not even to her mother or Christopher. Once the holiday was over, she forgot it completely.

They woke the next morning, reminding each other that it was Sunday and they didn't have to be anywhere. The realisation that at thirty-eight years old they had nobody expecting them, no children or partners making demands on them, was both liberating and worrying. It also made them both acutely aware that they could solve the matter for each other with a startling simplicity.

"This is nice," he said, stretching his arms towards the ceiling. "I like your little house."

Simmy tried not to read too much into these words. The prospect of his moving in permanently was far too distant, surely, to be taken seriously. One shared night did not a marriage make. And yet, she could not avoid the idea that just such a huge change might be on its way. Just as women find themselves jumping ten or twenty years ahead within seconds of knowing they're pregnant, she was mentally designing her wedding bouquet on the basis of waking in the same bed as a man.

"Breakfast," she announced. "Coffee." She then realised that she had quite a bad headache. The wine from the previous evening, she supposed. And a degree of dehydration. And the implications of what had happened. Real life was going to intrude at any moment, bringing stress and confusion in its wake.

"No hurry," said Christopher. "Stay here for a cuddle."

It should have been easy and obvious, just lying there together, skin to skin. There should be no reservations, no intrusive thoughts. Five minutes earlier, it might have worked. "Sorry," she said, with a sigh. "I've got a blinding headache. I need a pill and something to drink."

"Not a morning after pill?" he laughed.

She rolled out of the bed — which was not really wide enough for two — and looked down on him. He had used a condom, which he'd said had been in his wallet for well over a year, but in the sleepy small hours, there had been a further coupling that she had drowsily enjoyed without giving a thought to contraception. "You didn't — did you?" she said.

"I guess we both sort of forgot. It'll be okay. I don't think I'm very fertile."

"I don't think I am, either. It took me and Tony two years of trying for me to get pregnant." She forced a carefree laugh, which hurt her head. "But we're not doing that again."

"That's a shame. It was pretty darn enjoyable." He reached out for her hand, and held it tight.

"It was," she agreed.

He laughed, suddenly buoyant. "I feel wonderfully *free*," he said. "Knowing my dad isn't going to march in and start yelling at me."

She pulled away from him. "What?"

"I probably shouldn't tell you this, but just about the only serious talk I ever had with him was about you. He told me to keep my hands off you until you were old enough to know your own mind. Said it was all very well having a holiday flirtation, but if he ever caught me taking things further, he'd skin me alive. Or words to that effect."

"And you believed him? Why should it matter to him what we did?"

"Good question. He always seemed to have a thing about vulnerable young girls. It never made much sense to me."

"Well . . ." she said doubtfully. "He probably meant well."

"He's gone now, anyway. I can do what I like." He threw his arms in the air, and stretched. "At last."

She took a few steps towards the door, unsure of how to react. Something felt awry, as if a discordant note had intruded into their elation and suggested it was misguided, even perhaps somehow dishonourable.

"Funny old business, isn't it. Death and sex — they say they go together."

She was halfway down the stairs when he said this, and wasn't sure she'd heard right. The living room was airless and stale, with the empty wine bottle and glasses giving it a tawdry look. She spent five minutes whisking

216

away the debris, taking an aspirin, making coffee and toast, and wondering what would happen next.

Did Christopher take sugar in coffee? She had made it for him on Thursday morning, but couldn't remember that detail. Better take some up, just in case. She unearthed a wooden tray from the dusty top of a high cupboard and took the minimal breakfast upstairs on it.

In the bedroom, he was exactly as she'd left him, looking young and peaceful under the duvet. Her heart swelled at the sight of him. He really was very sweet. How she had loved him, more than twenty years ago! Every time she thought back, the memories intensified. She had mooned over him, waiting for letters from him, following his school career and making passionate wishes that they would somehow end up going to the same university. They did not. In the event, neither of them did degree courses. Gradually, other people came into their lives and their teenage love faded into nothing more than a rosy memory. This man here with her now was a different person, who happened to have shared some of his childhood with her. If a relationship were to develop, it would have to be built from scratch, as adults with past experiences and revised expectations.

Then his phone played a jingle, somewhere amongst the pile of clothes he'd left on the floor. "Must be yours," she said. "I don't know where mine is, but I'm pretty sure it's switched off."

He groaned gently, and reached a long arm towards the sound. "Can't reach it," he said. "Let it ring."

217

She kicked the heap closer to the bed, and then lowered the tray onto a corner of the dressing table, which was in fact just a chest of drawers with a mirror perched on top of it. Coffee slopped slightly. Her head was not feeling any better.

"Oh, it's Hannah," said Christopher, having finally laid hands on his phone. "She's not going to go away until I answer it." He thumbed the screen and put the phone to his ear. "Sis," he said.

The love/hate/resent/depend complexities of sibling relationships would always be mysterious to Simmy. She had witnessed Christopher go through all these and more in his interactions with Eddie, George, Hannah and Lynn and learnt almost nothing in the process. The little word "Sis" could mean a multitude of things, given the inevitable associations it must carry. "Mind your own business. Why should it matter to you?" he was saying next. "It's Sunday, for God's sake. Yes . . . I know. So what? How should I know the answer to that? Do it yourself . . . We have to get on with our lives . . . Yes, yes . . ." He rolled his eyes at Simmy, who had begun to wonder whether she should leave the room and let him speak in private. Then she turned mulish, remembering where they were. She should put on a dressing gown if she was going downstairs again. And she only possessed a very unflattering thing made of quilted nylon that would be old-fashioned on her mother, or even grandmother. Instead, she took coffee and a slice of buttered toast and climbed back into bed, squeezing up against Christopher and poking his shoulder.

"I'll call you about it tomorrow," he told his sister, and deactivated the call.

"How mean of you," smiled Simmy. "What did she want?"

"She wants to have a family meeting, but Eddie won't co-operate and she hasn't even asked George yet. She said I should speak to him. Pull rank as the eldest. She's the bossy one, not me. And even she is dithering about calling George. She knows he won't do anything she wants him to."

"What does she think it would achieve anyway?"

"Lord knows. It's probably something she's seen in a film, and thinks it's appropriate. She's got no idea, really. I suppose it's to do with deciding about the house, and the funeral, and all that stuff. Dad's car is sitting there out in the garage, and there'll be post to see to, and electricity and food in the freezer ... nobody's begun to think it all through." He was speaking slowly, the items coming to mind, one by one.

"The police probably wouldn't let you touch it for a bit, anyway. But Hannah didn't say all that just now, did she?"

"No — but it's obvious, now I put my mind to it. Lucky there are no pets to make decisions about."

"Is there food going bad in the fridge as well?" None of the implications of a house abruptly left empty had occurred to her before.

"Probably. Nobody's been taking a lead — until now."

"So there's quite a lot of sense in Hannah's suggestion after all. If each one of you takes one or two jobs, it'll all get done without too much hassle. Once the police tell you it's all clear, of course. You can't have a funeral until they release the body."

"They told me that. I guess it'll be this week sometime." He rubbed his face. "And there was me thinking I could just lie here all day and forget my troubles."

"There'll be your mother's things as well," Simmy realised. "Clothes and all those diaries and things that she kept."

"The police took some of the diaries. They thought it might help them work out who killed Dad."

Simmy winced. "That's not very nice," she said. "Makes me glad I don't keep a diary. What do they think they'll find?"

He said nothing, but his face revealed quite a lot. Worry, even dread, was evident.

"What?"

"It won't impact on the murder investigation, but there's sure to be stuff about the state of their marriage. It went through a very rocky patch a while ago. We all thought they'd split up. The girls were in a right old panic for a bit. They were still at school — or Lynn was, at least. I missed most of it, but Hannah kept me informed."

"But they patched things up?" Simmy wondered how much her own mother knew of all this. "It must have been around that time that my mum and dad moved to Cumbria. That's at least twelve years ago now."

"Right. They didn't have much choice but to stay together. Dad wasn't going anywhere and Mum could

220

never have survived financially on her own. That's what she thought, anyway. She'd have divorced him otherwise."

"But as you say, it can't have any bearing on the murder."

"No."

But they were both less than certain on that point, as became more apparent as they gave it some thought. "Your mum . . ." Christopher began. "She was quite closely involved at one point, according to Hannah. Stirring things up and making it all worse."

Simmy was tempted to defend her parent, despite a total lack of knowledge of the circumstances. "She probably meant well," was the best she could manage. "But I had a dream last night, which sort of carried on when I woke up. I remembered how depressed your mother often seemed, and how she complained about Kit such a lot. We all just carried on as if things were all right."

"That's what kids do. Anything else would be too scary. We were just glad that Angie was there to be a dumping ground. She seemed to cope with it all right."

"I think she must have been pretty annoyed with Kit, though. She's always been big on female solidarity. I wonder whether Fran's suspicions were ever proved right — or wrong."

He gave a little shrug. "We'll never know just what went on. I for one refused to pay attention to any of it. I had my own life to lead, and I didn't want to have to face the bad behaviour of my own father. I kept telling myself he deserved to be happy. There he was, in his fifties, keeping himself fit. He grew a beard and started going out more. Joined one or two clubs. Mum had her own friends and wasn't interested in going with him — big mistake. He'd always been fond of the ladies, and suddenly there he was, all sparky and full of himself. I think it was a bit of a midlife crisis, actually. I have a feeling he really went off the rails."

It fitted with much of what Simmy had been hearing about the man, although not very closely to her own experience of him. She couldn't recall ever hearing him make a joke. And he certainly wouldn't have seduced anyone with his affluence, given the modest salary he'd earned. "But it didn't last long?" she prompted.

"Long enough. Things settled down a bit, because we all got used to it, and Mum worked around it as best she could. Now Hannah says the strain of it was what killed her."

Simmy blinked. "That's a bit strong. What do the others think?"

"George probably agrees with her. Eddie wouldn't commit himself, and Lynn keeps her thoughts pretty close."

"And you?"

"I think it's too late for any recriminations. It's happened and we can't change it now."

They were still snuggled together on the bed, balancing coffee and toast precariously on their middles. "I'm still hungry," Christopher announced. "What time does the pub open?"

"I don't know. They'll start lunches at around twelve, I suppose. That's ages away yet."

222

"Less than an hour, actually."

"No! It can't be."

"We didn't wake up till nearly ten. It was a busy night."

She giggled. "The day's half gone already. How awful of us."

"Slobs. That's what we are. I could get used to it."

She gathered mugs and plates and put them on the floor. Then she turned and gave him a long considering look. The brisk efficient auctioneer of the day before was completely absent. Stubble was appearing on his chin, his hair was spiky, and his naked skin banished any hint of the world of work. She pressed her face to his chest, breathing in the natural smell of him. "You're like a flower," she mumbled foolishly. "A big wild flower growing in a humid forest somewhere. Something that has huge leaves and deep roots." She could see it quite clearly in her imagination.

"And you're like a lovely lustre vase. One of the undecorated Moorcrofts, I think. Worth a fortune. And quietly indestructible, unless treated with deliberate violence."

She wasn't sure she liked that image. "Some people might say we've got it the wrong way round."

"People know nothing. Isn't this strange?" he went on. "Our first night together, after all those years."

"We were far too young before. I'd have been terrified."

"And me. We'd have made a mess of it. I never forgot you, though."

223

"I have to admit I did, once Tony came along. I didn't have any space left over for memories of young love. He was pretty full on. Hard work, a lot of the time."

"Don't talk about him. He's an idiot."

"He is. I don't know what I was thinking, marrying him."

"We've wasted a terrible lot of time."

She deliberately misunderstood him. "Come on." She rolled out of bed, and grabbed a handful of clothes. "I'm going to have a bath."

"Can I come?"

"If you must." She wasn't sure she wanted him to, and it showed.

"I'll take the tap end, of course," he said gallantly.

It was a splashy, squashed business, and Simmy wasn't entirely sure she was ever going to want to have sex in a bath again. But Christopher obviously enjoyed it enormously.

They had roast chicken at the pub, not talking very much. The Mortal Man was Simmy's local, but she did not go there very often. It had a roaring fire, and the views towards the great fells just beyond Troutbeck were magnificent. Even in November there were walkers, with their boots and rucksacks. One couple came accompanied by a Lakeland terrier, which made Simmy think of her father.

"My dad loved the auction," she said. "He's going to treasure that dish he bought."

"I know. I saw his face. We like bidders like him. Usually they keep very po-faced. The dealers like to pretend it's all very boring. There are still a few who just flick a finger or even wink, when they're bidding. Silly, really. But it's a world unto itself. I feel like a novice compared to some of the old-timers."

"Is it as corrupt as they say? Ringers — is that the word? Fixing things up in advance and keeping prices low."

"The system makes some of that unavoidable. It's not really a very good way to sell things of real value. Not our sort of place, anyhow. Most of the stuff comes from house clearances, and isn't expected to fetch much. The job lots go for almost nothing, and there's often really good things down at the bottom of the box."

"Do you see the same items coming round again?"

He nodded. "All the time. Mainly, though, it's the unsold stuff. People just leave it till the next sale, and the next one after that. It all goes eventually."

"It has a sort of magic to it, doesn't it?"

"Absolutely. And we get people who're absolutely addicted. Housewives, who first came because they needed a rug or a big cooking pot, and just can't stop coming back. They buy all sorts of mad stuff. I often wonder what they do with it all."

"My granny lived near a big council dump, thirty years ago. It was in the days when you could go and take stuff. Nobody ever supervised or tried to stop her. She mainly took things for the garden, and ended up with a whole row of big old sinks, baths, dead

225

wheelbarrows — anything you could put plants in. It looked quite good, in a crazy sort of way. It all went back to the tip when she died."

Simmy entertained a brief thought of asking about his grandmother's jewellery, which Moxon seemed to think might have relevance to Kit's murder. But she pushed it away, as likely to wreck the atmosphere. The reminiscences so far were easy, friendly and unthreatening. A post-coital haze gave it all a warm glow. Christopher still hadn't shaved, and his hair remained untidy. They sat with legs touching under the table, and often lapsed into long silences in which they simply stared into each other's eyes. Simmy could not explain to herself what was happening, or what it might imply. She could do no more than remain in the present moment and savour every second.

CHAPTER
EIGHTEEN

They walked back to her cottage, only to find a familiar car squeezed against the hedge, leaving the barest room for passing traffic to get by.

"That'll be Moxon," Simmy sighed, before they got close enough to see inside the car. "Trust him to show up on a Sunday afternoon."

"You mean the policeman? The detective? Why would he be here?"

She caught the whiff of jealousy, and smiled. "Why do you think?" she said.

"I honestly do not have a clue," he responded swiftly. "If he thinks you can help him solve my father's murder, he must be nuts. You can't possibly know anything about it."

"I suppose that's true." Her mind felt cloudy, as she struggled to reconcile all the different assumptions surrounding Kit's death. "But somehow that's not how it feels."

The key to the puzzle then climbed out of the front passenger seat, and much was made clear. "That's Ben," she said. "Look — that's Ben." She ran the final few yards, intending to clasp the youth to her breast in relief at seeing him. But her quarry raised his hands to fend her off.

"Quite a little gathering, by the looks of it," said DI Moxon, eyeing Christopher impassively.

Simmy was only interested in Ben. "Are you okay now?" she wanted to know. "Did your mother . . . ?" She faltered, afraid of stumbling into murky waters. "I saw her yesterday."

"I know you did. And she's been behaving very weirdly ever since. What did you say to her?"

Three of them were clustered together on the narrow path to Simmy's front door. Christopher hung back, unnoticed by the others. Moxon seemed to think he had effected a fond reconciliation between Ben and Simmy, the way he stood over them, smiling like a benign uncle.

"Are you all coming in?" asked Simmy.

"Not me," said Christopher. "I'll be getting back now. Better see if I can keep everybody happy, Hannah especially."

The tetchy tone was impossible to miss. Simmy stepped away from Ben, to grab Christopher's arm. "It's been lovely," she said, not caring what the others might think. "Don't spoil it now. I didn't know these two were going to show up. You can stay a bit, can't you?"

His expression softened. "I don't think they'd want me to. I can see things are complicated. It *has* been lovely, but maybe the timing wasn't great. Best get all this stuff settled first, eh? I can recognise divided loyalties when I see them. And that's not a criticism —

it's the same my end, as well. Hannah really did sound serious, earlier on. I ought to go and see what she wants."

"All right, then. But phone me this evening, okay? Don't go all silent on me."

"You needn't worry." He looked into her eyes. "It's okay, Sim. Or it will be soon, I promise."

She felt an involuntary shudder ripple through her. "Don't say that," she whispered. "I'm not asking for promises."

He blinked, bewildered. "What did I say?"

"Nothing." She laughed and gave him a little push. "Phone me this evening and I'll try to explain."

Moxon and Ben stood side by side, shamelessly watching the affectionate parting. When Simmy turned back to them, they had very similar expressions on their faces. Benign tolerance seemed to sum it up, and she marvelled at how little irritation it made her feel. Rather, she was soothed and warmed by it. "Come on in, then," she said. "It's cold out here."

She made tea and found a rather dried-up fruit cake to offer them, all the while wondering what sort of conversation the three of them could possibly be about to have. Moxon showed signs of being present in a less-than-professional capacity. More of a facilitator, she guessed — bringing Ben back into the fold, using Simmy to reassure him. Although why the detective should be actively engaged in such a process was unclear. There had been several times when the man had deplored the youngster's reckless enthusiasm for the darker side of human behaviour. When Ben had fallen into genuine danger, his elders had all reproached themselves for it, in their various ways. So why should they now be making any effort to put things back to how they'd been prior to that adventure?

"You went to the auction, did you?" Moxon asked, after an uncomfortable silence.

She had forgotten all about her commission of the previous day. "Yes, I did."

"And?" he prompted.

"What do you want me to say? It was fun. Christopher was brilliant. Dad bought a lovely dish."

"Did he indeed?"

"It was a very nice day out. I had no idea it would be so exciting. The time flew by. Until Hannah accosted me, that is. She seemed in a bit of a state."

"Hannah Henderson? Daughter of the victim." It was Ben who spoke. "What did she say?"

"I can't remember all of it. She was angry about both her parents dying, which seemed fair enough. But she wasn't very nice to me. Said her mother always thought I was a perfect daughter. A paragon. I don't believe that's true, and even if it is, it wasn't my fault, was it?"

Neither of her visitors spoke. A nudging idea was bothering her, to do with Kit Henderson and women other than his wife. Quite how it connected to the topic under discussion was obscure. Then she remembered a possible link. "Christopher said his father warned him away from me when we were young."

"How young?" asked Moxon.

"Sixteen. We were in love, but we never did anything about it. I was fairly immature, I suppose. Kit was probably right."

"But it raises the notion of you as a figure on a pedestal, in the eyes of both the Henderson parents," summarised Moxon, with an intelligent gleam in his eyes.

"Yes," she agreed slowly. "How very strange that feels. I thought I was being included in a big family, as a natural thing — because it suited everybody. Now I'm wondering whether the whole set-up was organised for my benefit. Can that be right? All those holidays. I know my father never really enjoyed it. He must have been going along with it, for my sake."

"But your mother and Mrs Henderson were close friends."

"I suppose they were. They were very different people, though. Hardly anything in common. Fran always seemed to be in Mum's shadow, struggling to keep up." Again she remembered the belated awareness of just how unhappy the Henderson marriage had probably been.

"Class differences," said Ben, with a disdainful sniff.

"Probably. Although you can't exactly say that. We're nothing special."

"Both your parents have got degrees. The Hendersons probably left school at sixteen."

"They did," she nodded. "But they weren't stupid."

"How did the two men get along?" Moxon asked.

"I can't remember them ever really talking to each other, or doing things together. They weren't hostile, but you could tell they couldn't see much point in trying to be friends. It was all about the women and children."

"We still haven't got any handle on that jewellery," said the detective. "There's no sign of an inventory anywhere, and the sister, Mrs Lloyd, was unhelpful. Insisted there'd never been any jewels, apart from a cheap pearl necklace and a little watch with marcasite round it. Both lost somehow."

"Mrs Lloyd?" Simmy frowned. "Oh — Christine. Of course. She's very like Fran to look at, isn't she." Then she giggled. "Oh, what a fool. You never knew Fran, did you? Her sister was very British at the funeral, according to my mother. I didn't talk to her."

"I didn't know there was anything about any jewellery," said Ben, somewhat sulkily.

"Well, there isn't, anyway," said Moxon. "A red herring."

"A pretext for sending Simmy to that auction," accused the boy.

"I won't dignify that with a response," said Moxon, with steel in his voice.

Another silence fell, during which Simmy wished Moxon would go away and leave her with Ben. She was also missing Christopher, whose abrupt departure left her feeling abandoned. Unpicking events of twenty years ago seemed futile and Ben's comment on the jewellery raised her own suspicions.

As if reading her mind, Moxon got to his feet. "If I leave Ben here, will you take him home?" he asked.

She nodded, recalling the two pints of beer she had recently consumed. "Later on," she said.

"I've got driving lessons booked after Christmas," said Ben. "It's tedious having to cadge lifts all the time."

"You haven't got time," Simmy objected. "All those A levels! All that studying. You'll never fit driving in as well."

"Yeah, I will," he insisted. "I won't need many lessons."

Moxon paused on his way out. "Was Hannah Henderson with anybody?" he asked.

"Oh — yes. A man called Malcolm. He's got a wife called Cheryl, who was Kit's workmate from ages ago. They were at Fran's funeral. They're going on a cruise, so they'll miss Kit's funeral. Didn't I mention them before, along with a woman called June?"

"You did to me," said Ben with a smirk.

Moxon gave him another severe look, then said to Simmy, "And Hannah was with him?"

"She says he does a bit of antique dealing. I don't think there's anything else between them than that. She was quite angry with me," she finished.

"Yes. You said that. Can't have been very nice for you." His sympathy, as always, was genuine, and therefore unsettling.

"Oh well. I should be big enough to take it. I've got no reason to complain, really."

"And did you see anybody else you recognised, at the auction?"

"I don't think so. Dad didn't, either. But then, he was so fixated on Christopher, and the bidding, that he never looked at the other people. So was I, if I'm honest. Sorry," she ended lamely. "I wasn't a very good spy, was I?"

"Should have sent me instead," said Ben.

Simmy refrained from reminding him that he had in fact turned down her request for him to go. There was still a subtle sense of a young man in a state of convalescence. Simmy had been so worried about him over recent months that she could not believe that he was entirely recovered yet. The sudden knock-back at finding Kit Henderson's body couldn't fail to take its toll. "You couldn't have got there," she said reasonably.

"True. Which is why I need to drive. Melanie had her licence when she was my age. And the use of a car."

"I'm off, then," said Moxon. He threw Ben an affectionate glance, quite unlike anything that might be expected from a police detective. "You could do worse than take Miss Todd as your role model," he smiled. "I have a lot of time for that young woman."

The departure of Melanie from her position as Simmy's shop assistant had given them all some grief. She was now working in a hotel outside Hawkshead, forging a career path that brooked no opposition. None of the Windermere and Bowness friends saw very much of her these days.

"We all do," said Simmy. "She's a hard act to follow." Then, with an irrational glance around the room, she went on, "And where's Bonnie?"

234

"Not here," laughed Ben. "Corinne wanted her for something. That seems to happen a lot these days. I think she — Corinne, I mean — is worried that Bonnie's going to move out soon. She's mega fond of her, you know. Better than a lot of mothers."

"Better than Bonnie's mother," said Moxon feelingly. He knew more than was comfortable about the tangled troubles that surrounded Bonnie Lawson's family. "Bye, both. See you again soon, I expect." And he was gone.

They listened for his car engine, and then Simmy got up and closed the curtains of her front room. "Dark already," she sighed, before realising that she had been saying this every day like a daft old woman. "Soon be Christmas," she added, hoping to change the mood.

"Are you and Chris Henderson together now, then?" The question was bold and unambiguous.

"Um . . . well, it's early days, but I hope we are. We were a bit like you and Bonnie when we knew each other all those years ago. It's strange getting to know him again. He's sort of the same, but sort of different, now."

"You've both got baggage," he said knowingly.

She laughed. "You might say that, I suppose."

"You know — I've hardly ever been up here to your house." He looked around. "You've got it nice and cosy, haven't you? That is — it would be, if you lit the fire. Haven't you got any logs?"

"A few. I need to get more."

"Did you notice how smug and secretive Moxo was looking just now? Must have been something you said."

"What? No, I didn't notice anything like that. Are you sure?"

"Pretty much. He nodded quietly to himself, a couple of times. I think he's got an idea." Ben did not look entirely happy about his observations. "I wish I knew what it was. He thinks he's shielding me from being upset or whatever, but he's only making me frustrated and cross."

"Do you want me to light the fire, then? Are you cold? The heating's on."

"Don't do it just for me. Do you ever light it?"

"Not very often. Weekends, sometimes. It's a bit of a hassle." The wood-burning stove had been in the house when she bought it, and at first she'd taken pride in its efficient warming of the whole building. But then she'd run out of logs, and also of places to dump the ash that it produced, and almost forgotten its existence.

She wanted to ask him about Helen, and whether they'd managed a sensible conversation since Simmy's visit. But it was too hazardous an area to venture into without some sort of assurance that she wouldn't be overstepping an emotional mark. "Are you staying for tea?" she asked. "I need to wait a bit before driving. I had two pints of beer at lunchtime."

"It's only four o'clock," he pointed out. "I can stay till about five. There's an essay to finish before tomorrow."

"Right, then. So what do you want to do between now and then?"

He gave her a considering look, and she noticed almost for the first time how he'd matured in the year since she'd met him. She'd been automatically using the word "boy" when thinking about him, but now that seemed wrong. He was a young man, legally adult, in a close relationship and proving himself to be academically excellent. His interest in forensics and police work had not wavered in all the time she'd known him, his goals just as clear as ever. "I want to talk about dead people," he said. "If that's all right with you. Everyone seems to think I've gone soft or scared, or something. They're totally wrong. I wasn't bothered about seeing the Henderson man dead — only very surprised, and worried about Bonnie. I squatted down and really *looked* at him. And that meant I left traces for the cops to find. I admit I panicked when I realised what that could lead to. I mean — if I'd been on the forensics team, I'd have fingered myself as the killer." He smiled. "Should have known better, obviously."

"'Fingered'," Simmy repeated sceptically. "Never heard anyone actually say that."

"You know what I mean."

"Yes. Sorry. Bonnie was scared, as well. She really thought you'd be charged with murder."

"I know. But she'll be okay. She's working out her own theory of who did it. Apparently her main suspect is Lynn Henderson, or whatever her married name is."

"How does she work that out? Has she even *met* the woman?"

"Possibly not. She drew up a list of means, motives and opportunities, and that's who it flagged up. I'm not entirely sure of the workings."

"I'd have thought Hannah and George were a lot more likely. Hannah's angry about something, and George has never been very rational. My mother used to say he had a sinister look in his eye."

"He's certainly keeping out of the limelight, isn't he? Does anyone even know where he is?"

"Eddie probably does. I assume he's at home, minding his own business." Then she remembered Christopher's morning phone call. "Hannah's summoned the whole family to a meeting. I think it's this evening. Except she was scared to approach George directly, so wanted Christopher to do it. Eddie was being awkward about it as well."

"There has to be something in their past that explains the killing," Ben mused. "All these hints and winks about Mr Henderson and other women have to be the key to it. And his wife dying opened the way for whoever it was to get to him and do the deed."

"Bonnie thought they might have deliberately got you and her involved. If so, that points directly to Eddie. He had a good idea that she'd be turning up at the bungalow, and he might have worked out that she'd take someone with her. It would make a clever smokescreen."

"I thought that for a bit. But it's full of holes when you really look at it. The timing would have to rely on a lot of unpredictables. The person would have to keep Kit alive and talking if we'd turned up late. Someone else might have come to the door first. All those women who make pies for a man when his wife dies. There are whole armies of them, apparently."

238

"I'm not sure that's true," said Simmy. "Although Kit's probably the sort who would have them all running around after him."

"Definitely," Ben said. "And that's where we should keep our focus." He gave her another serious look. "Which is where my mother comes in," he said levelly. "You don't have to avoid that subject, you know. I bet she's said something to you about it."

"She has, yes. I don't know whether she'd got it right, though — about what you were thinking."

"What did she say?"

Simmy paused. "I don't think it would be helpful to tell you. It's not my business."

"Fair enough," he said, confirming her impression of a new maturity. "Let me start, then. It's really just an extension of what we were saying just now. Following the evidence can lead into very big mistakes. That's what shocked me so much. The facts are, one: my mother knew Kit Henderson years ago and had more to do with him than any of us knew at the time; two: she behaved very strangely when he was killed; three: she's got letters from *Mrs* Henderson tucked away in her desk."

"What? How do you know that?"

"I snooped," he said shamelessly. "On Wednesday evening. They're quite strong stuff, complaining about her husband's unfaithfulness, and not being able to trust him with any woman, even my mum."

"And she *kept* them? Isn't that rather weird?"

"She keeps everything. Says letters are the only genuine source of social history for future generations. Of course, she never gets any now. Nobody does."

"So?"

"So I asked her about it, on Saturday, without confessing to looking at the letters. I only read one or two. You can't get a moment's privacy in our house. Tanya was shouting for me as usual." He sighed. "Sisters are God's way of reminding us that we can expect a lifetime of trouble from women."

"Even Bonnie?"

"Probably," he said glumly.

"And what did your mother say?" She was finding it unusually difficult to keep him on the main subject.

"She said she could see how it looked, but she solemnly vowed that she had never had any sort of close relationship with Kit Henderson, and I should be more careful about forming suspicions without enough information. She's right, of course. What I took to be evidence was really the most flimsy bits of old history. Not facts at all, as it turns out. Made me see what a fool I can be sometimes."

"Have you talked about this with Moxon? Why did he bring you here, anyway?"

"That's quite a long story. He showed up at the house at half past one, when we were in the middle of a hunk of roast pork. Said he needed to go through one more time the details of what I saw at the bungalow on Tuesday. Checking where I went, basically, and what I touched. He's very hung up on that letter, or list, or whatever it is."

"Did you leave fingerprints on it, or something?"

"I don't think so, but I could have done. Anyway, he could see what bedlam it was at the house, so he drove me down to the station, which was more or less deserted, and then after a bit, he said he had something to ask you and did I want to come with him. So that's what happened. We'd been waiting for you quite a while before you and Christopher came sauntering home like . . . like Hansel and Gretel or something. Holding hands and not walking straight."

The simile gave Simmy a jolt. Hansel and Gretel were brother and sister, which in some ways fitted the relationship she had with Christopher. Were they too close for comfort? Was it unnervingly like incest to be in love with him? "Couldn't you have said Romeo and Juliet?" she asked.

He shrugged. "You're too old for either pair. I can't think of a good comparison, for the moment."

"Maybe Moxon wanted you out of his way. Did you think of that?"

"Not really. This case isn't like the others, is it? I am very directly involved. I found the body." He almost shouted these last words. "You can't get more involved than that. The irony is, that I would quite like to sit this one out, and just get on with all the other stuff in my life. I've got no theories about who killed the man. I might have been within seconds of seeing who it was, but those seconds may as well be weeks or months."

"Was there no lingering smell?" she wondered. "Something on the air?"

"Don't be ridiculous." But he grew thoughtful, and she could tell he was putting himself back in the bungalow, wondering whether he might have missed something as insubstantial as a hint of aftershave or garlic-scented sweat. "Nope," he concluded. "No smells."

"Does Moxon think my book is connected?"

"Book?"

"The one Fran left me. It's the only thing he could possibly find that makes me of any interest."

"I don't think he thinks it's significant. Where is it? Can I have another look at it?"

"I left it in the kitchen. Let me go and get it. Do you want more tea or anything?"

"No, thanks."

She fetched the book and they sat side by side looking through it slowly, page by page. "It is lovely, isn't it?" she said. "Even if it isn't worth anything."

"It might be worth something in a hundred years." He was running his hand very lightly over a picture of a tangled creeping plant covered in yellow flowers. "What's this?"

"Jasmine. It's a climber, but the artist has shown this one sprawling over the ground. The colours are more authentic than most of the others, although she's made the leaves the wrong shade of green."

He turned the page. "I know this one. It's a clematis."

"Right. But I don't believe you can get orange ones like that. They're pink, assuming that's intended to be a Nelly Moser."

"So there's something wrong with every picture — is that what you're saying? Do you think she did it deliberately?"

242

"If she did, we'll never know why. More likely, she was colour-blind, and didn't know what she was doing. Or the light was bad, maybe, if she did them in the evenings."

"She was Mr Henderson's mother-in-law — is that right?"

"Yes. Fran's mother. She did these in the 50s, apparently."

"Before her daughter was married, then. Before she knew Mr H?"

"Long before. He'd only have been a little kid when these were done. Why?"

He shrugged. "Nothing. I just thought there might be a message in here somewhere."

"There might be. Something like 'Nothing is as it seems' or 'Don't trust your senses'. Not very likely, though."

"And not very encouraging, if Frances knew that's what it meant when she left it to you in her will. That might suggest she was trying to put you off Christopher."

Simmy's heart lurched again. "That's way too convoluted," she protested. "For a start, Fran couldn't possibly have known that Chris and I were going to get together again. And if she did, she'd have approved. She always wanted that to happen . . . although . . ." she faltered.

"Although what?"

"Well, Chris told me this morning that his father warned him off me. That was directly opposite to what I always thought Fran wanted. I didn't think of that until now, even though I was really surprised. I was only sixteen. We were only sixteen. Kit probably just thought we were too young to get physical."

"You were," said Ben with some force. "Much too young."

She carefully avoided looking at him. This might be the answer to a question that had been nagging at her for some time: were Ben and Bonnie having sex? In most couples of their age, it would have been ridiculous to even query it, but Simmy had a growing sense that they were waiting for something, that celibacy had been a core element of their relationship all along. Now it felt as if she had confirmation of this suspicion. And she did not want him to know what she was thinking.

"Well, if there is a message, I can't hope to find it, can I? It could be anything."

He was frowning at the floor. "Maybe she had some kind of hunch that her husband was in danger, once she died. So she left you the book, to make sure you had to be in touch with the family again. That would give you and Christopher a chance of getting back together, and somehow, maybe, protecting the old man. Or even, in her mind, making something happen that would keep him safe. Except it didn't work, did it?"

"That's all terribly fanciful," she objected. "And if it was true, it must implicate one of the children. Offspring — whatever you call them when they're grown up. Hannah or George, most likely. But if that was right, why wouldn't she just contact the police and . . . No, that wouldn't work, would it?"

"Precisely. What could she say? 'One of my kids is planning to kill their father once I'm dead'? The police, for very good reasons, aren't authorised to interfere in any way *before* a crime is committed. I expect I've mentioned *Minority Report* once or twice, haven't I? It's a terrifying idea."

Simmy nodded vaguely. Something about working out who was likely to commit a crime and arresting them in advance. The very fact that it sounded so logical made it all the more dreadful.

"You know," said Ben, his eyes sparkling, "I really think we might be getting somewhere. It's all in the family. That's what makes the most sense. Isn't that what everyone's been thinking all along, one way or another?"

Before she could respond, there was a knock at her door.

"Probably my mum, come to collect me," said Ben. "I texted her a bit ago to tell her I was still here."

But it wasn't Helen Harkness. It was George Henderson, the missing brother, with a thunderous look on his small face, which was so like that of his father.

CHAPTER
NINETEEN

Simmy was pathetically glad to have Ben at her side, as the irate man marched into her living room. "Is Christopher here?" he demanded. "Hannah said this was where he must be."

"He's not. What do you want, George? Stop being so aggressive."

"Is this George Henderson?" asked Ben, standing up tall and solid. "I don't think we've met. I'm Ben Harkness. I found your father's body on Tuesday. I offer you my condolences."

Simmy almost laughed. It was so typically Ben that she wanted to hug him. But that would have spoilt the effect. George, who was perhaps half an inch shorter than Ben, was stopped in his tracks. "Thanks," he muttered. "It's been a pretty bad time for us, as you might imagine."

Simmy watched the two men get the measure of each other. George was thirty-five, already losing his hair. His skin was a hue that made you think of creatures that lived out of the sunlight. There was a crease between his eyes that made him look permanently angry. But in the eyes themselves there was a lost, bewildered look that Simmy remembered from twenty years ago. It had made her want to avoid him then, and it did still. Something had always been just a bit wrong with George — a fact that everybody knew, but nobody would admit. His fights with Hannah had provided an easy focus for their reproaches, and even offered an explanation. He had been displaced by two small girls, losing his role as youngest, and never quite finding where he belonged from that day on. But there might have been more to it than that, Simmy now realised. Something that concerned his parents, rather than his siblings.

"I gather that Hannah has called a meeting of all five of you," said Simmy, still marvelling that George had driven all the way up to Troutbeck, and somehow managed to find her cottage. "How did you know where I live? Why not just phone me?"

"I wanted to see you in person. What's going on between you and my brother? When did it start? I need to understand what everyone's doing. I thought when Mum died that was the worst that could happen. The world fell apart then. And now it's even worse." He sat down suddenly on the spot where Ben had recently been. "And *you* found him." He stared accusingly at Ben. "Dead on the floor of his own house. It's monstrous. Grotesque. I can't believe it."

"True, all the same," said Ben flatly.

"So who did it?" The man stared helplessly from one face to the other and back again. "Who would do that?"

Simmy could hear Ben silently answering *well, you maybe*, as she was herself. But looking at George, she

247

knew it could not have been him. Nobody could act as well as that.

"Sounds as if not many people really liked him," Ben said neutrally.

"That's no reason to *kill* him," George protested. "I mean, none of us really liked him, if we're honest, but plenty of people don't like their fathers — or don't *approve* of them, more like. It's probably the normal thing, if everyone was honest about it. No man wants to be like their father, when you think about it."

"That's true," said Ben, with a show of eagerness. "I grasped that only a little while ago. It's one of the curses of the human condition. All fathers want their sons to be a clone of them, but the sons want the absolute opposite. Tragic, really. Men are far better off just having daughters."

Simmy snorted a truncated laugh. "My father agrees with you. Thanks the Lord that he never had a son. Far too competitive, he says."

"Wise man, your dad."

"It's all in the Bible," said George heavily. "Cain and Abel, for a start."

Ben's eagerness burgeoned. "Yes! Although it gets a bit complicated in that instance. Abel's seen as the good one, for trying to please his dad, and Cain's the wicked evil murderer. I suppose your brother Eddie qualified as Abel — but which of you and Christopher is the killer, in that scenario?"

George's face grew red and mottled. "What do you know about my family?" he demanded. "You . . . you . . ."

248

"Careful," warned Simmy. "Ben's been following the case of your father's death quite closely, actually."

Ben went on. "It's a great story, when you think about it. The way I read it, Cain *pretends* to be as his father wants, in order to get the inheritance. Abel's rather slow and dim, unambitious as well. He doesn't deserve to be the one to carry on the line. But I can't remember what happens next." he frowned. "Something about the children of Cain, but I think that's just the title of a movie."

"He was marked by God and was a fugitive and a nomad all his life," said George. "The implication is that he was indeed the ancestor of all mankind, and they all carried his bad blood, capable of murder and lying and all the horrible things people do."

"Fascinating," Ben enthused. "I love Bible stories."

Simmy was undecided as to whether all this was a diversion, or a crucial insight into what had happened to Kit. Both, probably, she concluded. Diversions did, after all, end up taking you to the place you needed to be.

George was plainly reassessing the young man in front of him. "Are you a person of faith, then?" he asked, with a dubious tilt of his head.

"What? Oh — well, no. Really not at all. Sorry. But I don't think you can properly be a part of this culture if you're not familiar with the Bible."

"Almost no one of your generation would agree with you," said George, while Simmy also took exception to the remark. She had very little idea of who anybody was in the Old Testament, and even less in the New. In fact, she wasn't sure she could correctly identify material as coming from one rather than the other.

"You are, then?" she asked the man.

"I am," he said, with due gravity. "As I would have thought you'd remember from our earlier association."

"You mean when you were thirteen? Is *that* what was going on? I don't think I ever realised." She reviewed her memories of the solitary teenager, obviously tormented and enraged by turn. None of his behaviour had come across as noticeably Christian. "Did you go to church when we were on holiday? I don't remember that."

"They wouldn't let me," he said tightly. "And anyway, there wasn't a church that would suit me anywhere near. Wales is very Low Church," he added with a sniff.

"Smells and bells?" said Ben obscurely. "Isn't that what they called you in the olden days?"

"Possibly — about a century ago. Nobody cares enough to cast aspersions now."

"Was Kit religious?" Simmy asked suddenly.

"Not a bit. Didn't I just say they tried to stop me? They both behaved as if it was a sort of illness, right to the end."

The pain in his face rendered even Ben silent for a minute. Simmy acknowledged yet again how much he had grown up since she'd met him. A year ago he might well have asked excruciating questions about whether George thought his parents were in heaven or hell now, and would it work to pray for people who didn't believe in God. She wondered briefly at her own naivety when it came to matters of religion, given that she never gave the subject any attention at all. When her baby had died, there was no flicker of an idea that the poor little unborn soul might be surviving in some numinous realm, waiting to meet her in fifty years' time.

The silence inevitably led to a review of George's reasons for being there in the first place. Considering he could not have known that Ben would be there, it seemed fair to assume that he had wanted to speak to Christopher about something, having taken Hannah to be saying that their brother was liable to be tracked down in Troutbeck.

"You wanted to talk to Christopher, didn't you?" she said. "That's why you came up here. It must have been something important."

"I didn't like feeling left out — again."

Simmy blew out her cheeks at this. "It's your own fault, you idiot. You keep going off by yourself, not talking to anybody. You leave *yourself* out. You always did."

"Not any more. I've got nothing to be ashamed of. Nothing to hide. I'm tired of being belittled and made fun of because of what I believe. I'm free now, and I'm going to follow my own convictions with my head high."

"They'll be watching you, though, won't they?" said Ben, shattering Simmy's confidence in his new maturity. "Your parents, up in heaven — they'll still be keeping an eye on you."

"It doesn't work like that," said George stiffly. "You don't know what you're talking about."

"I know what Christians are supposed to believe. It's all pretty simple, as far as I can see."

"Stop it, Ben," ordered Simmy. "It's his own business what he believes."

In spite of himself, George looked glad of the intervention. "I'd be happy to explain it all to you sometime," he said. "But now I think there are more urgent issues. Until the person who murdered my father is caught and punished, none of us can get on with our lives. Each one of the five of us will have suspicion and gossip following us everywhere we go. There'll be sly looks and subtle digs, probably for years, unless the police come up with the actual killer."

"If that's all you've got to say, it's hard to see why you came all this way," said Ben, with a mulish glance at Simmy. "It's pretty much self-evident, surely?"

Simmy resisted the urge to chastise him again. He was right, after all. George seemed to be pointlessly blathering, further obscuring his real reason for being there.

"I told you — I was looking for Christopher."

"And we don't believe you, because you'd have phoned him, and found out he wasn't here, before coming in person. You didn't know I'd be here, so it's my guess — based on very sound deduction — that you came hoping to find Simmy alone. That suggests you had something to ask her or tell her that wasn't for anybody else to hear. And now, because I'm in your way, you're just wittering on, hoping that I'll leave before you do. Am I right?"

George gave him a dark scowl. "It's certainly true that none of this is your business."

"You know," said Ben thoughtfully, "when people say that it usually means they've got something they want to keep secret. And one of the many things I've learnt about murder investigations is that there aren't any secrets that can be kept. Definitely not one that has to do with the dead person — or people. Everything's fair game, even though it doesn't seem fair, I know. There's something yukky about it, but it's true, just the same."

"I've got no secrets," growled George.

"How boring it must be to be you, then," flashed Ben.

Simmy had stood enough. "Listen," she said loudly. "George — if you want to speak to me without Ben, we can go into the kitchen. Ben — play with your phone or something for a bit, okay. This isn't getting anybody anywhere, is it?"

Both men meekly did as bidden, despite Ben's umbrage at being told to "play" and George effectively being accused of wasting her time. She almost pushed him onto an upright chair, taking the only other seat for herself. "So get on with it," she ordered.

"Well . . . it probably isn't anything much. The thing is, Hannah told me she saw you at Christopher's auction yesterday, and it came out that she was with that Wetherton bloke. When I asked Lynn if that seemed strange to her, she got very agitated, and said that was sure to set all sorts of tongues wagging, and what was Hannah thinking of."

Simmy waited, assuming she was going to be asked not to spread unfounded rumours about his sister. It felt feeble and irrelevant, and mildly insulting, if that was all he'd wanted to say to her. She tried to phrase a response that would convey this without hostility, but he spoke again before she could get any words out.

"But that's not the important thing. It's that blasted book my mother left you that's really niggling us. All of us, apart perhaps from Eddie. Even Christopher can't see why she did it. I mean — the thing's so completely worthless. Why couldn't she just *give* it to you herself, months ago? She could have dropped it off at your shop or handed it to your mother at any time. But she made such a big thing of it, putting it in her will like that and leaving you that letter. Then, for good measure, she even puts it into the last-minute list she wrote for Dad."

Simmy was thoroughly disarmed. "I feel the same," she said, thereby doing some disarming of her own. "It really is quite peculiar."

"The list is *extremely* peculiar. It's impossible to imagine my mother giving that sort of instruction to Dad. Not while she was alive, anyway. And yet they say he was holding it, when . . . when he died. The police obviously think it's connected with his murder. They showed it to us, one by one. I'd never seen it before, and the others all say they hadn't either. Where did it come from? Why wasn't it attached to the will somehow? There's an implication that whoever killed Dad took it to the house and showed it to him — and that makes all of us suspect each other. Even the solicitor could be in the frame, if she asked him to

254

deliver it." He barked a sudden laugh. "That'd be a new one, wouldn't it?"

She was increasingly out of her depth during this rant. "How does any of that involve *me*?" she wondered. "What do you want me to tell you?"

"Just whether you've come up with any ideas as to what it might all mean. The book has to be a clue of some sort, don't you think? I thought I could have a look at it again. I haven't seen it since I was about ten, at Nanna's house. She used to get it out and show it to us, as proud as anything. That was it, I assume, in the living room just now? Were you showing it to that boy?"

"I was, as it happens. You're welcome to have a look. We can't see anything sinister in it — at least," she corrected herself, "you could say the whole book is a bit sinister. The colours are all wrong. Was your grandmother colour-blind, do you know?"

"I have no idea. She was a bit bonkers, in her last years, I remember. Kept wandering off and stealing cats from people. Family legend has it that she lived a very frustrated existence, never being able to do what she wanted. She never showed much interest in our family. My mum was one of three, and the other two were favoured over her, or so she said."

Simmy made no attempt to delve further. She was tired and confused, and wanted him to go. Moxon had more or less said there was no further concern over the apparently missing jewellery, so there was no sense of obligation to ask George about it. "Come and have a look, then," she invited. "If that's all you wanted to say." Why he couldn't have said any of it in front of Ben was unclear. Though there had been hints of family scandal, perhaps, and George always had liked to avoid any groups larger than two, she remembered. Mostly his favoured number was one, as she had already pointed out.

He followed her back to the other room, and stood over the table turning the pages of the big book. Nothing appeared to catch his eye, and he thumped it shut with a sigh. "You're right," he said. "The colours are weird, but otherwise it can't possibly have any significance. I never took much interest in it, from the start. But I think it's nice that you've got it now," he added generously. "You obviously appreciate it."

"I do," said Simmy.

Ben had been ostentatiously thumbing his phone ever since the others had rejoined him. He went on doing so, without looking up. Simmy realised it was close to five o'clock, and the day effectively over. She waited in silence until George understood that he ought to go.

"All right. Well . . ." he said. "I'm not sure that's got me anywhere, but you've been very patient with me. I always did like you, you know. I heard Dad telling Christopher to treat you decently, not take advantage or anything. It was hugely embarrassing, but I was glad he was watching out for you. I wasn't sure your own father even noticed what was happening."

"Nothing was happening."

"Until now," said Ben, without lifting his head.

Simmy saw her own flushed cheeks reflected in George's. He obviously didn't want to know. "Shut up,

Ben," she said. Then, "It was good to see you, George, even though it was for a sad reason. I hope you can find your way home all right?"

"It's Troutbeck, not Novosibirsk," said the incorrigible Ben. "Almost impossible to go wrong, I would have thought. Unless you intend to find a quick way through Kirkstone. That might see you upside down in a ditch, admittedly."

"I'll be perfectly all right," said George.

It occurred to Simmy that she could save herself the bother of taking Ben home if she got George to do it instead. She wasn't sure where he lived, but even if it was to the north, the detour to Bowness would only take him an extra fifteen minutes at most. She opened her mouth to make the suggestion, but was quickly forestalled by the youngster. "Don't ask him to take me home," he said. "I can call someone, if you don't want to do it. My mum texted to say she can't come until seven."

"Why — where do you live?" asked George.

"Bowness. Just a little way from where your parents were. But it's okay. I'm in no rush."

"Well, I *could*," said the man. "But I was actually going back up to Greystoke. Leonora's probably waiting for me."

"Your new girlfriend?" said Simmy. "She was at the funeral, wasn't she? I never managed to speak to her — you rushed off so quickly."

"Greystoke?" Ben interrupted. "Isn't that where Tarzan comes from?"

"It's a big estate near Penrith. I've got a cottage there, because I work for the family. The Howards," he added portentously. "I oversee the maintenance. There are three thousand acres," he said. "That's a lot to manage."

"That's a long way from here," said Ben.

George sighed and returned to Simmy's question about Leonora. "She'd never met Mum, so it didn't seem right to stay for the wake. She's been very supportive, though."

Simmy remembered talk about George's liver, and depression, and wondered if this Leonora knew what she was letting herself in for.

"Don't worry about me," said Ben loudly. "I'm not ready to go yet." He gave Simmy a look that quelled any further effort to unload him onto a man who might well be unstable, angry and possibly even a murderer.

She kept her peace and let the visitor go without further interruption. The moment the door closed behind him, Ben flopped back on the sofa, and said, "This is turning into quite an afternoon. Who's going to show up next?"

Privately, Simmy hoped that Christopher might miraculously reappear, before the day was completely finished. Or at least phone her. It felt like a long time since he'd made his precipitate departure, and she wanted to hear his voice. "Nobody," she said. "So get your coat, if you brought one, and let's go. If you stay any longer I'll have to feed you, and that's too much to ask."

He rolled his eyes and made a big production of getting up and looking for a coat. "Did I have one?" he wondered aloud. "I don't remember."

"It's cold out there, so I hope you did." But she knew he'd been dressed in the same clothes she could now see, with no additional layers. "You didn't, though, did you?"

"Probably not. This is quite warm." He plucked at the sweatshirt he was wearing.

"Come on, then. If you want to talk, we can do it in the car."

She could see that he very much wanted to talk, and silently wished he wouldn't. Christopher, Moxon and George had drained her of all ideas or comments concerning the fate of Kit Henderson and his family. Possibly, she and Ben might have got somewhere together, if George had not intruded when he did. But the impetus had been lost and now she wanted no more to do with it.

Ben, as happened a lot, picked up on her mood, and was blessedly quiet for the first couple of miles. Then he said, rather hesitantly, "Moxon does seem to have some ideas, this time," he said. "I keep seeing that expression on his face — as if he knew things that we didn't, and was quietly confident of getting the job done in his own way. I don't remember him looking so confident before."

"I didn't notice."

"Well he did. Sort of smug and superior, as well." He tapped a front tooth meditatively. "I think he thinks there's something about that book. We were almost onto it, when that man showed up. He's not very nice, is he? I'm never comfortable with religious people, are you?"

"Why — because they're so smug and superior?"

"Not at all. The opposite, if anything. As if they're just waiting to be offended and insulted, so they can come over all reproachful and forbearing. Actually, I suppose they can be a bit smug when they're doing that. All that moral high ground, and insistence that God loves them."

"Maybe he does."

"Yeah. With some of them, that's their only chance, isn't it? Of finding love, I mean."

"Hush, Ben. You can't say things like that."

"I certainly can, and I will. Belief in religion is a free choice, a matter of a person's own will, and that means it's fine to challenge and question it."

"Maybe, but you were making fun."

"That too," he insisted. "It's fair game. Besides, it'd take more than a few mild insults from me to shift them, wouldn't it? They've got God on their side."

"So why bother?"

"Good question," he conceded.

By which time, they were on the outskirts of Windermere, with only five more minutes to go. Simmy found herself musing on the way she was perpetually in the company of people who defied social conventions when it came to the expression of questionable opinions. Her mother would say, of course, that this was because *everybody* had questionable opinions, and only needed a safe ear into which to pour them. Which perhaps answered the original question. Simmy was unusually non-judgemental, or even passive. She let people say things with only a token protest. Ben hadn't said anything so bad about religious people, after all. It was the whole subject that chafed at her, with its minefields of offence and associations with ethnicity. Far better to steer clear of the entire business and leave others to wrangle over it.

"I'm not suggesting that the murder had anything whatsoever to do with religion," Ben said, just as they drew up outside his house. "Just to be clear."

"That's a relief."

"No — I think it must have been about something from the past. Something that got raised again when Mrs H died. And I think Moxo thinks that as well."

"Okay," said Simmy impatiently. "Well, it was nice to see you. Good luck with the essay, or whatever it is."

"Thanks for the lift," he said, with an air of disappointment. "See you in a bit."

She drove back onto the main road, knowing that there was no way she could avoid calling in on her parents. Her father was liable to notice her car passing the gate, even on a dark November evening, and insist on knowing where she'd been and why she hadn't stopped. Only one window in the whole house overlooked the road, but it would be just her luck that he'd be looking out of it at the exact moment she drove by.

So she found a space a few yards away and went to spend an hour with Angie and Russell Straw, who did, perhaps, know more than they realised about the reason Kit Henderson had died as he did.

CHAPTER
TWENTY

Russell had not seen the car. He was slow to come to the door and open it, making much of the double lock that he persistently applied, despite hopes that his neurosis was abating. "Daughter," he said with a weak smile. "Are we expecting you?"

"No, no. I had to take Ben home, and thought I'd drop in for a minute."

"Your mother's having a hard time with a duvet," he said. "A man vomited on it."

"The actual duvet? Not just the cover?"

"Seemingly so. Soaked right in, she says. A minor calamity, in the great scheme of things, but enough to upset a number of plans."

"Duvets have to be dry-cleaned. Has she got a spare one? Was it a double bed?" Simmy could not avoid an awareness that this could indeed be a major inconvenience, if not a calamity.

Russell shrugged and led the way back into the kitchen. "Simmy's here," he shouted up the stairs, as he passed.

Angie came onto the landing above them and said, "Send her up. I could do with some help."

Simmy joined her mother, who was flushed and flustered. Her sleeves had been pushed up her arms and her hair was in disarray. "Bloody people," she said in a whisper. "Demanding a whole new set of bedding at this time of night."

"Sounds awful. Have you got another double duvet?"

"Of course not. Normally I'd just swop them around, but by some fluke, all the rooms are full tonight, so I can't. I wouldn't mind if it had been a child in one of the little beds, but this is the biggest double in the house. It's a nightmare."

"Where are the people?"

"They've gone out for a bit, but they'll be back any second. The man's too ill to want to eat anything. They ought to have gone home, but they live in Kent, so it's a long drive. You don't expect to have to be a nurse in this job, but that's what I feel like. Who's to say he won't do the same thing again tonight, and *then* where will I be?"

"What are you going to do with the bed?"

"Give them sheets and blankets, instead. I never did like duvets, great unwieldy things. But I've got to get it into a bag for the cleaners, and wash the cover. The pillow's covered in it as well. I never saw so much sick. Why couldn't the bloody idiot make it to the lavatory? It's only about six feet away from the bed, after all."

Simmy took one side and they quickly had a whole new bed made up with pristine sheets and a handsome woollen blanket that she remembered from her childhood. It had covered her parents' bed for years.

"You've still got this," she said, fingering the honeycomb weave. "It's a lovely thing, isn't it."

"It is, and I'll sue that man if he throws up on it."

Downstairs again, Simmy was offered the customary leftovers from the day's meals. "We had a really nice chicken cobbler," said Russell. "I ate more than usual. Not much of it left."

Angie scraped the last morsels into a bowl and put it in the Rayburn. "Give it ten minutes," she said. "You can have bread with it."

"I was right about 'enounce'," said Russell.

"Pardon?"

"You remember. I was going through all the 'nounce' words. Pronounce. Renounce. Announce. Now I've discovered 'enounce' is a real word. It's not much used, and it doesn't have a very interesting meaning, but it does exist. Funny how happy that makes me," he finished ruminatively.

Simmy gave him a fond look, thinking how she could never quite match his expectations at moments like this. A better daughter would have found "enounce" for him, like a cat bringing a dead mouse to a beloved master.

"I've had quite a day," she said. "Non-stop visitors." Only then did she pause to ask herself whether she was ready to disclose the escalation of her relationship with Christopher. It felt much too early to do so, and surely she was too old to share such matters with her parents. On the other hand, if and when they found out, they

265

might feel wounded by her silence. Better to let it emerge casually, she felt, if that could be managed.

"Oh?" said Angie tiredly.

"Moxon brought Ben over. Then George Henderson showed up out of the blue. Everybody's fixated on that book Fran left me. Moxon seems to think it holds a clue to what happened to Kit. At least, Ben thinks he does. I'm not convinced. It's much too far-fetched, surely." She cast an anxious glance at her father, unsure as to the wisdom of raising the subject of murder again. His unstable state of mind was a perpetual impediment to straight talking; something still so new that she kept forgetting.

"That's daft," said Angie shortly.

"I know. But Mum . . . was there ever anything a bit . . . um . . . Jimmy Savile-ish about Kit? He didn't go for young girls or anything, did he? There are weird hints going around that might be suggesting something like that. I mean — he never laid a finger on me. And now Christopher says his father warned him off me, when we were sixteen. But there's definitely something fishy. You must know about it, if so. Has Moxon asked you? Or anyone else?" She thought of Helen Harkness, and the continuing uncertainty about how she and Kit had really been connected.

"Young girls?" Angie shook her head slowly. "Lord, no. There was more to him than that. It's only pathetic inadequates who go in for all that sort of thing. Kit wasn't pathetic in the least. And he had far too much sense. He liked women. Although . . ."

"What?"

266

"Well, some of them were quite young. The older he got, the younger they were. But not *really* young. Well over the age of consent."

"And you knew?"

"Only because Fran told me. He was never much bothered about covering his tracks. I know you never could see it, but he did have a sparkle to him, you know. Charisma. They couldn't resist him, once he'd got his eye on them."

"You make it sound as if there were dozens of them."

Angie laughed. "I'm only aware of three. And that's over a period of at least twenty years. Bad, but not desperately so."

"You knew who they were?"

"Vaguely. It was Fran's problem, not mine. All I ever did was listen to her going on and on about it. Sometimes I told her she should take a stand, but she never did. Said she couldn't face starting again on her own. To be honest, I don't think she lost much by it. She thought he was making a fool of himself, so by association she got tainted, but nothing too ghastly." Angie heaved a sigh and glanced at her own husband. "You never know how it's going to end up, after all."

"I had no idea," said Simmy. "I just thought Fran was getting bored with him."

A hollow laugh came from the chair by the Rayburn where Russell sat. "Comes to us all," he said, with a spiteful look at his wife.

Simmy did what she could to change the subject, but everything was connected to the Hendersons in one way or another. "Did he tell you all about the auction yesterday?" she tried. "Wasn't he clever to spot that lovely dish?"

"It's nice, but the fact is, it's much too big to be of any use," said Angie. "We can display it somewhere instead."

"Christopher turned out well," said Russell. "I always did like the lad, but I never had much hope that he'd make a success of anything. Now he's got all those people running around after him, and learning a whole lot about the business too, I suppose."

"Lots of shady characters, the way I hear it," said Angie. "And Christopher's only an employee, isn't he? He doesn't *own* the place." She went to the Rayburn and extracted the bowl of reheated cobbler. Simmy took it and ate it with relish. "Lovely!" she approved, before going back to the topic of conversation. "The auction is actually rather glamorous, in a funny way," she murmured. "Exciting, as well." She had a thought. "And we can call him 'Chris' now. It seems to suit him better. 'Christopher' is such a mouthful."

"Too late. After nearly forty years, I can't think of him as a Chris. I always imagine a woman, anyway. Probably because of Chris in *The Archers*, or Chris Evert."

"Plenty of male Chrises," Russell said. "All those men on the telly. Half of them seem to be called Chris. Moyles. Evans. Tarrant . . ."

Simmy closed her eyes and wished she'd refrained from saying anything. For herself, she was more than happy to shorten the name. She said it silently to herself, with a little smile. "He's the second in command, and the boss is close to retirement. He could easily be the top man before long. You should see him in action, Mum. It's hypnotic. You can't stop watching him."

"While people are swindling each other behind his back," said Angie. "I'd like to have seen it for myself, I must admit. Even though it all sounds a bit sleazy to me, if I'm honest. Far better to go to a car boot sale or a flea market, if you want something."

"I expect you're right — but there's a special romance to an auction. I can't explain it. The auctioneer adds an extra dimension to the whole process, I suppose."

"He's really just an agent, and you know how I hate agents," said Angie sourly.

"That boy, Ben," said Russell, apparently running through various young men in his mind, wondering about their welfare. "Is he all right? Didn't he intercept a killer? Or was that longer ago, in Hawkshead? Or what? I feel I ought to be worrying about him, for some reason."

"He's fine, Dad. And we can't go on calling him a boy. He's eighteen now, and very grown up."

"Surely not entirely a man, though? Youth might be the word." Russell mused for a moment. "Or young man. What do people say these days?"

"It's 'man' officially," said Angie. "That's what they say on the news. And then, when they add that he's only eighteen, I always think — that's not a man, you fool. But it's not really a boy, either," she concluded.

"Another gap in the English vocabulary," sighed Russell, with some satisfaction. "I bet Shakespeare coined something that we've forgotten."

"I'll ask Ben himself," said Simmy.

The modest meal was finished and Simmy could see that Angie was dropping on her feet. Guests were liable to demand an early breakfast on a Monday, all fresh and eager for their explorations, even in November. "I'm going now," she said. "Thanks for the chat."

"Good to see you," said Russell with a slightly unfocused smile.

"June!" said Angie suddenly. "That was one of Kit's women — or so Fran believed. She never had hard evidence, as far as I could see. But the name kept cropping up, mainly because we both thought it so awful."

Here we go again with the business of names, thought Simmy. It had taken her many years to grasp that it was a central passion for her mother. Nobody escaped without some comment, generally unfavourable, about the appellation chosen for them by their parents. But something snagged her attention. "There was someone called June at Fran's funeral," she remembered. "Probably the same person."

Angie frowned. "Was there? How strange. Why would she go? I wonder. What was she like? Which one was she?"

"I can't remember what she said. I barely talked to her. She was in her forties. Pretty. Lots of make-up. Most likely she worked with Kit at the carpet place, and was just a friend."

"Not Fran's friend," snapped Angie. "Probably gone to gloat. I don't remember seeing anyone like that. Probably kept out of my way, knowing what I know about her. The same as that Cheryl did."

"Nasty, nasty," said Russell.

Simmy laughed uneasily and made her departure.

It was only half past eight when she got home. The house was full of phantom men, the primary one being Christopher Henderson. Not just the bed, but the bath — both full of haunting images that made her smile and then wince slightly at the unaccustomed abandon they had seen.

When the promised phone call came just before nine, she settled down on the sofa, hoping for a warming end to the day, rounding it off nicely. After all, it had begun with cuddles; it should end with something similar.

But Christopher was all business. "We had that meeting after all," he started. "All of us except for Eddie. George told us he saw you this afternoon."

"Yes. So how did it go?"

"Oh — all right. Nobody could quite understand what it was for. We all kept interrupting each other, and Hannah wants me to phone the coroner's officer and pressure him for the release of Dad's body, so we can arrange the funeral. I can do that, I suppose. She issued us all with practical jobs, even Eddie in his absence. I also have to handle the sale of the bungalow, with appropriate consultation, of course."

"It should sell quite easily. People like bungalows."

"We'll get a bit of cash, eventually, though not enough to get excited about."

"Chris . . ." she began. "Last night . . ."

She heard a kind of splutter. "I know," he said quietly. "Sorry. I'm prattling, aren't I? I hate doing that sort of stuff on the phone. It feels a bit . . . deviant. I mean . . ."

"Yes, I know. But I did want to hear your voice, and know things are all right, and it wasn't all completely stupid."

"Things are going to be all right," he said. "There is nothing in our way, but our own hang-ups. And I don't think either of us is too badly afflicted in that respect."

"Your father's murder is in the way," she said, loud and clear. "We can't give ourselves any proper time or space until that's all settled."

"Oh?" There was a lengthy silence. "Is that because you're worried I might be the murderer? Because I can't see any other reasons for it being an obstacle."

"No! Not that. But whoever did it is likely to be somebody close to you. It'll be like a poisoned thorn in my thumb — and yours. We'll never be able to ignore it."

"Sounds a bit melodramatic."

"Well, isn't murder melodramatic? If that's not, I don't know what is."

"I suppose you're right," he said reluctantly. "But I won't let you go, Sim. I should have held onto you twenty years ago. I'm not making the same mistake again. Just you put that in your knicker drawer and keep it safe."

272

She giggled. "All right then. We'd better go before it starts to get deviant."

"I'll see you soon," he promised.

CHAPTER
TWENTY-ONE

She slept badly, and then had to be dragged into consciousness by the alarm clock, which she had sensibly set. The grey mornings could deceive a person into thinking it was still night at eight o'clock, and send you back to sleep for another hour.

The solitariness of her breakfast routine felt wrong. Despite being an only child, she did not regard the single state as natural. Over the past two years she had trained herself to accept it, but it had never suited her. The empty little house waiting at the end of the day was forlorn at best. It maintained a hollow place that should have another person in it. A place that was going to waste, more and more as time went by.

And yet she had laughed off all Melanie's efforts to find her a mate. When Ninian Tripp had crossed her path, she had treated him with a tentative lukewarm affection. He had made it clear that he had no intention of joining her to live in Troutbeck, and there was no space for her in his tiny Brant Fell cottage. Ninian was a free spirit, incapable of making and keeping a promise, obscurely damaged by past events. Nobody could seriously consider him as a viable life partner.

274

And now a man had, in a single night, awakened all the old yearnings. It was pathetic, she told herself. Nothing could happen as quickly as that. The dangerous delusion that they knew each other because of their early years together had to be given full consideration. There was a vast stretch of intervening experience that had made them both quite different people. She was even starting to think of him by a different name: not Christopher any more, but Chris. A stranger, then, who might well turn out to be altogether impossible to trust.

Outside, Troutbeck was quiet as always. Wansfell rose to the west, shielding the village from Atlantic weather, with a range of mirroring pikes on the other side of the valley. Many a time had Simmy marvelled at the wisdom of those early settlers who created a village in the most perfect spot. Invisible from most points, comfortably nestled between the dramatic hills and fells, it dreamt its way through the centuries with nothing to disturb it. The motley population comprised self-sufficient natives, the latest of countless generations of workers on the land, starry-eyed escapees from more hectic realms and a variety of others. There was space for them all, as well as those who bought property and then only spent four weeks of the year actually in it. Other houses saw an endless succession of holidaymakers, perhaps forty different sets in a single year. The pub and the shop saw them come and go, and scarcely bothered to take note of who was who, tired of asking the same questions of them, no longer caring what the answers might be.

Even Russell Straw, down in Windermere, had shown less interest in his guests in recent months. He had once taken great interest in discovering just who it was sleeping under his roof for two or three nights. He had rejoiced in collecting all their occupations. Solicitors and schoolteachers, social workers and software designers all gave him a thrill. Others, who withheld the information with politely tight smiles, were evidently spies or drug dealers, bankers or estate agents. Unpopular roles that were best kept undisclosed.

But the game became tedious eventually, and now Russell simply served them their breakfast with bland remarks about the weather.

Perhaps it was just because it was November, Simmy thought, as she drove slowly out of Troutbeck. Endings, challenges, a frisson of fear at what the winter might bring. Combined with the deaths of Fran and Kit, the decline of her father, the slow business in the shop, it was all decidedly depressing. And Chris was hardly going to manage to relieve it all by himself. It would be unreasonable to expect him to.

Bonnie was waiting for her on the threshold of the shop. "Hey, I didn't expect you today," said Simmy. "It's Monday."

"Yeah, but I had Saturday off, didn't I?"

"And here you are standing out in the cold. I am a bit late." They had discussed giving her a key, but it had never actually happened. "I expect I'd lose it," she said. "I've never been any good with keys."

"We could tie it to your phone," joked Simmy. "That would be the safest place." The notion of losing a phone was clearly ludicrous.

"Corinne dropped me off on her way to Barrow. She's visiting someone in the hospital."

"Oh? In the morning? Is that allowed?"

Bonnie's face contracted. "Actually, it's her mum. She's been there since Friday. They don't think she's going to make it this time."

Simmy wasn't sure what to say. Was the mother of a foster mother a significant figure, an honorary grandmother? Very likely so. "Have you been to see her?"

"Yeah. On Saturday. It was lucky you closed the shop, as it turned out. It's sort of sad, but she's not in pain or anything."

"How old is she?"

"Not sure. Eighty or something. Corinne's fifty, and she was the youngest."

"Oh dear."

"Yeah, well. It's what happens, right? Doesn't make sense to complain about it."

"We all do, though," said Simmy ruefully. "I suppose we all think it's some sort of massive mistake, when it comes to our own personal family."

Bonnie gave a little shake, as if to throw off this line of thought. "What about you? Have a good weekend?"

"Eventful. Friday seems a long time ago." And she gave her young assistant an edited account of the past two days, including the fact that she had seen Ben. "He stayed for ages at my place. Moxon brought him."

"I know. He called me when he got home. I heard all about it."

"He thinks Moxon's got a theory about the murder."

"Right. He told me that, as well."

They were setting up the shop as they chatted, ready for the new week. Poinsettias had arrived, along with some mistletoe. A week closer to Christmas brought a heightened acknowledgement of the upcoming festivities. "How many shopping days is it now?" wondered Simmy.

"Still more than thirty, if you count weekends. I don't think they say that so much now, do they? People do online shopping in the middle of the night, so it doesn't make much sense."

It made Simmy feel old. She felt a flash of empathy with really old people, who were seeing incessant change to aspects of their lives they had taken for granted for decades. Where would it all end, she wondered glumly.

Not a single customer had disturbed them by lunchtime, and only one order had come through on the computer. "Another one for Staveley," noted Simmy. "I quite like going there. I'll do it this time tomorrow."

There was a growing sense of being in limbo. On all sides there were issues waiting to be resolved. Even Bonnie's foster-granny, or whatever she was, was apparently waiting to die, fading painlessly into oblivion. Simmy wondered whether she should encourage the girl to talk about it, or leave it out entirely, so as to provide a sanctuary from the whole business. Best to take her lead from Bonnie herself, she decided.

And all the time she was more than half expecting somebody to come bursting through the door with news, demands, appeals — something that would shift the inertia and lead to a dramatic conclusion. It could be Moxon, Christopher, Eddie, George, Ben — even Angie or Hannah were possibilities. But not one of them appeared.

Instead, she received a phone call.

It was Helen Harkness. "Two things," she began briskly. "First — Kit's funeral. I suppose I'll have to send the bloody man some flowers, if only because it was my son who found him. Can you put me in a pending tray or something? A spray of neutral colours, thirty quid or so?"

"Neutral colours?" It was the first time Simmy had heard the phrase in relation to flowers. She envisaged dried and dead blooms in sepia, beige and grey. "Like white?"

"Whatever you think. Pale, anyway. As far as you can get from flamboyant and intrusive."

"All right." That made two orders in the imaginary pending tray. She wondered whether her software had a heading for such situations. Probably not, she decided, and wrote it down on a notepad with a pen.

"And second," said Helen, relentlessly, "thanks for having Ben yesterday. He was gone much longer than I expected. I hope you had a good talk?"

"Did he tell you any of it?"

"You're joking. He won't even give me a clue or two to help me guess."

"Did he at least mention that we had George Henderson with us for a lot of the time?"

"He did not. You mean one of Kit's sons, do you?"

"The third one, yes."

"What did he want? Where does he live?"

"I'm not entirely sure what he wanted, other than to stop feeling left out. And he lives miles away, practically in Penrith."

"Is he married?"

"There's a girlfriend, called Leonora." Simmy waited in vain for a comment on the name, as would undoubtedly have come from her mother. The fact that it didn't come brought a very slight sense of relief.

"Oh, well," said Helen, sounding as if she wanted no more information about the Hendersons. "That's all I wanted to say."

Simmy was listening for the buzz of a disconnected line, when the woman added, "That Hannah's a piece of work, isn't she?"

"Pardon?"

"She's put a whole lot of stuff on Facebook. Wilf showed it to me this morning. Talking about finding the birth mother who gave her and her sister up, wanting to make up for lost time. She must be mad. Doesn't she realise that all sorts of people are going to pop out of the compost heap and claim her as theirs? I mean — *Facebook*, of all things!"

Wilf was Ben's older brother, who occasionally involved himself peripherally in Ben's obsessions, but mostly got on with his much more ordinary and contented life. "I never knew they were adopted until a few days ago," said Simmy. "I'm still trying to get to grips with it."

"Oh, I keep forgetting how well you used to know them." A short pause, then, "How could you not know? Did they keep it such a secret?"

"My mother says not. She thinks I was just incredibly unobservant."

Helen laughed, and with a brief farewell, the expected buzzing sound filled Simmy's ear.

"Was that Ben's mum?" asked Bonnie, two seconds later.

"It was. She's ordered flowers for Kit's funeral, when it happens. I imagine the body will be released any day now." Another unanticipated aspect of floristry was a rapid acquisition of the arcane details surrounding un-expected deaths. At least half a dozen customers had explained the role of the coroner to her, and how frustrating the delays and obfuscations could be. The most recent — four or five months earlier — had been a long rant from a man whose ninety-five-year-old mother, having died slowly in hospital, was referred to the coroner *without the family being told*. This last was the sore point. Simmy had glimpsed a world riddled with suspicion, where the son had perhaps poisoned his aged parent with a slow-acting substance, and no way was the hospital doctor going to let him escape retribution.

"It could happen, though," Melanie had said when hearing the story.

"So could a lot of things. Surely you agree that it's based on a kind of insanity, which does no good at all? All it does is impede a process that's already impossibly slow and inefficient?"

"Maybe," said Melanie.

Bonnie would be more inclined to agree with Simmy, surely? Much of her life so far had been spent working round officialdom with its mistakes and failures to understand. But Bonnie was as yet ignorant of matters involving a coroner. "Released?" she echoed.

"That's right. They have to be sure there's no more evidence to be found on — or in, I suppose — the body, before they let it be buried or cremated."

"Mm," said Bonnie, showing no sign of wanting further information. Simmy looked at her, trying to assess the degree of squeamishness behind the single syllable. Any girlfriend of Ben Harkness was unlikely to get away with much in the way of female vapourings, but Bonnie did have genuine issues around the more visceral aspects of life. She washed her hands a lot, and never wore the same clothes twice without cleaning them. She had suffered from severe anorexia and missed a lot of school as a result. She had needed to be protected from the sight of Kit Henderson's bleeding body.

"Right, then," Simmy sighed. "There must be some work we can do." But when she looked around the shop for inspiration, she could see nothing that was not already in perfect order.

"It feels weird, doesn't it?" said Bonnie. "Just standing around like this, waiting for something to happen. It's not exactly *productive*, is it?"

"I'm not sure I ever feel particularly productive," Simmy admitted. "I'd say we were more of a service industry than a manufacturing one, wouldn't you?"

Bonnie looked blank. "Is that what 'productive' means, then? I thought it was just . . . making good use of the time." She frowned. "Product — right. Now I see."

"My father would be proud of you," laughed Simmy.

"So would Ben." Her eyes grew glittery with the ecstasy of her adoration. "There was *so much* I had never even thought about. Words. History. Poems. Science. It just goes on and on — and he knows all of it. *How* does he? He must have started when he was two, to have learnt such a lot."

"He's a prodigy," said Simmy carelessly. "Some would say he's a freak of nature, with a brain three times as big as most people's."

"No, it's not. He's just . . ." As she sought for the words, the choked sound of the doorbell announced a customer at last, along with a belated realisation on Simmy's part that there was something she could usefully have filled the past ten minutes doing. She could have climbed on a chair and examined the problem with the silly thing.

Two men came in. They were both quickly recognised by Simmy, and neither was especially welcome.

"Mr Wetherton," she nodded to the older one. "And Jack — that's right, isn't it? Hannah's husband." They must be bringing news of Kit's funeral, she supposed, and more orders for flowers. She had no idea at all what Jack's surname might be. She still thought of

Hannah and Lynn as Hendersons, having failed to attend their weddings or note the gender or date of their offspring.

"Right first time," said the younger man. He was mid thirties, with dark colouring and a lean outline. Not entirely unlike Kit in his prime, Simmy noted. She had only met him once, at Fran's funeral, holding a child in each hand, in an attempt to keep them quiet. They were the only children present, and Simmy had caught a number of disapproving glances. Only after an hour or so did Simmy learn that the children belonged to Lynn, not Hannah, and their father was a man named Barry, who was being obsessively attentive to Kit, while neglecting his daughters.

"She's good with names and faces, I see," remarked Malcolm Wetherton. "Once seen, never forgotten, obviously."

"Not really," she demurred. "After all, I am a very old friend of the family, so anybody connected with the Hendersons is bound to make an impression on me." Just how this man was connected remained obscure. He kept popping up, as a husband of a friend, and then a friend in his own right. If he was pally with Hannah's husband, that at least probably removed any lurking doubts as to how he'd come to be with her at Saturday's auction. This association prompted her to ask, "Did you buy anything on Saturday? My dad got a lovely dish. He was terribly pleased with himself."

Jack blinked and looked from face to face. "What's all that about?"

284

Uh-oh, thought Simmy. Maybe things were not so innocent after all. But Wetherton smiled easily, and said, "We were both at Christopher's saleroom in Keswick. Didn't Hannah tell you?"

"Not that I recall," said the husband, finding himself in a classic situation, universally recognised. "*Did* you buy anything?"

"Not much. I was selling mostly. Got a nice price for a painting I picked up at a car boot. Probably worth three or four times as much again, but I'm not complaining."

Jack met Simmy's eye, and gave a conspiratorial wink. "Crazy business, if you ask me," he said. "The same things going round and round, everyone trying to make a profit. When will anybody just buy the picture because they want to hang it on their wall?"

Malcolm Wetherton shrugged. "Who knows?"

"Chris is a good auctioneer, don't you think?" Simmy asked, with a craven desire to speak his name and hear him praised by these men.

"The ladies like him," agreed Wetherton. "Just like his old dad, in that respect."

"Which brings us to the reason we're here," said Jack deftly. "Flowers for the funeral. We're thinking it'll be the end of next week, paperwork permitting."

"Okay," said Simmy. "Tell me what you'd like." She glanced at Wetherton, wondering whether he had suggested the advance flower order, since he had already done the same thing himself, several days ago. The suspicion popped up that he was using it as a regular pretext for coming into the shop; if so, he was singularly unimaginative.

"I told Jack I'd already ordered mine," he explained. "We met in the street just now and I thought I'd come with him. We've got some matters to discuss after this."

"Have we?" Jack blinked. "What're they, then?"

Wetherton looked at Simmy and said nothing. A moment's awkwardness was dispelled by Jack pointing to random flowers standing on the floor in buckets, and suggesting the general shape and colour of his funeral flowers. "There won't be a joint one from all the children, then?" she queried. "That's the most usual thing. Like you did for your mother."

"That would make more sense," he agreed. "But when Hannah suggested it last night, George said he'd already decided to go in with Eddie, and the rest of us could do what we liked. She told me to get on with it while I had the chance."

"Seems rather a shame," Simmy began before catching Bonnie's eyes on her. Standing by the table holding the till and the computer, the girl evidently had something she would have liked to say.

"What?" muttered Simmy.

"Two new orders just popped up."

It was obvious that this had not been the main thing that Bonnie had wanted to convey, but Simmy played along. "Oh good. About time, too." She briskly took all the necessary details from Jack, including his surname, which turned out to be Latimer. "So she's Hannah Latimer," she said. "I never knew that."

"Sounds rather nice, don't you think?" said the man, as if he could take any credit for it.

"And you've got one child — is that right?"

"Right. Kieron. He's five. Lynn's got Christa and Ginnie. We see a lot of them."

"Christa? Was that after Kit?" She could scarcely believe that her mother had failed to trumpet this piece of blatantly unimaginative repetition on the part of the Hendersons.

"What? Oh — no. At least — it never occurred to me that it might be. She's Christabel, officially."

"Still quite similar," said Simmy.

He didn't look as if he was following her fixation on nomenclature, especially as his companion was showing signs of impatience. "Okay, mate," said Jack, genially. "Just because you've got no kids shouldn't make you so antsy when someone else talks about them."

Simmy repressed a shudder. Reference to childlessness was a perpetual minefield. Who could say what disasters and disappointments lay behind the Wetherton story, just as they did with her own?

"Time enough yet," said the man. Simmy remembered, with a slight effort, that he was married to the woman called Cheryl, who looked to be over forty, and he was well into his fifties. Good luck to them, then, she thought, with a surprising little pang of excitement.

Wetherton led the way to the street at a pace beyond the advisable in a crowded flower shop. Simmy and Bonnie both watched with in-held breath. They only exhaled when the door closed behind both men.

"So what was that look for?" Simmy demanded.

Bonnie made no attempt to play dumb. "You were talking yourself out of business, telling them they should just send one lot of flowers. You'll get twice the money if they do five separate ones. At least. Nobody's going to spend less than forty of fifty quid, are they? And even the most fabulous joint effort wouldn't come to more than a hundred and fifty. Likely to be a lot less. I worked it out while they were talking," she added, modestly.

"You're right. I wasn't thinking. Or rather, I *was* thinking how much work it would be if they all came to me. Remember that Hardy funeral, in the spring? It nearly killed me, doing all those wreaths and sprays and whatnot. Maybe George at least will go to someone in Penrith. Although I suppose Christopher —"

She interrupted herself with a slight gasp at the flood of euphoria that accompanied his name. It was entirely involuntary, coming as a physical shock.

"What's the matter?" asked Bonnie. "You look as if you're having a heart attack."

"I sort of am," Simmy grinned. "But a nice one."

Bonnie put both hands over her face, exaggerating her astonishment. "Stone the crows," she said. "Wait till I tell Ben."

"I think you'll find he already knows," blushed Simmy.

CHAPTER
TWENTY-TWO

By Monday lunchtime the sense of limbo had become a permanent state. Despite visits from two people linked to the murdered man, there was no suggestion of a resolution. Moxon had apparently not solved the case, or if he had, he wasn't sharing his triumph with Simmy. After the previous evening's chat with Christopher, she found herself expecting another call. In fact, so deeply had she fallen for him that hourly calls would have barely sufficed. She checked her phone so many times that Bonnie noticed.

"Hasn't he called you?" she asked, with excessive solicitude. "He must be busy."

"Yes."

"You've got it bad, haven't you?" the girl went on, ignoring any protocols that might have inhibited her. "Are you worried about him at all?"

"Worried? No. I'd phone him if I was. And I'm not just waiting for a call from him. There are plenty of other people who might want to talk to me."

Bonnie nodded with infuriating understanding.

The repeated slackness of the business gave her too much time to obsess. Her idle mind roamed over a host of awful possibilities. Chris might have been arrested for killing his father; but if so, she would have heard somehow. If he had changed his mind about Them — as she thought of herself and him — he might well stay quiet about it for a while. "I *could* phone him, I suppose."

"Of course you could," said Bonnie warmly. "Why don't you?"

Because I don't know what to say, was the inescapable answer. I can't expect him to traipse down to Troutbeck all the way from Keswick every evening, especially in November. And then get up at some unearthly hour to traipse back again. It was infeasible and unreasonable. And if she wasn't calling to arrange something like that, then what else would she talk about? Sweet nothings sat badly with the workplace, in both cases. "Better not," she said. "I'll leave it till this evening."

"You're worried he might be a suspect, aren't you? Just like I was with Ben last week. It's horrible, isn't it — having such ideas flying around?"

"That's what happens when there's a murder," said Simmy. "Although it hasn't been like this before. I didn't know any of the people involved until I had to take flowers to them. It's different when it's a family you've known all your life."

"Or *think* you've known," said Bonnie acutely. "I expect they've all changed quite a lot since you last spent any time with them."

She thought about it. "Yes, they have," she concluded. "Lynn and Hannah especially, because I never saw them past the age of about twelve. But Eddie and George, as well. I wouldn't have recognised either of them if I'd met them in the street. Funny how different they are now. Eddie's whole *shape* has changed. They used to look fairly alike, with Fran's long face and straight hair. But now you'd never guess they were brothers. George has got much darker, for a start." She thought again of the surprising passion for religion that George had revealed, and which she should apparently have noticed all those years ago. "I am so unobservant," she sighed. "I seem to have missed practically everything that was going on, back then."

"Eddie's the one I'm most doubtful about," said Bonnie. "After he sent me down to Bowness the way he did. I still think that he had a hidden motive."

"Chris said he was the one refusing to go to a family meeting last night," Simmy remembered. "You'd expect it to be George who'd rock the boat, not Eddie."

"Ben says he's sure neither of them's the killer." The girl's voice carried a dash of disappointment. "No motive, that he can see."

"When did he say that?"

"Last night. We were on the phone for an hour. That's longer than usual," she added, as if expecting reproach. "Corinne wasn't very pleased about it, for some reason."

Simmy guessed that it might be helpful to keep the topic going, now it had been broached. "She might have wanted you to talk to her instead. About her mother or something."

"Come off it. I was *there*, wasn't I? I wanted to go down and see Ben properly, but I stayed at home to be with Con, because she was expecting the hospital to phone. They didn't, obviously. It's going to be like that until the old lady dies. Nobody seems to have any idea when that might be."

"She might even get better."

Bonnie shook her head. "No. They're sure that won't happen. She's been unconscious since Friday. Everything's shutting down — that's what they said." Again the small spark of excitement at the reality of death was forcing itself into the open. "It's a very weird business," she finished with a sigh.

Simmy agreed. "My mother said that she didn't even recognise her dad when he was dying. She said it could have been any old man, and she never entirely believed they'd got the right one. I remember her coming home all wide-eyed with the shock of it. I was seventeen."

"He can't have been very old, then."

"He was seventy-nine, I think. He had a stroke."

"Families," said Bonnie with a wealth of world-weariness that made Simmy smile.

The two new flower orders were going to make Tuesday almost busy. Certainly by recent standards they produced a welcome change of pace. One delivery was to a street only a few hundred yards away, and the other to Newby Bridge, at the southern tip of Lake Windermere. "You can do the local one if you like," she told Bonnie. "They want it sometime tomorrow."

"Can I?" Bonnie blinked in surprise. "Are you sure?"

"Why not?"

"No reason. It'll be exciting. I think."

"What's the matter?"

"I might feel a bit daft carrying a bunch of flowers up the high street, that's all."

"You're joking. Have you forgotten you're working for a florist?"

"Sorry. Who's the person?"

"It's a couple. Mr and Mrs Hughes are celebrating their silver wedding anniversary. This is from their two children, Brendon and Dymphna. That's a good name."

"Don't start on names again," begged Bonnie. "Silver's twenty-five, isn't it? That means they should be about fifty, right? Why aren't they at work during the day?"

"Don't ask me."

"I know — they could have been living together for ages, and only got married when they were forty or something, so now they're old and retired. And their children are middle-aged. Because they were born ages before the mum and dad got married. That happens, you know," she ended solemnly.

"I'm sure it does," said Simmy, finding herself unable to think of an example known to her personally. Not for the first time, she was forced to see herself as a sheltered innocent in a world where rules were being broken on a daily basis. Her mother adapted to social change much more readily than she did herself.

Ben surprised them by arriving shortly before two, which was much earlier than usual. "The tutor's sick," he explained laconically. "Suits me nicely. We've got to settle this murder *now*. No more messing about. We'd have cracked it yesterday if that pesky George hadn't shown up when he did."

Simmy sighed and Bonnie whooped.

"I thought Moxon was on top of it," Simmy said.

"If he is, then that's fine. All the better, of course, if we come to the same conclusion as him. I bet we will. He seems to be a bit brighter these days."

"And he won't like it if you get in his way, will he? If he's got it worked out already, why should we waste time covering the same ground?"

"Good practice," he told her with exaggerated patience. "Besides — you don't look very busy."

"Three orders for tomorrow. I should be making them up this afternoon."

"Go on, then. You can talk at the same time, can't you?"

"If I have to."

"Okay. So — first off, we need to think about all the people who were at Mrs Henderson's funeral. It all starts with that, you see. When she died, everything changed for the family, and somehow an opportunity opened up for whoever it is that hated Mr H enough to kill him. That's my first premise," he explained patronisingly.

"First premise," repeated Bonnie, who looked as if she ought to be taking notes. "The funeral."

"Right. And you, Simmy, were there. So you can supply the list."

"No way. There were *hundreds* of people there." She knew full well that this was a shameless exaggeration.

"I think not. Probably only about sixty or seventy, from what I heard. Don't forget I live near most of them. A chap at college's mother did the catering. She said they ordered food for seventy, and that pretty much everybody there was local. If we count you and your parents, all the Henderson offspring, one or two neighbours —"

"Are you saying we can discount the neighbours?" Simmy queried. "If so, why?"

"No, I'm not saying that. Just that we have them listed already. I want you to think of the rest of them, the ones I can't even guess."

"Wait a bit, then. Let me get started on the Staveley flowers. I'll take them first thing tomorrow." She gathered up the assorted blooms and foliage, ribbons and wires, and disappeared into the cool room at the back.

"Hey! I can't hear you out there," protested Ben.

"Yes, you can if you try. I'm not coming out, anyway, until this is done."

"It only takes her ten minutes," said Bonnie. "Do you want a muesli bar?"

"No, thanks. I had the full works in the canteen, for once. They're making quite a good job these days, for a change."

"Canteen!" she scoffed. "School dinners are school dinners. What was it?"

"Spaghetti bolognese, with a remarkable variety of vegetables. I didn't even recognise some of them."

"Brave," she approved.

Simmy heard most of this banter from her back room, aware of Ben's barely suppressed impatience. "Are you making a list?" she called. "Of the funeral guests, I mean."

"Good thinking." He found a notebook and pencil in his bag and started to write. "Family . . . neighbours . . . Straws . . ." he muttered. "Who else?"

"Fran's sister Christine, and her husband. A group of women from the WI. She was their secretary, apparently. Another group of younger women. I sat with them. June was the name of one of them, and Cheryl the other. They were with Hannah." She was still talking in a raised voice from the other room. "I think there was some talk of June being one of Kit's bits on the side. My mother said that was Fran's suspicion, anyhow."

"Why would she go to the funeral?" Ben nibbled his pencil. "What would she care about the wife being dead?"

"She might have liked her," said Bonnie. "It goes like that sometimes. My mother had a boyfriend who was married. She often said she liked the wife better than the man." She adopted an expression of wise tolerance for the foibles of humanity.

"Hm," said Ben.

"I think she just went because she lives so close by," said Simmy. "Or was that the other one?" She tapped her head in an effort to shake the memories loose. "Yes, that was Cheryl, not June. You probably know them by sight. She said she knew everybody."

Ben returned his attention to Bonnie, who was waiting for a response to her own remark. Her mother, as Simmy had gradually learnt, was irredeemably deplorable. Everything Simmy had heard about her only added to this conclusion. Only after considerable damage wrought on the child by the succession of boyfriends did the authorities remove her and put her under the infinitely preferable care of Corinne, at the age of nine. The foster mother had made this child a special project ever since.

"Who else?" Ben asked Simmy, who was finishing her bouquet with a fake satin ribbon.

"I can't think of any names. I said the Wethertons, didn't I?"

"No."

"Yes I did. The Cheryl woman is married to Malcolm Wetherton, who keeps coming in here. He's some sort of antique dealer. He was at the auction with Hannah."

"And Cheryl?"

"No. I haven't seen her since the funeral."

"Hm," said Ben again.

"There's nothing happening, is there?" Bonnie complained. "We're just carrying on as usual, and nobody bothers with us. There's absolutely *nothing happening*."

"So we make something happen," said Ben calmly. "Once we work out who the killer is, we flush them out." He closed one eye in profound thought. "I think it was most likely a woman," he said. "One of the daughters. Or that June woman. What's she like?"

"I only saw her for a few minutes, and she barely spoke to me. Didn't seem very friendly. Early forties, big brown eyes, lots of make-up. That's all I remember."

"You think it's a woman because the murder weapon was a pair of scissors," she accused him. "From what I heard, it seems terribly violent for a woman to have done it. And Kit was pretty robust. He'd have fought her off."

"Enraged women can be just as savage as men."

"Scissors?" murmured Bonnie. "Is that what it was?"

Ben sighed and threw an exasperated look at Simmy. "I was hoping she didn't have to hear the details," he said.

"Gosh — sorry. I assumed you'd have talked it through with her minutely by now. Isn't that what you usually do?" Then she realised that in one previous case Bonnie had been centrally involved and Ben had not yet quite accepted that her subsequent recovery had been somewhat faster and more complete than his own had been. Not even Corinne seemed entirely sure that Bonnie had not suffered invisible harm from the events in Hawkshead. Everyone had rallied around Ben, perhaps overlooking the needs of his girlfriend.

"I'm not sure I'm happy with the idea of making something happen," Simmy demurred. "What if you've got the wrong person?"

"I haven't got anybody yet. It could be a person we haven't met or even heard of." Again he chewed the pencil. "But I don't think that's very likely. There's a strong feeling of claustrophobia about all this. The

298

family are all still clos
time. Even Christoph
the world. They're a
Not like my family,"
he thought this a m

"I never though
Simmy slowly. "But
suppose — having th
images filled her mind othe
Hendersons, if she and
permanently. Would it be like
all the year round, for decades?

"They're sucking you in as well," said Ben, with
acute look. "So — let me ask you this: if it had to be
one of them who killed their father, which would you
opt for?"

"I'm not answering that," she returned indignantly.
"It's unfair and totally unscientific. What happened to
forensic rigour and following the facts?"

"You can prove anything with facts," said Bonnie,
with a laugh. "Isn't that what people say?"

"Only stupid people," snapped Ben. "Without facts,
everything collapses."

"So don't ask me daft questions like that," said
Simmy. But already the answer had come clearly to
mind, slightly surprising her. Eddie — that's the one
she would choose. Eddie Henderson, who came and
went even less predictably than his brother George.
Eddie, the middle son, watchful and self-effacing.
Eddie, she felt, was capable of almost anything.

to be George," Ben accused
ur face."
ng," she flashed back, realising too
n trapped. "George isn't subtle or
get away with killing anybody. He'd
re with the weapon in his hand until
und him. He'd confess the whole thing
ack on his religion to save him."
So it's the other one — what's his name?
Not one of the girls, then?"
Shut up. You're not being fair. I don't want it to be
any of them. I'm perfectly sure it wasn't any of them, in
fact."

"In fact," Bonnie repeated, with a mulish glance at
Ben. His sharp response to her contribution had been
wounding, but she wasn't cowed by it. "Is *she* allowed
to use the word like that?"

Ben leant towards her and took her hand.
"Apologies," he said. "You know I don't think you're
stupid."

"Accepted," she replied, with a little bow. "Now, how
are we going to make something happen? I like the idea
of that." She wrinkled her whole face. "But what can
we do?"

"Think it through. Set people against each other. You
saw what I did just now with Simmy — making her
reveal what she thought, even when she didn't want to.
That's the sort of thing I have in mind."

"Okaaay," said Bonnie slowly. "I'm sure you can
manage that." Her loyalty was unalloyed, and Ben
preened under it.

"You're not going after Eddie, are you?" Simmy worried. "He's probably perfectly innocent."

Ben smiled. "He probably is. But *somebody* isn't."

"Who?"

"I'm not there yet. I might need to talk to Moxo again first."

"He's not going to tell you anything important, is he?" said Simmy sceptically.

"He might. He must remember how helpful I was, when there was that business in Ambleside." There was a hint of wistfulness in his tone. Moxon had never dismissed Ben's efforts to assist with investigations as most professional police detectives would, but neither did he allow him to get too close. It struck the man as almost perverse, the way Ben had actually discovered bodies, and been in the exact spot at the exact moment, more than once. There was an uneasy respect between the two that had grown over time.

"That book you were left," Bonnie interrupted. "Full of those weird pictures. Could there be clues in there somehow?"

"Absolutely impossible," said Ben. "They were done seventy years ago or something. And how would it work, anyway?"

"Except we were talking about ways that it might mean something," Simmy reminded him. "Not the actual book but the fact that she gave it to me in the first place."

Ben shook himself. "Think!" he commanded. "Both of you." Then he visibly followed his own instruction, his eyes flittering from side to side. "That meeting last

301

night. The one Hannah called for all the siblings. Did it happen?"

"Yes, they all showed up except for Eddie, and Hannah gave them all a job to do. Christopher is supposed to be chasing the coroner's officer today, so they can get on with fixing the funeral."

"Urghh! Family meetings," Bonnie groaned. "Never a good idea."

Ben and Simmy met this with equally blank looks. "Doesn't happen at the Harkness household," said Ben.

"And our family's so small, we wouldn't know we were even having a meeting," said Simmy.

"So you don't think they started accusing each other of murdering their dad, then," said Ben.

"Of course they didn't," snapped Simmy. "And even if they did, they wouldn't tell anybody, would they? What if one of them confessed to the killing, and the others all agreed to cover it up and provide alibis or whatever?"

"What if they *all* did it together?" said Bonnie in a hushed voice.

"I don't think any of them did it," said Ben. "But they might well have worked out who did, if they got their heads together."

"Then they'd tell the police," said Simmy.

"Or maybe they'd go for revenge more directly. That George looked capable of something like that."

"I could phone Chris, then," Simmy offered, feeling warm at the prospect. "What do you want me to ask him? I don't actually think there's anything more he'll tell me, after last night. Just that Hannah was bossy as

302

usual and they don't sound particularly united as a family."

"Just see if anything new's developed today," said Ben.

"Okay," she said doubtfully, and got her phone from her pocket.

"Are you going to do it *now?*" Ben looked impressed. "Won't he be at work?"

"What if he is?"

Ben's parents were both old-fashioned professionals who had firmly and absolutely banned any contact from their children during working hours, unless somebody was actually dying. In his world, you just didn't break that edict. But Simmy had no such inhibitions. Her mother had worked in offices of various sorts, welcoming the interruption of a personal call. To a lesser degree, the same was true of her father.

So she phoned Chris, using the mobile number he had put into her phone over lunch at the pub. He answered cheerfully, with no detectable undercurrents in his voice. "Hey! I was just going to call you. Must be telepathy."

"Are you having a good day?"

"Quiet. Typical Monday. Although a man came in just now with the most gorgeous piece of Carlton I've ever seen. Tree and swallow pattern. Perfect condition. I nearly swooned, it was so lovely."

"Nice," she said weakly, having no idea what he was talking about. "Has Eddie shown up yet?"

"He wasn't *missing.* And yes, he sent us all an email saying his exhaust fell off. It was a bit of a drama apparently. Looks as if we all had a busy day yesterday," he added, with a little laugh.

"Well today isn't at all busy here. Although Hannah's husband came in this morning, with Malcolm Wetherton. Apparently your dad's funeral is pencilled in for the end of next week. Is that right? Did you get some sense out of the coroner's officer that quickly?"

"Actually, he called me at nine o'clock and I passed it on to the others. We're not at all sure of the date, though. It might be longer. None of us can concentrate on another funeral so soon. I think we're all still pretty numb about it. I certainly am — I keep letting other things distract me." The same little laugh came again. Simmy knew perfectly well what it meant, but was doing her best to resist any response, with Ben and Bonnie listening so intently.

"I'm not surprised," she sympathised. "Everyone must be wondering what the police are thinking, and what questions they might ask next."

"Oh, I think they're done with the questions," he said, oddly airily. "After all, it's almost a week now."

"Yes, but — Chris, your dad was *murdered*. Somebody deliberately *killed* him. You must want to know who it was."

"Yes, of course I do. We said all this yesterday, didn't we? It's too big, Simmy. That sounds daft, but I still can't help feeling I won't like it when we finally know who it was. It won't change anything, will it? I can't say I'm especially keen to know the reason for it, either. I know my father was no angel. Quite a few people might have reason to hold a grudge against him. Once the

304

whole business is solved, and out in the open, it's not going to look very good for the Hendersons, is it? As a family, I mean. We'll be *tainted*. So forgive me if I don't want to get mired in all that mucky stuff."

Simmy met Ben's eyes, wondering how much he could hear. "Mucky stuff?" she repeated, suddenly remembering the flashback she'd experienced in the middle of the night, in bed with Chris. It all kept coming back to the same thing, until now it felt inevitable, barely even surprising.

"Never mind," he said. "Listen — I can't get away this evening, but I could come tomorrow, after work. Would that be all right?"

"Lovely," she said. "And you can tell me all about Carlton — whatever it is."

"You don't know? My God, you've got a lot to learn, my girl."

"And I bet you have no idea what gypsophila looks like. Or crocosmia. Or syringa."

"Touché," he said with yet another carefree laugh. "See you tomorrow, then."

"Did you hear any of that?" she asked Ben, when the call was ended.

"Not really."

"He's worried that his father was doing something nasty, and when the story comes out, the whole family is going to be tainted." She frowned. "But he didn't *sound* particularly worried about it. He kept laughing."

"Yes, I did catch some of the laughing. Sounded like relief to me. As if he was worried, but now he isn't."

"No, Ben, you've got that wrong," Bonnie interrupted. "He's just happy that he's got together with Simmy after all this time. It's love, that's all."

Simmy experienced a jumble of emotions: embarrassment, joy, confusion and more. "Stop it," she said. "Leave my personal life alone, will you? You're as bad as Melanie, and that's saying something."

"No, but we're *happy* for you," persisted the girl. "It's *good*."

"All right. But it's also *private*, okay? Leave me some dignity, that's all I ask."

Ben was waiting for the mushy stuff to stop, so he could get back to the more important matter. Simmy quickly put his waiting at an end. "Everything keeps pointing the same way," she said. "Like all roads leading to the same place. Kit was having an affair, and now somebody's punished him for it."

"But who would care enough to kill him, other than his wife?" asked Bonnie. "I mean — who else would have got hurt?"

"The mistress, obviously," said Ben, slightly scathingly. "If he dumped her, or broke promises — especially after his wife had died and he was free — then the woman scorned would be pretty annoyed about it, wouldn't she?"

"So how do we find out who that was?" asked Simmy. "My mother might help, I suppose. She's already mentioned a woman — girl — called June. But I think that was ages ago. And she was at Fran's funeral. How would that work?"

"We're getting closer," said Ben excitedly. "I can feel it."

Before Simmy could say anything to subdue him, the same husky note that had been irritating her increasingly over the past week announced a newcomer.

CHAPTER
TWENTY-THREE

"The man himself!" Ben cried, as triumphant as if his own magic wand had achieved the visitation.

Moxon cast his eyes to the ceiling in amused exasperation. "Nice to be made so welcome," he said.

"We're brainstorming," Simmy said.

"Well, good for you. I came with one quick question, actually."

"Fire away," Ben invited.

"A question for Mrs Brown."

Ben waved a graciously permissive hand, and Moxon sighed. "All right, then. Have any of the Hendersons mentioned that list to you? The one I showed you."

"The one he was holding when he died?" Ben interrupted eagerly.

"Right," said Moxon patiently. "So?"

She had to think.

"Well, yes, I talked to George about it. And Christopher might have said something, although I can't remember if he did."

"But you didn't know anything about it before Henderson was killed?"

"No, no. Absolutely not."

"Hm. I was afraid you'd say that."

"Why?"

"Well, it seems strange that she should have such firm wishes, and yet say nothing to any of the family."

"Maybe she did. There's no reason any of them would talk to me about it, is there?"

"So what are you thinking?" asked Ben, obviously puzzled.

"I'm thinking there's implications here that we haven't altogether got a grip on."

"And it was written by Fran? You're sure of that?" Simmy said.

Ben and Bonnie had drawn together, her hand on his forearm. "It was," the detective nodded.

"What did it say, exactly?" asked Ben.

Moxon hesitated. "I can't tell you, you know that. I showed it to Mrs Brown, but you two — well, you know how closely involved you are. It would be highly embarrassing if I had to disclose in court that I let you see it."

"Can I tell them roughly what it said?" asked Simmy.

"I can't stop you," he smiled.

"And you can stop calling me Mrs Brown," she said. "I thought we'd got past that a while ago."

He smiled and nodded again. "Sorry. Force of habit. Professional protocol."

"So?" prompted Ben.

"It was a list of requests from Fran to Kit. She wanted him to get a dog, buy a new car, plant some trees and one or two other things I can't remember."

"Trees?" Ben repeated. "In that little garden?"

"Quite sensible ones, really. Cherry, hazel, juniper . . . they'd all fit, even if the juniper might make it rather dark after a few years."

"So where did it come from?" demanded Ben. "The woman had been dead for weeks. And she wouldn't *post* it to him, would she? He must have found it tucked away in the house somewhere."

"He was holding it when he was killed. There were no other matching pages anywhere in the house. It reads quite strangely when you really look at it." Moxon paused for dramatic effect. "We think it was in fact sent to someone else, who then took it to the bungalow, and there was some sort of argument or confrontation, at the end of which Mr Henderson was violently murdered."

"You don't say 'violently murdered'," muttered Ben. "That's a tautology."

"No, it's not, Ben," said Bonnie. "If you poisoned somebody, that wouldn't be violent, would it?"

The young man gave his beloved a full-beam smile and Simmy said, "My father would be proud of you. Knowing what a tautology is, I mean. If you ask him nicely, I'm sure he'll adopt you."

Everyone chuckled, including Bonnie.

"The page," said Moxon. "We showed it to all the sons and daughters, and they all said they had never seen it before. We did it simultaneously, to avoid any conferring. They were all quite convincingly bewildered, by all accounts."

"Which one did you interview?" asked Ben.

310

"None of them, as it happens. It was done by an assortment of constables and sergeants, on Friday morning."

"Nobody said anything to me." Simmy found herself slightly miffed at this. She had spoken to all the Hendersons but Lynn since Friday morning. She had spent a night of passion with one of them, for heaven's sake.

"Right. That's all I wanted to know." He appeared more satisfied than disappointed. "Do you think your mother might have any further light to throw on the matter?" he asked, far too diffidently for an experienced officer of the law.

"Well, she was telling me about someone called June, last night. I suppose it's the same woman who was at the funeral, with a friend of hers. Cheryl Wetherton, married to Malcolm. He keeps turning up here, for various reasons. There was another woman as well, who joined them later on, and seemed to be their friend, but I don't know her name. They were all sitting together, with Hannah, when I left. They seemed a bit out of place, somehow. Not related or anything. And a bit young to be proper friends. Older than the offspring, younger than the parents. Kind of in between, like early or mid forties." She felt herself babbling, trying to be helpful and probably just throwing up an accidental smokescreen.

"Yes, I have all those names from the list of mourners," said Moxon. "At least, I think I have. Mr and Mrs Wetherton, certainly. And I believe there was a Mrs Ford and a Miss H. Jewel."

"Good memory!" applauded Bonnie, who was apparently finding it difficult to make a single helpful contribution, and was feeling rather left out as a result.

"I've had a week to memorise them," he smiled at her. "I could easily recite the whole list. Sixty-eight people, counting the vicar and the organist and the woman from the hospice."

"And my parents, and a whole lot of Hendersons," said Simmy. "Yes — we've just been trying to get that same list together here. I don't think I managed more than about thirty-five, though."

"We hadn't finished," said Ben.

"I think you know who did it," Bonnie suddenly challenged DI Moxon. "You're just trying to gather evidence now. Won't you tell us who it is?"

Ben and Simmy both held their breath at this piece of impertinence. Then Ben said, "He can't. That would be slander, apart from anything else."

"You're wrong, anyway," said the detective. "There are still quite a few people under suspicion. I don't have anything definite on any of them. Although . . ." he lapsed into a moment of silent contemplation. "Now, I'm getting an idea." He squared his shoulders. "Beck View — next stop, Lake Road," he said. "I suppose they'll be in, will they?"

"I couldn't say," Simmy told him. "Afternoons are their free time. But I don't imagine they'll have gone anywhere in this gloomy weather."

He was off without another word, leaving the threesome all looking at each other for enlightenment.

"Who's Miss H. Jewel?" asked Ben. "You never said anything about her."

"No idea. How many names begin with an H, anyway?"

"Hermione."

"Helen."

"Hilda."

"Hester."

"Harriet."

"Hazel!" said Simmy. "Hazel Jewel. Cheryl Wetherton. June something." She waited. "Think about it, kids. Think hard."

Both young faces gazed blankly back at her. "It's all thanks to my mother," Simmy said. "And her obsession with names. I bet she'll latch onto it, the same as I just have, once she starts talking to Moxon."

"What? What is it?" Ben was shouting furiously, unused to coming second in anything that required intellectual activity.

"That list of trees that Kit was holding. Cherry, Juniper and Hazel . . . get it now?"

He mouthed the words twice over, then "My God! Cherry for Cheryl, juniper for June and hazel for Hazel. So — you think all three of them have been discarded by the old man, over the years, and got their revenge on him together? They *all* killed him?" He frowned. "They'd never get away with it, if so. Everyone knows that criminals betray each other, every time."

"Why should it be all of them?" Bonnie asked. "Why not just one, with the others not knowing anything about it?"

"And what about the fact that *Fran* wrote that list?" Simmy wondered. "And turned the names into trees that she wanted Kit to put in the garden. Which is quite a nasty thing to do, when you think about it."

"Very," Ben agreed.

"So — she must have sent it to somebody, and that person took it to show Kit, and then killed him," Bonnie summarised. "Is that right?"

"That's what it looks like," said Ben. "But there have to be other interpretations. And what other trees or plants were on that list? And did Kit get the message?"

"Other interpretations?" asked Simmy.

"Well, let's do some more brainstorming. What if Mrs H did send — or give — that list to her husband directly? And it made him think fondly of one of his old girlfriends? So he invited her round for old time's sake, and she was so outraged she bumped him off?"

"Doesn't quite ring true," Bonnie demurred. "She wouldn't have gone in the first place unless she still had a soft spot for him. Or unless she went with the intention of killing him, taking her sharpest pair of scissors with her. That seems a bit unlikely."

"It *all* sounds a bit unlikely," sighed Simmy. "None of it's bad enough to justify murder."

"We'll have to be clever, if we're to get Moxon the evidence he needs," said Ben. "It's no good just talking about it — we need to take some action."

Simmy had been content to go along with the theory that someone other than any of Kit's offspring had killed him. More than content — it came as a great relief. But she could not entirely dismiss the anger in

Hannah's eyes, or the volatile behaviour of both George and Eddie.

"What do you suggest?" she asked, worriedly.

"First we find their addresses, or phone numbers. Then . . . I don't know . . . pretend to be writing a piece about exploitative relationships with older men. Invite them to disclose any experiences they might have had." He rubbed his nose doubtfully. "That sort of thing."

"It'd be awfully time-consuming," said Bonnie. "And surely they'd never fall for it."

"The only one of us who could come close to being a journalist or social worker or whatever is me," said Simmy. "And I flatly refuse to do it."

"Okay. I'll keep thinking." Ben looked at his watch. "I'll have to go now. Two essays to get background material for, and a lot more besides. The truth is, I don't have much time for this sort of thing at the moment. I'm not going to have, either, until next June."

"So let Moxon do it," said Simmy. "Nobody expects you to solve all his murders for him."

"But I *want* to," he wailed childishly.

"I know you do —"

"But we can't always have what we want, can we?" Bonnie interrupted. "Don't be such a baby. Once you get these exams all passed, you'll be solving murders every day of the week."

He grinned and threw an arm around her shoulders.

It was half past three when Angie Straw charged into the shop like a bull. Simmy actually trembled for her

315

china — the nice pots made by Ninian Tripp that sat around the floor with flowers in them.

"What have you been telling that detective?" she demanded. "He's been wasting my time for almost an hour with a lot of nonsense about women with names like trees. Rowan! I ask you. What sort of idiot calls their child *Rowan*? It's the tree that witches gathered around, or something."

"It wards *against* witches, actually," said Bonnie, who was standing as tall as she could against the sudden onslaught. While directed largely at Simmy, it definitely included her as well. "I've got a stepbrother called Rowan."

"Don't tell me — he was born a girl, and kept the same name." Angie was in full spate, randomly offending anybody who crossed her path.

"No. He was always a boy," said Bonnie, mildly enough to cause the irate woman to falter. "He's the son of my father's second long-term partner. I've only met him twice."

Simmy was merely waiting out the storm. While doing so, she had time to grasp that Moxon had arrived at the identical conclusion as she, Ben and Bonnie had done. The list in the dead man's hand was a tricksy way of referring to women from his past. Why her mother took such exception to this remained unclear.

Finally, it felt safe to ask, "Why did that make you so cross?"

"Because it makes Fran look so bad, obviously. Not only was she a humiliated wife, putting up with all his peccadilloes, but now they think she arranged his death somehow."

"What? Where did that come from?"

Angie shook her head impatiently. "That was the clear implication of his questions."

"So what did you tell him?"

"That all I knew was that Fran sometimes had cause to complain about her husband's flirtations with younger women. It was all in the past — nothing for at least eight or ten years, as far as I knew. It was nonsense to think there was any sort of convoluted conspiracy to kill him after she'd died. In fact, the idea is disgusting."

"Are you sure that's what he was thinking? Wasn't he just trying to get the facts clear in his mind?"

"Oh, you *would* defend him. You're much too fond of your pet policeman."

"Shut up, Mother. He's married, for a start. And I've never — you *know* I haven't."

"So, who is Rowan?" asked Bonnie. "Somebody's child?"

Angie looked oddly cornered. "Actually, he's the son of that June woman, whatever her name is."

"How do you know that?" Simmy demanded.

"Because there was a fuss when he was born. Fran got a letter. It was all very unpleasant for a while."

Simmy just stared at her mother's face, projecting her own sudden suspicions and insights onto it, while knowing that there was a mirroring understanding in the older woman's eyes.

"Do you know where they live?" she asked.

"Not exactly."

"You can ask Christopher what the surname is, Sim," said Bonnie. "Then we can easily find the address."

"Even easier, I can let the police do it for themselves. I assume you've told them all this already? They'll have found her by now. We don't have to do anything."

"What about the others — Cheryl and Hazel?"

"I told him all I knew about them too."

Simmy remembered Moxon's account of how the police had interviewed all five Henderson siblings at the same time, using a team of junior officers. A somewhat larger team than she had thought they had access to, in this quiet and law-abiding part of England. They could be doing the same thing again, with the women so helpfully identified by Angie Straw.

But she thought probably not. There could be little point, surely, unless Moxon suspected them of working together, and thus capable of alerting each other to police interest. That could happen, she supposed. She wished Ben hadn't gone home; his quick-thinking and lateral approaches could be helpful now.

And then she asked herself — why should she care, anyhow? What was it to her? The answer hit her in the midriff, making her feel stupid and strangely treacherous. She had a new lover, and both his parents had just died. His troubles were her troubles, and she had no choice but to do all she could to assuage them.

"They all came to the funeral," she said. "Why would they do that?"

"Your detective asked that as well," said Angie. "I don't think he found my answer very enlightening."

"Why — what did you say?"

"I said there was such a thing as female solidarity, and they probably all had a degree of respect for Fran. Possibly even sympathy, if they'd come to see Kit as he really was. When my mother was in her thirties and forties, men behaved like Kit did as a matter of course. They had other women. They ran off leaving their wives destitute. They just did as they bloody well liked. And some — like Kit — didn't catch on to the fact that times had changed. Women in my generation were not going to stand for it. Some of them still think they can get away with it, of course. Some of them always will."

"And Kit did get away with it, didn't he? Fran stuck with him."

"He stuck with her, more like. He let them all down — girlfriends and wife. And the kid."

"What kid?"

"The one called Rowan. His mother swore blind he was Kit's, you see. That was what caused so much trouble."

CHAPTER
TWENTY-FOUR

It was all rather banal, Simmy thought frustratedly, as her mother filled in a few more details. A story one heard over and over — the humiliated wife, remorseful husband, confused offspring and sympathetic friends offering a range of conflicting advice.

"Fran ended up just trying not to think about it, but I don't believe she ever forgave him," Angie concluded.

"Is any of this enough to explain Kit being murdered?" Simmy wondered.

Angie merely shrugged. Bonnie, who had been openly listening to the whole conversation, said meekly, "People can get themselves very worked up. If they'd been planning it for a long time, they might just, sort of, pass a point of no return. Don't you think?"

"I can't imagine it at all," Simmy admitted.

"I can, just about," said Angie. "Rather as Bonnie says — it would be like losing face, not to do it after promising yourself you would."

"Are we saying it was June, then?" Simmy finally asked. "How old is this Rowan now?"

"Oh — must be at least sixteen. It was ages ago now."

"And where is he? Does he know the story? Who does *he* think is his father?"

"I have absolutely no idea. Fran hadn't mentioned him for years. He could have gone to Australia, for all I know."

"More likely he's still living with his mother and doing his GCSEs," said Bonnie. "Somewhere not a hundred miles from here."

"You're probably right," Angie nodded.

"Well — are we going to *do* something about it?" Bonnie was jigging on the spot. "At least we can call Ben and bring him up to date. He'll be furious if we don't."

"The Wethertons live in Bowness," Simmy said. "I remember her saying at the funeral."

"So what?" Angie said.

"Well, we're focusing so much on June, we're forgetting the others, especially Cheryl. And whoever Hazel Jewel might be. I'm sure we've got the answer, and that makes me feel so useless hanging around here, when we haven't even got any customers. The Hendersons were our *friends*, don't forget. For all those years — you and Fran telling each other everything, and now there's me and Christopher . . ."

"Ah! Yes. I was meaning to ask you about that. Russell told me how you were making cow eyes at him on Saturday."

"I was not making cow eyes, whatever that might mean. He ignored me completely. And I was watching Hannah half the time, anyway." She paused. "I wonder *why* she was with Malcolm Wetherton. I never really believed what she told me. And her husband obviously didn't know about it until I mentioned it this morning."

Bonnie spoke up again. "We're missing something, aren't we? We've got all the pieces, but we're not putting them together right. Oh, I really must call Ben."

"Wait a minute," Simmy ordered. "Let's just concentrate for a bit, first. Mum — this *has* to be about their marriage — Fran and Kit's — and something he did that was bad enough to make someone kill him. Moxon thinks Fran sent that list to someone, as an incitement to murder. Which makes *her* guilty, in a way. And what about that book she left me? Does that have something to do with it?"

"Please stop talking," begged Bonnie. "There's a little voice in my head, trying to tell me something, and you're drowning it out."

Mother and daughter stared at her, half offended, half intrigued. After a long silence, Bonnie began to speak. "They *all* had possible reasons for wanting to kill him. He betrayed everybody, didn't he? Even the men who married those girls later on."

"What? Which girls?" asked Simmy.

"June. Cherry — the girls he probably seduced and exploited when they were too young to know what to do about it. Then if he dumped them, they were probably scared to start again with men their own age. Not exactly damaged goods like in the olden days, but a bit like that. Ashamed, maybe, or even still in love with him. And maybe when Fran died, years before anybody thought she would, leaving him available, they'd either be afraid he'd start on them again, or furious because

322

he *didn't*. Am I making sense?" she finished humbly. "I'm just doing what Ben says we should — putting myself in everybody's shoes."

"Sounds fine to me, so far," said Angie, with the same sort of expression that Moxon adopted when facing Ben Harkness.

"Then there's his daughters. They're both adopted — right? So they already feel just a bit funny about him, possibly. I'm not saying that's a thing, in general, but with these two it might be. If they see him carrying on with women who aren't terribly much older than them, they'll be forced to think of him as a man, as well as a father — if you see what I mean. And Simmy says he was always flirting, everywhere he went. That's embarrassing for daughters — maybe worse than embarrassing. Unsettling. And then they'd see what it did to their mother, and it would all get rather sick and cause all kinds of emotional problems. Don't you think?"

"I think you're being fantastically clever," said Simmy. "It *was* like that. I remember now, even though I'd pushed it all out of my mind. You must have it all much clearer in your mind than I have, Mum. I just focused on Christopher and ignored everything else that was going on. But I remember how miserable Fran was sometimes, and how Kit was always trying so hard to be funny, and nobody ever laughing."

"Lynn laughed," said Angie. "She always laughed at his awful jokes. Russell used to say she must be simple, to find such things amusing. Of course, Russell was miffed because she didn't understand his sort of humour."

"Poor old Dad," smiled Simmy. "With his complicated puns. I don't think any of the Hendersons ever understood when he was trying to be funny."

"So that leaves the three sons," went on Bonnie, throwing a cautious look at Simmy. "George was always fighting with Hannah, right? What about the others?"

"What about them?" asked Simmy.

"How were they towards their dad?"

"Eddie hated him and Christopher despised him," said Angie, almost without thinking. "Fran used to agonise about it, blaming herself." She sighed. "God, what a can of worms we've opened here. All those myths about blissful family holidays by the sea, and really it was all pretty grim. I can't think why we ever agreed to go along with it."

"The triumph of hope over experience," said Bonnie. "Ben taught me that one. Dr Johnson said it about marriage. It applies to other things as well."

"It's not really true, though. We just got into the habit, and I did like having so much time with Fran," said Angie. "Plus we thought it would be good for P'simmon to see how big families behaved. We felt guilty at not giving her any brothers or sisters, so that was our way of compensating. And Christopher was always so good with you," she addressed her daughter. "It seemed unkind to deprive you of that friendship."

"Eddie hated him and Christopher despised him," Bonnie repeated. "What about George?"

324

"George just wished he would go away. I sometimes imagined he kept a voodoo doll to represent Kit, and spent all his time sticking pins in it." She gave the girl a straight look. "Not one of them would harbour such bad feeling for so many years before killing him," she said firmly.

"They might, once their mother was dead," said Bonnie, every bit as firmly.

"Not Christopher," said Simmy, rather faintly. "Absolutely not him."

"It must have been Hannah, if it was any of them. But why should it be? What are we thinking?"

"The other thing to consider is whether there was more than one person involved," went on Bonnie relentlessly. "They could have fired each other up, kept each other on the mark. It must be easier then."

"Hannah and Lynn?" said Angie. "Could be."

"Cherry and June? Cherry, June and Hazel? Isn't that where we started?" Simmy shook her head. "I can't even remember all the theories we've gone through in the past twenty minutes. We've slandered just about everybody we know."

Another silence saw them all stymied for further action. "I have to get the flowers ready for Newby Bridge tomorrow," said Simmy. "And the other local ones. I'll be here until six at this rate."

"I should go," said Angie, with an alarmed look at her watch.

"Bonnie — you can go if you like. I'll close up a bit early and crack on with those orders. Let's leave it all for now, and have a fresh look at it all tomorrow."

Angie passed a hand over her brow, and Simmy realised how exhausted she was looking. "Mum — go home. Put your feet up for a bit before supper. Or get Dad to cook it for a change. You've been doing too much."

"I'll call Ben, and tell him what we've been saying," said Bonnie.

"Fine — but do it when you get home. I just want a bit of peace and quiet for an hour."

"If you ask me, the police will have everything done and dusted by bedtime," said Angie. "We've just been guessing, while they're out there in the real world, doing their job."

"Probably," said Simmy.

At last she was left alone. She locked the door behind them, and then she determinedly fetched the stepladder that she kept folded up in the cool room, and climbed up to see to the croaky doorbell. As suspected, it had a disagreeable collection of cobwebs, dead flies, dust and even a few feathers all wrapped around the pinger that was meant to strike the small metal bell. It took seconds to remove, leaving open space between the two parts. She climbed down, unlocked and opened the door experimentally. The bell chimed loud and clear, a sweet note of optimism and promise.

"There," she muttered. "That should bring some customers in."

Outside it was dark but clear, with street lamps casting warm yellow beams along the main street, turning Windermere into a Dickensian scene of quiet shops and stray passers-by. Simmy wished Christopher could be by her side, looking out on it all.

But before that, she intended to have a gift for him; a gift that might possibly be ready within the next hour or so. At some point in the talking and surmising that had just taken place, she had seen the truth. Or so she hoped. She would walk down to Bowness, and find out for herself if she was right. But first, being of a risk-averse disposition, she sent a text to Ben telling him where she would be. Then she sent another to Christopher, asking him to call her at eight o'clock that evening. After that, she turned her phone off.

The walk down the hill into Bowness took roughly ten minutes. She did not hurry — the time was well spent in preparing what she would say.

But the plan went wrong almost from the start. Just as she was passing the Baddeley clock tower, which marked the line between Windermere and Bowness, she encountered the very person she had set out to find. It was too much of a miraculous coincidence to be credible, especially when the woman said, "I was just coming to find you."

Simmy kept her counsel, and merely said, "Oh?"

"Actually, it was your mother I really wanted. I know her B&B is just up here somewhere. I thought you might be there as well."

"She's terribly tired," said Simmy. "I don't think she's really up for visitors. And isn't it rather a bad time, anyway?"

"It's the only time I could manage," said Cheryl Wetherton, looking very flustered. "We're off on our cruise tomorrow, and I wanted to drop in and ask if one of my cousins could stay there after Christmas."

"Why not just phone her?"

"I know. I should have. But I thought a little chat might be nice, as well. I wanted to ask her something a bit personal."

"What time are you leaving tomorrow?"

"Soon after nine. We're flying from Manchester. I can't really believe it — me on a cruise. I've never been anywhere. This is my first passport. Of course, Malcolm says I deserve it, that it's about time something nice happened. We've had another disappointment lately, you see." She lowered her gaze, and Simmy waited for the all-too-predictable revelation. "We've been doing IVF, for a baby, and the third attempt has just failed. I'm too old. I keep *telling* him we've missed the boat. It's all my fault, I know. I was just so . . . *scared*, for so long. But I don't mind too much, really. I've never been the type who craved for a baby. I'm just so grateful to Malc for taking me on, as he did."

"Well, you won't have time to have a proper talk with my mother," said Simmy briskly. "She'll still be doing breakfast at nine. I can take the booking details if you like. As for the other thing . . ."

"It was about Kit Henderson," said Cheryl. "But it isn't important. He's better off dead, you know. He did an awful lot of damage to people like me." She flushed. "I can't tell you anything else. It's all over with now. I've got Malcolm to look after me, and Kit can't bother me ever again."

328

"Was he bothering you, then? After you were married?"

"Oh, no. Not at all. It was just *knowing* he was still there, just a few streets away, that I could never quite forget."

"Was he the father of June's child?" Simmy burst out, her suspicions forming an unstoppable volcano inside her. "The boy, Rowan, is Kit's, isn't he?"

"What? Who told you that?"

A man's voice broke into their intense conversation, there on the pavement. "Cherry? What's going on?"

"Oh, Malc — how did you find me? I was going up to see Mrs Straw, and bumped into Persimmon. I was just saying, it's not such a bad thing that Kit's dead. You know you think so as well." She seemed to Simmy in that moment quite blithely oblivious to the poor taste behind her words. She tucked her hand between her husband's arm and chest, squeezing close to him. "It's not important. We can go home and make sure everything's packed."

Simmy took a deep breath, but it did little to calm her shivers of apprehension. "Cheryl — did you kill Kit Henderson?" she asked. "Because it really looks as if you of all people had the most reason to hate him, and want him out of the way. June, too, perhaps, but I think it must have been you."

"Shut your mouth, you bloody stupid woman," said Malcolm. "What insanity is this? Cherry wouldn't hurt a fly. She's only just managing to feel like a normal woman, after being exploited and abused all her life.

You're right she has good reason to want the man dead. But *she* didn't do it, you idiot."

"Malc, don't," begged Cheryl. "She's just talking nonsense." She laughed, sounding genuinely amused. "I mean — it wasn't just me, was it? Kit was the same with loads of girls. It was just that I — I was different. I took it all much too much to heart."

Simmy heard a line echoing inside her head, spoken by Wetherton on Saturday: "The ladies like him, just like his old dad." That's what the man had said about Christopher and Kit, and nobody had taken much notice. But now it reverberated, combining with the hypotheses that she and Ben and Bonnie and Angie had all created and tested in recent days.

"You did it, then," she said, calmly. "As revenge for what he did to Cheryl. Wasting the best years of her life, leaving it too late to have a baby. *You* did it. Didn't you?"

The man gave her a long complicated look. "In your dreams," he said. "Now leave us alone before we sue you for slander. We're off to the Caribbean tomorrow and nothing's going to stop us."

"You killed Kit Henderson with a pair of scissors. Fran sent you a set of instructions for him, encouraging you to go and wreak vengeance, not just for yourself, but for her as well. You read it out to him, put it in his hand, made him see what damage he'd done to at least four people, and told him how his wife knew about it all, and wasn't willing to just let it all go. She turned the names into trees to make a sick joke out of it, and maybe protect her children. You sat there drinking tea

330

with him, and then you stabbed him where you knew it would hurt. Did you stand over him while he bled to death? Did you put a hand over his face to muffle his screams?"

"That's enough, Simmy," said DI Moxon, stepping out from the shadow of a nearby tree, like Orson Welles in *The Third Man*. "I think we can take it from here."

"No-o-oo," screamed Cheryl. "No, no, no. Malcolm, tell them they're crazy. Malcolm, oh Malcolm."

Epilogue

Two Weeks Later

"We were right about our low fertility," Simmy told Christopher. The chronic post-menstrual depression that had become a permanent feature of her life was more acute this time. She had become more and more hopeful with every passing day since the first night with Chris. At least, her rational mind had kept away from the subject, but her body and instincts had yearned and clamoured for fulfilment.

"Ah," he said warily. "Do I detect disappointment?"

"Apparently so. I'm thirty-eight, Chris. And I need a baby. Preferably two."

"It's only been two weeks. How can we know what sort of parents we'd make? I'm the son of a philanderer. I live twenty-five miles away. How would it work?"

She looked around the hall; the same hall in which she and all the Hendersons had drunk tea after the funeral of their mother not many weeks earlier. Now her husband had been cremated in like fashion — but the family had agreed that the two sets of ashes should not lie together. "After all, she set Wetherton onto him," said Lynn. "What a dreadful thing to do."

"She never forgave him for the damage he did to Cheryl," Angie had summarised. "And to herself. For a long time, she hated Cheryl most of all, until she realised what a victim the wretched girl had been all along. He threatened her with dismissal from work, and all kinds of other things. Then he promised her he would always love her."

"You can't know that for sure," objected Simmy.

"Oh, but I can," Angie corrected her. "Cheryl came to see me yesterday and poured it all out. Apparently I'm the closest thing she can find to a sympathetic ear."

The funeral was soon over, the mourners there on sufferance, unsure whether or not they should be regarding Kit Henderson as so reprehensible as to deserve his fate.

Simmy had closed the shop at lunchtime, seeing Bonnie go off to the funeral of her foster-mother's mother, in the other chapel at the crematorium, twenty minutes before that of Kit Henderson. She had almost flown to Christopher's side at the first opportunity, heedless of what anybody thought of them. She was impatient for them to get free of the defilement that hung around the Henderson family, and begin their headlong romance, which was twenty years overdue.

"We can make it work," she told him firmly.

"All right, m'lady," he smiled. "Who am I to argue with a woman who can catch murderers single-handed?"

"I didn't catch him single-handed. The clue was really in that letter your mother enclosed with my book. It just came to me, somehow — female solidarity, the way Fran was with letters, all the things my mother had been saying about Kit, and there she was taking the time and trouble to make sure I had something of her own mother's. It sounds whimsical, but everything just fell together and made a complete picture."

"A picture that nobody but you could see." He frowned. "I still don't entirely follow."

She tried again. "It was the *tone*. The letter to me was so warm and affectionate. But that list with the trees and so forth, was utterly different. Cold, callous, not a hint of affection. It was not the sort of thing a dying wife would leave for her husband, unless it had an ulterior motive. Well, Ben and Bonnie and my mum all came to that conclusion on Monday, and decided it pointed to June, because of her boy, Rowan."

"Who is not my half-brother, incidentally," said Christopher. "That was proved conclusively when he was nine."

"But he might have been, by the sound of it. But I started thinking about the Wethertons, and all I'd heard about them, and decided to confront Cheryl. I was wrong, though — I was sure it was her, not her husband. He practically told me my mistake, standing there by the clock tower. And Ben sent Moxon to find me, which wasn't difficult, seeing as we were only about a hundred yards from the police station."

"I still think it shows you to be a formidable woman," he insisted, "which is just how I like you."

And he gave her a long sensual kiss, right in front of twenty people.